THE WORKING TOOLS MURDERS

WILLIAM WENDYLL

ISBN: 978-1-956019-76-6 (paperback)
ISBN: 978-1-956019-77-3 (ebook)

Canoe Tree
Press

4697 Main Street
Manchester Center, VT 05255

Canoe Tree Press is a division of DartFrog Books

ACKNOWLEDGMENTS

Thanks to my lovely wife, Rowella, for providing me with the inspiration to write this book. On the evening of 17 March 2020, in Penang, Malaysia, it had just been announced that the country would go into a period of lockdown to combat against the Coronavirus outbreak, Rowella asked me:

"What on earth are you going to do with yourself for the next few weeks? I know you too well; you will drive me nuts!"

ONE

The early morning spring dew hung in the atmosphere and shrouded the outside lights of The Shoulder of Mutton public house, in the village of Cooper's Wood in the Yorkshire Dales. Fortunately, these lights, as dim as they appeared, contributed to the portable illuminations provided by the local police. Several people, dressed in what looked like overcoats over pyjamas, stood outside the main entrance to the pub. The landlord, Bill Cooper, stood alongside them as he focused on the police officers and medical examiners in the gateway of the derelict Ackroyd Clay Brick factory.

In the distance, coming along a lonely and quiet Station Road, Bill recognised the car that was headed towards them. It came to an untidy stop just outside the main gate. Bill shouted over to Matt as he got out of the car, just as a large van pulled up alongside to obscure Matt's line of vision. Matt's eagerness to get to the crime scene showed that he had never heard Bill's voice.

"What's this?" asked Bill.

"Stuff f'news, f'telly," said the driver.

"Park yonder," said Bill as he pointed farther along the road. The kerb stones set around the outside of the building had moved crooked over the years.

"Some more," shouted Bill. "Go on... farther."

Bill turned back and walked towards the entrance. He caught sight of a bystander.

"Bloody telly men. The draymen don't come until next week. Brewery will have my head on a chopping block. Solid oak they are," said Bill, his thumb pointed back over his shoulder.

Inside the factory premises, a team of white-suited officials was already at work. Some attended to the usual paperwork and recorded measurements, made notes, and detailed sketches, scribbles. Others were busy as they made the most of the early morning darkness, and luminol was sprayed with photographers at the ready. A couple more collected samples of hair and any other particles that may have been unknowingly left behind. Matt weaved his way between the CSIs and headed towards two guardian constables.

"Good morning, sir," they said together.

"Morning, lads," replied DCI Matt Baxter. "Who the hell has been phoning me at this time of the morning?"

"The boss from the station was trying to reach you, sir. He said he had something for you to look at. Said he would try the walkie-talkie and to let you know he will come along here later in the morning," said Ryan, a detective inspector, who recently joined the regional police force from down south, Billericay in Essex to be exact.

"Here's the body, sir," said Ryan as he moved aside.

"Oh, my goodness!" Startled by what he saw, Matt started with the industry-standard first question: "Who found the body?"

Ryan pointed to two constables standing nearby.

"These two uniforms. They drove past here a few hours ago and they said they noticed it looked as though someone had tampered with the gates. They suspected something as the gates were intact when they passed by earlier in the evening, around seven," said Ryan. "They thought it was odd as it's been empty for months."

"Good police work. Well done, lads," complimented Matt. "Any ID?"

Ryan passed him an almost empty wallet, which contained some old business cards.

"We found this over there, sir. It looks like the attacker emptied it and threw it away," said Ryan.

"What? A mugging, in a derelict brick factory?" said Matt as he returned the wallet to Ryan.

"Well, they probably tried to make us think it was a mugging, sir, but look here," said Ryan as he pulled back the victim's coat sleeve to reveal a rather expensive-looking wristwatch.

Matt's eyes widened as he leaned forward.

"Strike, is it?" he asked.

"No, sir. I've seen a few of these; this one is pukka," said Ryan.

"Anything else?" Matt asked.

"Sir, just this." An outstretched arm handed him a folded single sheet of white paper with what appeared to be a list of items printed on it.

"We found this in the inside pocket of his overcoat, sir," said the constable. "Doesn't look like much, maybe a tour guide or narration of some sort."

Matt pointed to an evidence bag as he focused his thoughts elsewhere.

"Send it for prints and examination with the other stuff. Anything on the weapons?" asked Matt.

"We started a search, boss," said another constable, "but we would like a few of the white suits to disappear before we can give it a good looking over."

"I agree, and by that time we will have enough staff up and about to get stuck in . . . after they have been over the road, of course," said Matt, as he showed exactly what he referred to.

However, contrary to Matt's statement, more police officers had already arrived on the scene, which he noticed as he walked away. He also noticed an outside broadcast station was being assembled, and a few reporters, arms stretched out, holding OB microphones, started their way over to him. Matt quickened his pace as he noticed Bill waving at him and he squeezed in through the main door. Bill slammed the door shut behind Matt, which provoked several reporters into knocking loudly on the old oak door.

The Shoulder of Mutton is an original coaching inn that dates to the 18th century. Travellers frequently used it on the branch routes off The Great North Road stations at Doncaster and York. The pub has its fair share of legendary highwaymen tales passed on by the local village population.

Whenever someone mentions highwaymen, Dick Turpin immediately springs to mind. Famous for his legendary holdups on the London to York route. However, as time went by, people understood it was one of Turpin's associates, "Swift Nicks" Nevison, that actually performed the holdups.

But other highwaymen also made legends. Down in the great city of London, the French-born Claude Duval never made it north, as he was far too busy charming the wealthy ladies of the city, while he robbed their husbands at gunpoint. Even though they were part of a holdup, the wealthy ladies admired the impeccable manners of this highwayman.

And let's not forget the illicit activity of the three Dunsdon brothers from the Oxford region, known as "The Burford Highwaymen," who provided us with the colloquialism, Tom, Dick, and Harry.

Bill went behind the serving area and reached for a whisky tumbler, into which he dispensed a measure of a rather nice single malt whisky.

"Here, mate; it's never too early for one of these when you've just been through something like that." Bill turned and dispensed another measure, this one for himself. Bill, an ex-forensic pathologist, often recalled his active days, and he still found it quite difficult not to get involved.

"See that dozy bugger driving the van? He nearly smashed through the cellar doors," said Bill.

"It's still early, mate. Too early for some," said Matt. He looked at his phone screen.

"Aye, reckon. I heard a copper say the victim looked a right mess," said Bill as he took an early morning sip.

"It wasn't pleasant, Bill. Gruesome . . . a right mess. Can I ask a favour, mate?" asked Matt.

"Sure, you can. How can I help?" replied Bill.

"We need to set up a secluded interviewing area for an hour or so, later in the day. Just to interview your staff and the overnight guests. I wondered if we could use that little corner of your lounge area. You know, instead of taking them all down to the station. By the way, Bill, how many guests did you have last night?" asked Matt.

"Full house we were. Three regulars, a lad and a lass up from Derby, I think she said. We also have a right pretty lass staying here, doing some arty stuff for one of them country life magazines. She's been here since Tuesday afternoon. Lovely girl," said Bill.

A quieter knock. Ryan entered and held a chisel in front of him. It appeared to be new.

"Sir," he started, "one of the team found this."

"Someone found a chisel . . . in a brick factory," said Matt.

"Hang on, mate," said Bill. "That factory has been empty for a few years now and that looks like a brand-new tool to me."

Ryan put the tool in an evidence bag and glanced at Matt, then at Bill, then back at Matt, and finally made a glance at the whisky bottle on the shelf.

"The first one I have been on, sir," Ryan started the conversation. "What do we do now?"

"Well, first, we have one of these," said Bill as he put a glass of whisky in front of him.

"Cheers, Bill, Guv," said Ryan. "We didn't get any of this in Billericay!"

Ryan's Essex accent was unmistakable when he was amongst the local villagers and his workmates. He had recently decided to relocate as he preferred a much quieter life and wanted to get away from drug dealers, knife crimes, and counterfeit watch traders.

"I don't envy the examiner's job today, mate. You saw him yourself. He looked like someone cut his throat and smashed his head in just to make sure he was dead," continued Matt.

"The reporters are getting a tad anxious, sir," said Ryan, above the sound from the main entrance doorway.

"Let them wait . . . thanks mate, come on lad," said Matt.

They left the pub through the second entrance that led to the rear car park, thus they were unseen by the reporters. Fortunately, Ryan had parked up in the car park and they set off to Cooper's Wood police station.

As they arrived at the village station, they met Chief Superintendent Myles. He works out of Leeds and covers most of North Yorkshire but as he lives nearby, he had already been alerted of the late-night discovery.

"What the hell are you doing here, Baxter? Didn't you get my message? We have received a report regarding an abandoned vehicle over in Mount Ashton Retail Park. Somebody said it might have some connection to the stiff over in the old brick factory. What is wrong with your two-way, flat battery? You'd better get over there straight away and see what it's all about. And keep quiet with the reporters. We're not ready for the news yet!" said Myles.

"Bugger! Mount Ashton is at least an hour away and then an hour back. I quite fancied one of Connie's famous full English breakfasts, Ryan. By the time we get back, those hungry arses from Derby will have eaten the lot! By the way, who took the call on the two-way?" said Matt.

No response from Ryan as he hurried into the driver's seat. For Matt, the possibility of not having breakfast seemed to be more important than police communication at this stage.

The twists and turns of the road over the hill to Mount Ashton could be quite scary during the daytime, let alone so early in the morning. The last hairpin bend led them into the main road through Ashton village, and toward a newly developed retail park. Flashing blue lights showed the location of the abandoned vehicle. Two constables got out of their patrol car to meet them. Matt pointed and made a hand gesture to switch off the annoying illuminations.

"It's a rental, sir," said the constable. He passed the rental agreement to Matt.

"A6, is it? The name of the hirer is David Illya, and there is another named driver, Tamara Illya," Matt read aloud. "Husband and wife, probably. Spring break touring the Yorkshire dales?"

"Illya, that's an unusual name, isn't it?" said Ryan.

"It is indeed. Remember that TV show, way back, ah, probably before your time, Ryan?" added Matt.

"It sounds Russian or Ukrainian, out that way. Where did he fly in from? That might help us," said Ryan, reading the fine print on the rental agreement. "Nothing, so that's all we have; just a name."

"Young man, as you progress through the force, you discover a name can be so much more than just a name," said Matt.

"They picked it up at Heathrow, whoever they were, or are, yesterday morning. We will get onto the car rental company; they might have their flight information in their records. Have you looked in the boot yet?" said Ryan as he walked to the rear of the vehicle.

"Nothing in the boot, just a briefcase on the back seat. There was a notepad, calculator, two power banks, some business cards, and a receipt inside. The receipt is for one of the power banks," said the police constable.

"Business cards; are they the driver's cards or others? What's the address on the receipt?" Matt asked.

"That's odd. There are three different business cards here for this David Illya guy, the driver on the form; look. The others could be people he met in Kuwait, Jordan, Cairo. Very odd, boss," said Ryan as he examined the cards.

"Why did the super say someone thought there was a connection of this vehicle to the dead body? Big assumption if you ask me, sir," submitted Ryan.

"Yes, there are some odd things here indeed, Ryan. They purchased one of the power banks yesterday in Leamington Spa. Why did they need two? The car comes with a charging socket; look . . . rather strange, don't you think?" said Matt as he pointed to the socket.

"What if he had more than one phone? What if he had more than two phones, sir?" said the constable.

"There has to be something more to suggest a link of this abandoned car to the dead body," said Matt.

"Ryan, the depart mileage on that hire agreement, can we compare it to the mileage on the clock?" Matt looked at every option.

"How, sir? No ignition key and it is a keyless start?" he replied.

"So why would someone hire a group five motor in London, drive it north to the middle of Yorkshire, leave an almost empty briefcase inside and then leave the car unlocked and just disappear?" asked Matt to his colleagues.

With no response from the constables, Matt and Ryan set off back to the village. Matt Baxter had something on his mind; he glanced at the dashboard clock.

"Can you drive any faster, Ryan? My internal alarm clock is going off," Matt said. He referred to one of his morning habits.

"Can you hold on, sir? There is nowhere to stop until we reach Shackleton Bottom, and then there's just that old petrol station, run by that old man and his weird son," said Ryan.

The heavy branches from the tall trees hung over the narrow road and blocked the streetlights. As they entered the village they saw a road signpost, partially obscured by unkempt foliage:

We come t
SHACK ETON BO TOM.

Almost immediately after the signpost was a compound surrounded by a broken wooden fence. The occupants kept the five bar gates permanently wedged open with some concrete blocks. Two unlit lights stood at the gate entrance. Loose wires hung down from the top of the lamppost and blew recklessly with the early morning breeze. The car skidded to a halt. Undoubtedly, the noise of the tyres on the gravel surface woke the occupants of the house within the compound.

Matt quickly got out of the car and probably moved faster across the forecourt than Ryan had achieved over the hill. After a few minutes, he returned to the car.

"Right, come on, lad; let's get over to the Shoulder; we might just make it in time," said Matt as he got back in the car.

About twenty minutes later, they arrived back at the crime scene. It was still busy with police, medical staff, and the press. He asked Ryan to drop him down the side of the pub at the same door where he had exited earlier.

Also, if anyone asked about a statement, he should tell them they will make one at about ten o'clock. The empty bar room Matt had left just two hours earlier was now full. Obviously, the staff and crew must also have heard about Connie's well-known breakfasts.

"Hey up, where the heck did you get to?" Bill whispered in Matt's ear.

"I will tell you later. Can we have two Full English, please? Ryan is just parking up," said Matt.

"Yes, I reckon Connie's got yours warmed up already. Give me a minute," said Bill as he walked away. Ryan arrived.

"I ordered us some breakfast. Bacon, sausages, black pudding. I hope you are not one of them vegans!"

"If I were I would have found a way to tell you the first day we met, sir," said Ryan with a smile on his face and they laughed together, probably for the first time during their brief acquaintance.

Within a few minutes, a few of the crowd started whispering to each other whilst pointing towards Matt and his colleague. Matt was just about to stand up to make an announcement when, just then, a constable walked in and bent down to whisper in his ear. Matt's eyebrows raised in surprise, and he stood up and walked behind the bar. The reporters stood and tried to get a view of what now occupied Matt.

Matt held a bag in his hands, and somewhat discreetly, he showed the contents to Bill. It was a mallet, wooden handle, three-pound wooden head. He looked up at Bill, who stood opposite him.

Mallet, chisel, mallet, chisel! Why does that ring a bell? thought Matt. Bill's face gave him the answer as he made a slight nod. As Freemasons, they were both reminded of these tools as being part of their Masonic ritual.

Bill raised his eyebrows, his eyes widened. "No twenty-four-inch gauge?" he asked.

TWO

"Nope, no twenty-four-inch gauge," replied Matt.

"It could be a coincidence, mate," said Bill.

Matt unfolded the rental agreement and passed it to Bill. Ryan joined them.

"This is where we were earlier; a brand new A6 abandoned on that new retail park over the hill," said Matt.

"Bloody hell, Matt," exclaimed Bill. He spotted a significance straight away. "Look at the name!"

"Aye, the guy off the telly, Illya Kuriyaki something or other... *The Man From U.N.C.L.E*, back in the seventies," said Matt.

"No, not that," he continued. "Something else. David and Tamara?"

"Tamar was the name of David's only daughter. Her half-brother Amnon raped her. David never punished him and a few years later, Tamar's own full brother Absalom killed Amnon," said Bill.

"Which David?" asked Ryan.

"King David, the one in all the stories that you hear in the morning assembly at school," said Bill.

The look of bewilderment on Ryan's face showed he did not have a clue what they were talking about.

As he opened the main entrance door, Matt prepared himself to meet the reporters, by now, all showing signs of impatience. A brief statement led to questions from the crowd, which followed the typical pattern. The reporter from the *Yorkshire Times* asked a question, Matt answered. Then the same question, phrased differently, was asked by the *Northern Daily*. Matt answered. Then, almost the same question was asked by the next reporter. Matt answered. *That's enough of that*, thought Matt, well known for his low patience threshold.

The team of police officers gathered for a briefing, after which they split up to attend to their assigned duties.

"We will meet back at the station this afternoon, five o'clock, for an update," shouted Matt. "Ryan, can you go back to the station and get on the blower to one of your mates for them to contact the car rental depot? See what they can find out for us?"

"Why? The car came from Heathrow. Never mind. I will see what I can do." Ryan realised Matt was not too familiar with the south of England region.

"I'll meet you back at the station shortly," said Matt. "There is something I need to attend to here first. Bill, have you got a minute, mate?"

Together, they made their way to the crime scene. Matt's thoughts were focused on the wounds of the victim. How the two instruments could have inflicted them. He needed one more look at the wounds, as he stopped the medical examiners before they bagged up the body. It was still a mess and hard to see, but he put his two fingers near the wound on the neck.

"Nasty, don't you think, Bill?" said Matt.

"It doesn't look like a clean cut at all. I can't imagine a knife would make such a wound," said Bill.

"Look at the head injury, though; hold on to your breakfast, mate," said Matt.

"Yes, I see what you mean. Awful; thank you," said Bill as the examiners prepared the corpse. Matt and Bill returned inside.

"The problem here is you and I can see a coincidence between the two weapons and the name of the abandoned car driver. But there is no correlation between the two. The person who had driven the car up could have attacked the victim. Then again, the two cases could be completely independent of each other. It only means something to us because of our Masonic knowledge. We recognise the connection, that's all. To anyone else, there is absolutely nothing in common with any of it." Bill was right.

Matt agreed and reminded Bill that he would return to interview the staff and his guests. A glance at the wall clock as Matt took from his pocket a nicely carved meerschaum calabash.

"Hey! Not in here, Sherlock." Bill pointed to the door.

"Ah, well, it is almost ten o'clock, anyway. I must dash, mate; our Penny's car is in for service," he said as he departed.

Two long blasts on the car horn let Matt's wife, Penny, know he was out-side waiting for her.

"Right on time," she said as she got in the car.

"Come on, Penny, look lively. Where is it this week?" asked Matt.

"We're playing at Barbara's this week, then lunch at the Shoulder," said Penny.

Matt set off along the meandering country lanes that would take them to Bab & Monty Hudson's Dogs Home.

"Have you not heard the news?" asked Matt. "Two bobbies were on night patrol through the village, and they found a dead body in the old brick factory."

"Oh my God!" exclaimed Penny. "Man or woman?"

"It's a man, and it doesn't look like a mugging. Whoever the attacker was, left him penniless but wearing a three-thousand-pound watch," explained Matt.

"I hope Bill is keeping the pub open. It's May-Ling's birthday, so we have planned to go there for lunch after our game," said Penny.

"You should be all right; no need for him to close. Anyway, you know Bill, he will milk it if he can. Business is business," said Matt. He slowed and dropped Penny at her destination.

"I will be in there later. I have some interviews to do," said Matt. The door slammed shut. Twenty dogs or more started barking.

"No wonder Monty keeps leaving her," Matt said to himself, and off he went and made his way back to the station.

Matt entered the station through the two swing doors in his usual noisy way.

"What have we got?" shouted Matt as he walked in.

"Not much, sir. I have contacted the car hire depot in Heathrow, but they were funny about giving information over the phone. So, I contacted Thames Valley and they are going to send someone in there. I have emailed them a copy of the rental agreement and a case note," explained Ryan.

"Good lad. Anything on hotel bookings in the region?" Matt's next question.

"A list of people for you to call here, boss," he said as he passed several notes to Matt. "The Royal in Ingleton had a reservation for last night and tonight for a David Illya. Get this, though: single occupancy and he never checked in."

Matt raised an eyebrow when he heard this. Two drivers on the car rental, single occupancy at the hotel but never checked in. He spun around and stared at Ryan.

"Something is missing about the abandoned car," Matt said in a manner showing that he needed some help.

"Why was it left unlocked by the driver?" volunteered Ryan.

"Yes, why indeed?" asked Matt. "It makes little sense. Keyless start or not?"

"Hang on!" exclaimed Ryan. "Luggage, sir; there was no luggage in the vehicle. If he hadn't checked in, his luggage would still be in the car."

"Or in someone else's car," added Matt as his thoughts deepened.

"So, we have determined where the driver of the abandoned car intended to stay. Now we have to find out why he didn't stay," said Matt.

"The medical examiner says it will be mid-morning tomorrow before they can get a report out. We have the estimated time of death: anywhere between eight and midnight. Doesn't give us much at all, I am afraid," Ryan admitted.

Matt sat and dialled the first number on the list of many. About twenty minutes later:

"I have to go back to the pub now and start interviewing. I popped back to see if the super had anything further for us on a connection between the two cases."

"Start going through the business cards, Ryan. Get a junior to search the companies on the internet. Anything. The smallest detail could be significant for us on this one," Matt said as he made his way to the exit.

It was more like the eve of a national holiday in The Shoulder of Mutton. Customers occupied all the tables in the bar, and the lounge side was also almost full. Matt never realised how many people attended these crime scenes. The staff had already rearranged the furniture in the designated interviewing area. Bill had even moved in some Chinese-style wooden curtains as a barricade from outsiders. Matt knew what he had to do would not be easy, with so many reporters and other nosey people around.

The interviews were with the two members of bar staff who had been on duty last night and then the guests. But first, the manager from the security contractor for the factory had arrived. Bill seated him in the pre-arranged area.

"His name is Baldwin," said Bill. "I can't recall seeing him around the factory site before, but then again, he's the boss, you know."

Matt introduced himself and continued with the interview.

The factory has been empty for two years and is always in darkness. But Matt wanted to know more about the apparent lack of security at the site.

"It's all about costs, financing it; is not cheap to place night or even day guards. This is rural territory. The costs for security are high compared to the risk involved," explained Baldwin.

"How difficult would it be to hook up an electrical supply to light up the reception area at the front of the building?" asked Matt.

"Very difficult these days. We would need permits and approvals from the electricity department. Plus, we would need permission from the council, the health and safety guys," replied Baldwin.

"What? To get the power on for an hour?" exclaimed Matt as a somewhat rhetorical question.

Baldwin nodded his head.

"Sorry, but I don't understand. The factory, yes, is unused but it still has old stocks, machines, tools, and equipment inside. There is a value to protect there?" asked Matt.

"No, sorry, Mr. Baxter. How would anyone remove the equipment or a pallet of house bricks without being seen? The equipment is old technology. That's why they ended up closed down anyway, if you ask me," explained Baldwin.

"So . . ." Matt hesitated. "I don't mean to appear or sound rude here, but what does your company provide? The factory is not producing; no one ever comes. As you say, it's the middle of the rural countryside."

"You should know that the company was never actually liquidated so the authorities don't appoint a receiver or a liquidator. The old lady owner decided on the level of security she felt was needed and we supply the personnel," said Baldwin. "She said she wasn't ready to pay for full-time security, didn't think it was needed. We have an officer who makes rounds in the area and will visit the site every two to three days to make a routine check of the premises. He completes a log sheet and files it in our offices."

"So that brings us to who opened the gates?" asked Matt.

"I have checked before I set off from the office this morning. All the keys were in the safe, and we have not opened the safe since the day before yesterday," replied Baldwin.

"Where are your offices exactly?" asked Matt.

Baldwin extended a business card to Matt. Bill looked at it over Matt's shoulder as he hovered around.

"Heckmondwike," said Matt as he read the card.

"Den-deh-den-derder-den-deh-didder-dehdeh," Bill hummed aloud as he picked up some empty glasses.

Matt and Baldwin stared at Bill.

"Arthur Wood, he was the composer of the theme tune to The Archers on the radio. He was born in Heckmondwike," explained Bill, as if everyone ought to know this piece of trivia.

A word of thanks from Matt and Baldwin left.

Bill sent in the first of his staff, a young girl, Emily, who had worked at the pub for the last two years. She answered Matt's questions and provided an alibi. Her boyfriend collected her from the pub at about 11:30. They went for a kebab for supper in the next village, Ribblesdale, about four miles away.

Next was Charlie; he had worked at the pub for almost three years. Not so easy with Charlie as he admitted he walked back home after he left the pub at about 12:30. He stayed back and had a nightcap with Bill, as they had a few points to sort out for the next few days. Charlie shares an old farmhouse with a couple of his friends who are both overseas on holiday. He left the pub through the entrance to the car park, as this is normal procedure for the staff after-hours.

Matt checked this story with Bill, who collaborated with what Charlie had said. When asked what they had discussed, it was about the guests coming and going over the next few days. It is the Cooper's Wood village festival on the first Saturday of April. Guests have booked the rooms in the pub weeks in advance. Hence, they planned for room cleaning, laundry collections, and food. It seemed reasonable.

Matt made a start on the guests staying at the pub.

Martin and Lesley Thorpe: regulars. They often stayed as Martin has business in Leeds, and Lesley is a keen hiker. They were both in the lounge all night with some friends. Martin had recently won a big contract from the Leeds company. Lesley was quite pleased, as it meant more return hiking trips for her. Their friends booked a taxi and went home around eleven, and Martin and Lesley went to bed and had a good night's sleep. Bill confirmed afterwards that they had consumed a fair amount of alcohol. This could be a reason for their absence outside earlier in the day.

Anthony and Maria Banks: a regular couple. They are self-employed and semi-retired. They like to relax as they travel quite a lot and visit the region regularly. They sometimes stayed for more than a week. Last night, they had an early dinner in the bar and then took a bottle of wine to their room. They were seen outside the pub earlier.

Cyril and Sylvia Jones: another regular couple. They often come up from Wales, as Sylvia's elderly mother still lived in the village, and they like to come and see her every six or eight weeks. They were both out all night, presumably visiting Sylvia's mother. They had been seen outside in the early morning.

Robert and Janet Smalley: their first time. They live in Oakwood, Derby. Janet had recently lost her mother, so they felt they needed to get away for a few days. The previous evening, they claimed that they had met some friends over in The Rainbow pub in Mount Ashton and didn't return until around 1:00 a.m. Bill remembered hearing some noises around that time and he looked outside to see them getting out of a car. They were also outside in the early morning hours.

Finally, the young woman, Phoenix Istaza. She entered the lounge, stood still, and appeared totally innocent as she looked around the room for the intended meeting place. Bill beckoned her and pointed to Matt. She was dressed elegantly casual—her own style. She wore a simple cotton, very well-tailored blouse and denim jeans that fitted and looked better than any attempt by a window dresser on a mannequin on Regent Street or Fifth Avenue.

As Bill had mentioned earlier in the day, she had checked in to the pub on Tuesday. She works as a freelance artist for a German lifestyle magazine. She also does some design work for a fashion house in France. Being exhausted, the previous evening, she had a light meal in her room and fell asleep early. No one had seen her outside in the early morning hours.

It was almost half-past three. This would give Matt enough time to get to the station to prepare for the review meeting. Matt thanked Bill for his cooperation, and as he departed from the pub, he bumped into one of the guests again.

"Oh, I forgot something, Miss Istaza. When you have a minute, could you let me have a copy of your passport, please?" said Matt.

She tried to shout after him, but he was off through the door in a second. The door closed, and she turned to Bill, adopting her most innocent face and body posture.

"Don't worry," said Bill. "It's procedure; you're not from around here. Pass it over, and I will make a photocopy for you."

"Here you are, love," said Bill as he returned her passport. "You're leaving us tomorrow, are you?"

"Yes, I am afraid so. I have to move on to the next location of my assignment," she said, "but I cannot find the key to my car. I don't suppose anyone has handed one in, have they?"

"Nothing so far, sorry. Where did you last have it?" asked Bill.

"It was with me last night when I parked up. I thought I could have dropped it in the car park as I came in," said Phoenix. "I have checked outside again, now after the police interview."

"You looked a bit ruffled when you came through last night, love. Looked like you had been in a barny with your boyfriend," said Connie, who had joined them in the bar area.

"Ruffled . . . ?" asked Phoenix.

"Aye, ruffled, love, as in 'ruffle your feathers,'" said Connie.

Phoenix shrugged her shoulders and thought to herself, *I was not wearing any feathers. How odd the language they speak in this region!* Then she considered what or who was "barny"?

She looked embarrassed at finding herself in this predicament. But this girl knew how to turn on the charm; no doubt about that.

She had such a sweet smile. Yet when it broadened across her face, it was as though all her facial features contributed to the smile. Her demeanour, at first, appeared to be of shyness. But she could soon change and present herself with great confidence.

"I would love to stay longer, as I do like it here, with genuine, down-to-earth people around me," she said. "My work means I spend a lot of time in Paris, Frankfurt, and London, so I don't have so much time for the city people. I love the countryside and the open air, so much better than the city. Unfortunately, I have lost most of today because of the lost car key and police interview."

"We're chokker anyway, love," said Bill.

"Chokker?" asked Phoenix.

"Chokker block. It means full. Full to the rafters." Bill had to explain.

Very odd language, indeed.

The other officers arrived in the briefing room, and they settled down in front of the big whiteboard. The whiteboard remained white. There wasn't a single photo, map, or even a name or scribble mark on there yet.

A few more telephone calls for Matt to make before he announced: "Right, gather around. What do we know?" Matt started the meeting.

A lack of response from everyone showed that there was not much progress made on this case so far at all. Even the door-to-door interviews had produced nothing significant.

Matt opened an evidence bag, which contained the wallet removed earlier from the body. He spread the cards, one by one, out on the table. Ryan then spread out the business cards from the briefcase in the abandoned car. He placed the business cards on the table aligned to the first batch.

"Sir, Michelle has been searching for the companies on the internet. I think we have our first breakthrough. Look at this," said Ryan.

"These are from the car—business cards, company name, MESOL. Look, with offices in Dubai, Jeddah, and Bahrain, all with the driver's name. Now, from the victim, several business cards. Look, a personal card for this Tamara person. But I can't work the address out; it seems they don't show the country."

He scrutinised the address on the card.

"Balat Al-Rashid Building, Sultan Suleiman Street, Musrara. It sounds like the Middle East to me. Arabic. Isn't Musrara in Abu Dhabi?" he asked.

"And the phone number, look a GSM +49, that's Germany. Try it, Ryan," said Matt as he passed the card over.

"It's just ringing out, sir," said Ryan.

"Anyway, it's better than nothing at all. We can try again tomorrow. Let's stay positive," he said. "Now, we've all had a long day. Four o'clock this morning, most of us started. Let's call it a day, get a good night's rest, and come back bright and early tomorrow morning," said Matt.

"Let's hope we have something on the board by then," said Michelle, leader of the support officers.

Matt stood up and moved toward the door; he stopped. "Hey, Ryan, how are you with chatting up beautiful young Mediterranean girls? And I mean beautiful." Matt made Ryan a proposal. Or was it an offer he couldn't refuse?

Matt briefed Ryan and told him to go to the pub later that evening. To see if he could contact the attractive girl staying there. Invite her for a drink, dinner, kebab, put it on expenses but not to get drunk and throw up over her Jimmy Choo shoes.

"If anyone fancies a pint, I am off to The Shoulder for a couple. Then I am heading home for a nice dinner and an early night." Matt picked up his jacket and headed out of the door. He stopped, turned around, and pointed at Ryan. "You'll still be on duty. This is not Surrogate Lovers Limited. And don't milk the exes!" Matt said before he headed off towards the pub.

"Hey up, Matt, anything new?" Bill asked as he pulled a pint of beer.

"Nothing, mate. Hey, where's that French girl? Is she still here? I asked for a copy of her passport, and I don't want her to disappear without leaving it." Matt's eyes focused on the foamy head on the pint of beer.

"It's here." Bill reached up to the top shelf for the piece of notepaper.

"Thanks, Bill. Ryan will be in later. Do you mind passing it to him? Don't let the girl see you. I will lose it if I take it now," explained Matt after he glanced quickly at the paper.

"Will do. And she is Maltese, not French." Bill started his next pull. "She intended to leave tomorrow, but she has lost her car key," said Bill.

"I don't know what she is, mate; it was difficult to get anything out of her during our interview earlier. So, she came here by car and lost her key?" Matt asked. He was now halfway down his first pint, and it was delicious, besides being well deserved.

"Yes, it's parked around the back. Nice motor it is, mate. One of those new German ones, Porsche sports SUV," said Bill.

"I better have a quick look at that," said Matt as he went towards the side entrance that leads to the car park.

There, in the corner, a new Porsche Cayenne Turbo S E-Hybrid Coupé. A cashmere beige paint job with Spyder Design wheels. *Now, that's a beauty*, he thought.

A closer inspection revealed she may well have travelled alone. But why were there two power bank phone chargers on the front passenger's seat? That struck a mental note. *She must have a hell of a job or good business to afford to run one of these*, he thought as he returned inside.

"Your Penny was in here earlier, had lunch with that dog's homeowner.

Babs something, Barbara somebody," resumed Bill with a new topic. "Those two pretty Chinese lasses came in with them," Bill continued.

Matt, not paying much attention, said, "Aye, they had been playing that Chinese checkers game, Mah Bong, something or other. Did I hear that other pretty lass come back in here now a few minutes ago? Bill, did you see her?"

"Yes, I did. She came through the lounge entrance into the other room. She darted straight upstairs to the bedrooms. I called after her, but she seemed to ignore me. It looked like she had been crying," said Bill.

The door opened, and in came several of Matt's colleagues. They also needed a drink after work, because of their early start and strenuous day. Ryan had to dash off home to prepare himself for an eventful evening, about which he had been very secretive.

"Get their drinks in, please, Bill, my tab," said Matt.

His colleagues were the perfect distraction Matt needed for him to make further investigations on the female guest.

An old building like The Shoulder of Mutton, unfortunately, featured old creaky floorboards. As Matt ascended the wooden staircase, it proved quite tricky for him not to give his presence away. Added to this, he didn't even know which room the girl was in. This attempt could become quite embarrassing if any of the other guests were to find him snooping around. Suddenly, around the corner, a door opened, and he positioned himself out of view.

Then he heard a voice: "*J'avais l'intention de me rendre à Londres en voiture demain mais je ne peux pas partir maintenant, ce sera samedi ou Dimanche. Au revoir.*"

It was the girl. She headed downstairs. Matt was close behind her and when he reached downstairs, he used the lounge door exit. He made his way back around the premises and through the car park and entered through the bar door. Bill was so busy, he never even noticed Matt's movements.

Phoenix was over near the fireplace in the bar. Bill served her a glass of wine on a tray. She must have something, this girl…

Matt joined his colleagues and blended into the conversations. All the time, he tried to catch the eye of the girl.

She checked her phone frequently. *Nothing unusual for a young woman these days*, he thought as he made his way over to greet her.

"Hello," said Matt, as he sat down beside her. "I got the copy of your passport, thank you, and I wanted to apologise if I appeared rude to you this afternoon. It's not often we find a dead body around these parts. So, you said you work for a German company. How did that happen?"

Phoenix threw back her long wavy hair, smiled, and placed her slender fingers on top of Matt's hand. "Hello, Mr. Baxter. There is no need to apologise. I understand completely. I don't think murders often happen anywhere, do they? And as far as my job goes, I work with a French fashion magazine company, and we have an office in Germany. I work with both offices. It's a very interesting job. I love art, fashion, and clothes, and I get to travel. I got the opportunity through my father's contacts," she said.

"Who said it was a murder?" asked Matt. He raised an eyebrow.

"Sorry, I assumed it was a murder with all the activity and the number of police and medical people around all day. Oh dear, does that make me look like a suspect now?" she said.

Matt frowned.

"By the way, miss, I must also ask you to leave your forwarding address with us before you move on from here. The landlord, Bill, said you are leaving tomorrow. So, please leave your permanent home address if you don't mind," said Matt.

"By all means. Let me write it down for you. Do you have one of those sexy black books that we see police officers use all the time on the television? You know, with the black elastic strap…" said Phoenix as she mimicked stretching the black elastic strap.

She's quite a naughty girl, this one, thought Matt as he handed her a blank piece of paper. He winked as he tapped the end of his nose with his sexy black book.

"By the way, is everything all right, miss? Bill mentioned you looked a little upset when you returned a few minutes ago," said Matt.

"Yes, I am fine; thank you. I was hoping to meet up with someone over the weekend in London, but he has to leave tomorrow," she explained.

"Boyfriend, eh? I am sure he will be there waiting for you," Matt said, trying to comfort her.

"Not a boyfriend, but someone special in my life. By the way, there may be a change to my schedule, as I cannot find my car key. I will be here tomorrow, or at least until I can get my car started," she said.

"Please let me know if you need any help, Miss Istaza. Is it a keyless start?" asked Matt.

"Yes, it is. I hate them," said Phoenix. "I have to get back home to Paris before Monday. But my office wants me to attend one more assignment near here before I leave to go back," she said.

She delivered her broad smile again as she handed back the piece of paper.

"There, my Paris address and phone number and also the number for my German office. And please, call me Phoenix. All my friends call me Phoenix or Julie," she said.

"So, if you work for a company in France or Germany, why do you own a right-hand drive vehicle?" Matt was intrigued.

"Oh, the car outside," replied Phoenix as she pointed back over her shoulder. "That's the family car that we keep in London. When I go back to Paris, I am most likely to take the train through the tunnel, so I will leave this car at our apartment in London. The train is so easy, two and a half hours and I am at Gare Du Nord and my apartment is in the 16th anyway."

She pointed to the address on the paper and used this very casual reference to the fact that she lived in one of the most exclusive and swanky areas of Paris, the 16th arrondissement.

"I will be here all evening, of course, with no car. Unfortunately, for me, it's a nice dinner and an early night. It doesn't seem to be such a lively place around here," she said.

"This is the Yorkshire Dales, miss. Life is what you make it around here," Matt said, and with that, he excused himself as he stood up and walked towards his colleagues. He stopped and turned back towards Phoenix.

"By the way, where does Julie come from?" asked Matt.

"From my school days in Paris. Some of the students were from Asia, and they had difficulty pronouncing my name. A girl from Thailand called me Julie. I reminded her of Julie Andrews from *The Sound of Music*, with my hairstyle," explained Phoenix. "It stayed with me over the years, I guess."

As Matt turned towards the bar, Bill stared at him.

"Single malt, Matt?" he chuckled.

"Give me another pint, and then I am off home. Penny is waiting for me." Matt grinned.

What on earth is going on with this girl? Matt thought as he started his next pint.

Not long after, Matt said farewell to his colleagues and gave a polite nod to Phoenix. She returned the gesture. The rest of the officers also left. Some planned to go home, and some planned to go for dinner elsewhere to celebrate a birthday.

So now the pub was almost empty, and Bill's attention turned to the beautiful girl, all alone, by the fireplace.

Message alert on Bill's phone:

> RYAN WILL COME 2NIGHT. MAKE SURE HE MEETS THE GIRL. WATCH HIM FOR ME!

Bill smiled to himself and put his phone back in his pocket. Connie walked behind the bar.

"What's making you giggle away like a teenage schoolboy, as if I didn't know? You're still the same as when I met you thirty-five years ago, Bill Cooper," were Connie's first words.

She stared over towards Phoenix.

"Nay. Right. If you're staying down here for a bit, I want to go and freshen up for this evening. If that young Cockney copper, Ryan, comes in, buzz me upstairs, please, Connie," said Bill as he left the bar area.

Now, almost all alone, Phoenix stood up and walked towards the bar. She sat down on a high stool as she finished her glass of wine.

"Good evening. May I have another glass of wine, please?" said Phoenix as she placed the glass on the bar counter.

"Of course, love," said Connie. "Has my husband been misbehaving? I understand you are leaving us tomorrow. Where are you off to, love? Anything on your car key yet?" asked Connie, three questions in one sentence.

"Well, I was due to go to London, but without a car key, it looks as though I am stuck here, and I will have to find another hotel. Is there anywhere nearby? I don't want to go to that posh place over the hill; it's too far and I don't like the road," said Phoenix.

"You're in luck, love. We'll have an early checkout. Their plans have changed, and they have to leave first thing tomorrow," explained Connie.

"That would be wonderful." Phoenix handed over a gold credit card. "Put the charges on here, please," said Phoenix.

Connie delivered a fresh glass of wine with one hand and took the card with the other. After a few minutes, she returned the card with the transaction slip.

"I've booked you in until Sunday, love. We have a village community day on Saturday, and that might be a bit of fun for you, something different. If not, and you leave on Saturday, we will refund the charges back through your card. Don't worry, love," said Connie.

Phoenix wouldn't worry about this.

"I hope I can get some more work done during the next few days. I cannot do anything without transport. The car man in London said it would be tomorrow before they can get someone over to attend to my car," said Phoenix.

The conversation turned to the upcoming community day. Women's talk, as Bill put it: what to wear, shoes, dress, if one outfit would even be enough for the entire day. Connie found herself in a very relaxed situation. So much so that she poured herself a glass of wine and continued the conversation. Not long after, Bill returned to the bar, dressed in fresh clothes and smelling of Old Spice.

Bill and Connie found themselves busy enough with the evening trade, so Phoenix turned her attention back to her phone.

But not for long as Ryan Clarke entered with a clear announcement, as the door banged shut after him. He made his way to the bar and ordered a gin and tonic with lots of ice. He raised his glass towards Phoenix: "Good evening, cheers," he said.

And as Phoenix lifted her head to expose a magnificent long slender neck, he almost dropped his glass. *My goodness*, he thought, *the boss wasn't wrong about this one.*

"Good evening, cheers," she replied and smiled back at him.

Ryan recognised her beauty immediately and was speechless. He trembled as he started his gin and tonic.

Bill entered behind the bar and nodded to Ryan. "Hello, Ryan. Are you well?" he said.

"As well as can be expected. Thank you, Bill," replied Ryan.

"Oh, you are different," said Phoenix, as she tipped her glass towards Ryan.

Ryan turned around and looked over each shoulder and turned back again. "Sorry, are you talking to me?" said Ryan.

"Yes. Your voice is different," she said.

"Yes, I am from Essex," said Ryan. He explained the geography of London and the rest of the south of England.

With formalities over, their conversation went on. The major topic of the lost car key came up again.

"You phoned them in London. Why?" asked Ryan.

"That's the address on the website. I forget where they said their repairmen would come from, two hours away," said Phoenix.

"That could be anywhere. Manchester. One and a half hours, Leeds is an hour. Ooh, it might be Sheffield; that's about two hours." Connie joined the conversation.

"Yes, that's it," exclaimed Phoenix.

"I hope you don't mind me saying, but you have a very unusual name," said Ryan. "Where are you from?"

"No, I don't mind at all. I often get asked. The name Istaza is actually Maltese. My parents named me Phoenix at the request of my grandfather." She was getting bored already.

Several deliberate leg movements and she completely distracted Ryan. Had he noticed that she hadn't even answered his question?

"And now, home is where, Phoenix?" asked Ryan.

"I travel a lot with work, which I enjoy, but when not away, I live in Paris," said Phoenix.

"You lucky girl. May I buy you a drink, Phoenix?" asked a very polite Ryan.

"Yes, please, excuse me while I visit the ladies' restroom," she said as she glided herself off the high stool.

Bill was straight over. "You best watch yourself with her, lad. A ball of fire, that one, if you ask me," he said. "Here, your boss asked me to pass you this; it's a copy of her passport. You better hide it before she gets back."

"Matt said she was a tasty piece, all right, but I never imagined this." Ryan showed his excitement.

"Hey, you're working. Don't forget, young man," Bill said in his voice of authority, an index finger pointed straight between Ryan's eyes.

"Hey Bill, this copy only shows her name and passport number, mate. And it's not very clear. Can you get us another copy with date and place of birth, you know, the usual stuff?" said Ryan.

He timed it right as Phoenix entered back into the room and returned to her stool.

"Well, if you don't have plans, may I invite you to join me for dinner here this evening?" asked Ryan.

Before she answered, "Come on, let's have another drink and then go through to the dining room," Ryan looked for Bill to refill their glasses.

Oakwood Lodge was the first of a row of four cottages that looked down over the village of Cooper's Wood from the front. They provided beautiful views over the Yorkshire Dales from the rear. The drawback of this was that they could get hit by chilly winds from both directions in the winter months. Matt and Penny sat with their feet up and a bottle of wine between them as Penny watched her favourite TV show. Matt pretended to be interested.

The credits rolled, and Penny, who seldom wanted to hear about Matt's work, made this an exception. The abandoned car threw up more mystery to her than the discovery of the dead body.

The conversation got around to the guests staying at the pub. In particular about an attractive young lady that had checked into the pub a few days ago. Matt informed his wife that he had interviewed her already.

"See the motor she drives, Penny? Beauty," said Matt.

"Her or the car?" asked Penny.

"Ryan is meeting up with her tonight at the pub. See if he can get any information out of her. It seems odd that she arrived on Tuesday, stayed at the pub for a couple of nights, and in the factory opposite, a brutal murder takes place. When I interviewed her, it was tough to get anything out of her. Funnily enough, she barged into the pub earlier this evening and shot upstairs. Bill said it looked as though she had been crying," said Matt.

"Poor Ryan, bless him. If it's the same girl Barbara and I saw this afternoon sitting outside the pub, he has got his hands full there. A beautiful girl, she was. Lovely long, wavy, dark brown orangey hair; not auburn, more titian."

Matt stared at her. *Titian. What on earth is titian?*

"She had a long slender Audrey Hepburn neck and legs up to there and back again."

"Yep, sounds like her," said Matt.

Penny looked at him from the corner of her eye.

"I even heard her say the word 'beastly,'" said Matt. They both laughed as he topped up their wine glasses.

THREE

Bright and early next morning, Matt Baxter arrived at the station. He pinned several pieces of information from the previous day on the whiteboard.

In the middle of the board, Matt placed a photograph of the deceased. Small yellow sticky notes covered the forehead and neck wounds. He also pinned copies of the car rental agreement and the various business cards. He added a list of the names of the guests who had stayed at the pub. Other than the coincidence of the business cards, there was almost nothing to go on. Using a marker pen, Matt wrote:

Weapon(s):
chisel
mallet

Matt considered the weapons and how they may have inflicted the head wounds. It didn't need any elaborating, but Matt's mind was still going over how someone could inflict the wound to the neck. He couldn't take away the thought of the third of the three first-degree Masonic working tools. The twenty-four-inch gauge, how? Or, as Bill pointed out, it could just be a big coincidence. But Matthew Baxter does not believe in coincidences in the crime world, ever.

Not long after, the rest of the team had gathered, and the last one who arrived was a tired-looking Ryan. Matt carried on, but he wondered about the outcome of the previous evening's meeting.

As expected, it was a quick briefing.

"Let's pick up where we left off yesterday. Get out there but be back here at three o'clock this afternoon," Matt shouted above the noise of tables and chairs moving. "Not you, Ryan. You're coming with me." Matt growled at him.

As they drove off in Matt's car, he reached underneath the dash and pulled out the cherry light, which he stuck on the car roof.

"Rush hour," he said to Ryan with a wink.

"How did you get on last night?" asked Matt.

"Well, I got there, as you said. I went into the bar, and there, sitting on a high stool, this beautiful girl. You were right there, boss. She put on a very good display of her merits, I can tell you." Ryan explained.

He still sounded quite excited by his experience of the previous evening.

"Not all that . . . what did you find out from her? Work, background, parents. She's from which country? Where is she going? Where does she live?" asked Matt as he shook his head in disbelief.

"Oh, sorry, sir; you want the boring bit." Ryan smiled and winked. "Okay, boss; you know about her work, anyway. She lives in Paris when she's not travelling and that's something to do with the clothes and fashion work she does. She said nothing about her family and when they came up in conversation, she avoided the topic."

"She told me she doesn't speak any other European languages, no French, German, or Italian; nothing."

"She speaks French, and not bad either. I heard her on the telephone upstairs in the pub yesterday evening," said Matt with a very glib tone to his voice.

"Well, if you knew that, sir, why did you ask me to find out?" asked a confused Ryan.

"To see what she is like at telling the truth," replied Matt.

"We had dinner together and enjoyed a very stimulating and varied conversation. We talked about several subjects, ranging from jazz music to modern street art. From adventure sports to watching old Laurel and Hardy films," replied Ryan.

What on earth is he going on about? thought Matt. Laurel and Hardy films. Ryan must have dreamed that she was even interested in Laurel and Hardy films.

It was about an hour's drive to reach the medical examiner's office. At once, they dressed in their clean white room suits and entered the examination area to see the body. It wasn't the first time Ryan had been exposed to this scenario, as the procedure was part of police training. The extent of the brutal inflictions was now more visible, which came as a bit of a jolt to Ryan. It was a good job last night's grilled trout stayed in place.

The examiner showed them around the body and highlighted the wounds. It appeared Matt's assumptions on how the murderer had used the weapons were quite accurate. He showed the wound on the neck. This was the initial attack, and it was inflicted with a very odd-shaped, sharp weapon, but not a knife or a blade. They had analysed the condition of the cut flesh around the wound. Severe bruising occurred in the same area of impact. The murderer had intended this attack to take the wind out of the victim and shock him only. The fatal blow was to the forehead. The examiner recognised several fractures around the surface. This showed that the attacker delivered more than one blow. Examination of the weapons showed up minute traces of blood on the chisel point. The attacker had wiped the weapons clean with some type of cleaning agent or chemical. These weapons had already been sent to another department for further analysis. Unfortunately, the weapons showed no fingerprints.

As they left the examination room, the examiner called over to them. "I assume you have arranged for DNA samples of all the overnight guests who stayed at the pub that night. We will also need DNA samples from the landlord, the landlady, and the bar staff. We will email our full report to you after lunch," said the examiner.

"Get one of your assistants over to Cooper's Wood as soon as possible to collect the DNA you want. It's only an hour in the car," said Matt as they walked out.

"Typical," said Matt as they reached the car.

Matt dropped Ryan at the station, and then he made his way over to the pub. As he arrived, Bill was placing the Today's Specials blackboard outside the main entrance.

Matt also thought about how he could get a closer look inside Phoenix's car.

"Morning, Matt; how are you today?" The usual friendly greeting from Bill.

"Can't grumble, mate, can't grumble. Got a pot of tea there, please, Bill? I understand Miss Malta is staying for a couple more days," Matt inquired.

"Yes, she has extended until Sunday," explained Bill as he disappeared into the kitchen area.

"So much for needing to be back home by Monday. By the way, can you let me have a list of the home addresses of your guests who stayed over on Wednesday night; just for our file, like?" asked Matt.

"I have made it already, mate. I knew you would need it," said Bill as he passed over a piece of notepaper.

"By the way, the CSU will come over later. They need DNA of you, the staff, and the guests; well, from those who are still here," said Matt.

Matt heard a female voice; it was an accent he had learned to recognise.

"I told you yesterday. I can't find the key. No, it's a keyless start. I hate it. I need the key to open the door. They said this morning sometime . . . Shef something, someone said last night, it's got something to do with a day of the week . . . yes, that's it. Wednesday. Last week, what for? Okay, how was it? Of course, I will let you know. Love you too." Phoenix had still not sorted the problem with the car key.

"Good morning, Miss Istazi. May I assist you in any way?" Matt offered.

"These damn keyless start cars!" she exclaimed. "The dealer in London said it would be today before they get someone here," she said, very distraught. "Where are they?"

"The dealer will have called their regional office and they will get their service people on it. It will take a couple of hours, three at the most. They will reset the locking system and provide you with a new key," explained Matt.

"Bill, bring me another cup and saucer, please, mate. I have company." Matt beckoned to Phoenix to sit and join him.

"Now, Ms. Istazi. When are you going to tell me the truth, young lady?" Matt started.

A startled Phoenix immediately turned to him and screwed up her eyes. "I am telling you the truth. I have nothing to lie to you about," she said.

"A freelance artist; working for a French fashion magazine and driving a hundred-thousand-pound motor car. And you claim you cannot find the ignition key. Are you sure you have been completely honest with me?" asked Matt.

"Mr. Baxter, you invited me to drink a cup of tea with you. I assumed it was a gesture of goodwill to destress my current anxiety. I didn't realise it would be another interview, and if I had known, then I would have ordered my own cup of tea," she exclaimed as she slammed down the cup and walked away.

Bill had observed everything from inside the doorway. He stared at Matt.

"She'll be all right; she's stressed!" exclaimed Matt. "I'll ask our desk officer to get onto the Porsche dealer in Sheffield and see what we can do for her. Wait for her to calm down a bit and let her know, please, Bill."

Matt returned to his newspaper and he hoped for another chance later in the day.

"l will tell her. She's moving into the big room in ten minutes. She will be busy for a couple of hours, I bet. I have never seen so many clothes for one girl. The cleaners are getting the room ready now. I'll call you if anything changes," shouted Bill as he walked away.

But Matt thought it would still be worthwhile to be in the area when the technicians arrived to sort out the car.

There was still the question of the abandoned vehicle. Ryan had arranged for someone to go to the rental company at Heathrow airport this morning. That report should be back later in the day and could show where he arrived from. A lot of travellers get their tickets sent to their phones these days, but there was no phone found either.

Whoever hired the car drove up past Oxford and stopped off at Leamington Spa, so they took the scenic route to avoid the M1. If he set off with a full tank of fuel, by the time he reached this area, he would be almost empty. That meant that he would have filled up before going any farther. The only petrol station he would see as he came through this way was the one at Shackleton Bottom. It is doubtful the driver knew this region, so he wouldn't have taken a chance with the car being so low on fuel. For sure, he would have filled up there. Matt looked at his watch. He wondered if he could be over to the petrol station and back again before the technicians arrived. It's worth a try. *Better than sitting here, drinking tea all morning*, he thought.

The petrol station at Shackleton Bottom always appeared the same.

Beyond the rickety main gate entrance, it comprised a two-pump forecourt and a shop. The shop was always well-stocked with cardboard cartons of all types of tinned food. It was perfect for picking up anything needed for a camping holiday.

On the left-hand side was a small workshop identified by two old wooden doors, wide open. A stack of tyres held one door open and a spinning KEYS CUT WHILE U WAIT sign held the other door open. It was a joke within the community that they might have a key cut here but doubtful they would risk any car repairs. On the other side of the forecourt, the right side, there was a two-storey accommodation where the father and son lived.

The old man walked with a stooped back caused by lifting boxes of baked beans, day after day. The son, the weird one, as claimed by many locals, always sat alone on the forecourt. He would stay in his chair for almost the entire day, wearing his headphones as he listened to, presumably, music.

Matt Baxter arrived in his Range Rover, and he parked away from the fuel pumps. Whenever a vehicle arrived for fuel, there was always the same routine.

"*Customer, Dad!*" shouted the young man as he stood up out of his chair.

"Pump won't reach," he shouted to Matt as he got out of his car. Matt ignored him. The son then commenced a debate about who was going to serve the client. Matt couldn't tolerate such a lengthy debate and he interrupted their discussion.

"Does either of you recall seeing an Audi A6 come here for petrol sometime on Wednesday afternoon?" he started.

"Uh, this abart th' car, cops found t'other side o' hill," said the old man. He had a broad Yorkshire accent.

"Answer the question, please," said Matt.

"Any ID?" said the son. Matt ignored him.

"Yes, someone came in here and filled up on Wednesday afternoon. I remember it was about three o'clock, teatime. He used the toilets while Tom filled his tank," said the old man.

"How did he pay for his petrol?" was Matt's next question.

"I remember he paid using a card. I remember it well because he showed me his phone. It was very smart, and he said he could pay me using his phone, but I wouldn't accept it. Anyway, he was all right with paying me and gave me his card."

Tom fidgeted with his headphones and awkwardly placed them on his head as he went inside the small workshop, only to reappear a few seconds later, once more adjusting his headphones. Matt noticed his unusual behaviour.

"May I see a copy of the card transaction receipt, please?" requested Matt.

"Yes, sure you can. Come in and don't worry about our Tom," replied the old man.

The old man looked through a box full of card receipts, and Matt wondered just how many customers they serve here. After all, it was quite remote.

"Did the lady with him use the toilets also?" was Matt's next question.

"Lady, lady, there wasn't a lady with him. I never saw a lady. Did you see a lady with him, Tom?" asked the old man.

Tom shook his head. "Nah, Dad."

"Here it is."

The old man passed the credit card receipt to Matt, to which he examined, "May I take a copy?" and Matt lined up his phone.

"Of course, you can. Is there anything else? Do you want any beans?" added the old man.

"Did he say much, talk about the weather, where he was going, where he came from?" Matt opened up the interview, as the old man seemed helpful enough.

"Please, sit down, and I will put the kettle on and make a cup of tea," offered the old man.

Matt scanned around the tea-making area and hoped the tea was going to be brewed in a teapot and poured into cups. While waiting, Matt excused himself and went to make use of the toilet. When he returned, a cup of tea had been poured and waited for him. He sipped the tea; it was dreadful, made in the cup. He shivered.

"He wasn't from around here, that's for sure. We could tell by his accent, as it sounded funny. I cannot remember hearing it before and I mentioned it to Tom? He said he had driven up from London and he was tired. He also asked me about Ingleton as he had booked in that posh hotel there, about thirty miles, other side of Ashton," explained the old man. "Anyway, I told him he is on the right road, keep straight and go over Mount Ashton hill. He got in his car and drove off. Pleasant enough chap."

"He drove away smartish. I said to Tom he will soon slow down when he reaches the bends in the road," concluded the old man.

"Did he sound French or German, the accent he spoke with?" asked Matt.

"No, not German. I recognise German as we get a lot of them in here. We also get French and Italian. No, this was odd. It reminded me of the crazy guy from about twenty years ago. We often saw him on the television. He had a moustache, held a big cigar in one hand and a rifle in the other hand," described the old man.

"You've been most helpful. Thank you very much and thanks for the tea," said Matt as he stood up.

"That Wednesday was a very odd day. First, this foreign chap comes here. Then later in the afternoon, around five o'clock, it was the first time I haven't had to fight with Tom over who will pump the petrol." The old man started another story.

"This very smart-looking woman came here; she got out of the car, took our Tom's breath away, mind. Tom talked to her, and we could tell she is also not from around here, and I don't mean she is from Hull or Liverpool. Tom said she was Italian, or Spanish."

"Can you have a go at remembering the car she was driving, or at least the colour or type of car, estate, was it?" asked Matt.

"German," said the old man. "I am never sure which brand these days. I can remember the colour all right . . . a right nice light brown it was, mind you, it suited the lady driver. I will say that. She had the most beautiful dark brown-orangey hair." Some more valuable information from the old man.

"Milky coffee, our Tom calls it; don't you, Tom?" he said. "The car . . . not the hair, he has another description for that; don't you, Tom?"

"Anything else you can think of?" asked Matt.

"Aye," he said. "We closed about quarter to eight that night; football was coming on at eight. A few minutes after the kick-off, we thought we heard some noises outside. It must have been on the telly, as when Tom looked outside, he said he couldn't see anything."

"And Tom didn't sleep well that night, did you, Tom? Mind you, it's not surprising if he was still thinking about the Italian girl. But he said to me, the next morning about eight o'clock, he heard a car come to a screeching stop outside. A man jumped out and ran to the toilets. He wasn't in there for more than two minutes and he came back out, got in the car, and they drove off."

What a very useful visit; they notice everything, thought Matt as he announced his farewell. The old man seemed to be harmless enough, and he had provided some very useful information. Not so sure about the son though.

As Matt walked towards his vehicle, he noticed Tom was bent over down the side of the workshop, near the rotating *keys cut* sign. What on earth was he up to?

"Oi!" shouted Matt.

"Plug come out," replied Tom as he stood up, holding an electrical plug in one hand, his trusty smartphone and headphones attached in the other.

What's he up to? Doesn't the wind make them rotate, thought Matt.

———————————

Matt returned to The Shoulder of Mutton, by now it was almost lunchtime.

"You ought to bring your bed in here," said Bill as Matt walked towards the entrance.

Matt smiled back and gave Bill a thumbs-up hand gesture as he entered the pub.

Phoenix was sitting by the fireplace, where she waited for the car technicians. She saw Matt as he approached. She immediately stood up and apologised for her behaviour earlier in the day. She had received two pieces of bad news in a short period recently, and she was distraught. Matt didn't push her on details and thought it would be foolish to create a scene and have her walk away again at this stage.

He sat down near the window and ordered some lunch while he read a few messages on his phone. No attention from the girl. After a few minutes, her phone rang.

"Oh, wonderful, yes, that's right. In? In what? Yes, it is an old pub. I don't know the village so well, but it's opposite an old factory." She paused. "If you need it, I can share the location on maps. Oh, no data connection here, I see, okay. Yes, come past the railway station and about 600 meters, it's opposite. The railway line continues through the old brickworks. Yes, quite large, but the car park is behind. You will see some picnic tables in front. Thank you. I will wait outside," said Phoenix.

"They're almost here," she said to anyone who was listening, and she held her phone close to her chest.

"Let me know if you need any help, miss," offered Matt.

"Thank you. I will wait outside, so I don't miss them," she said as she passed Matt's table.

He adjusted his seating position, so he had a view of oncoming vehicles. *An excellent morning's work*, he thought to himself. If it hadn't been so early in the day, he would have had a pint!

Less than five minutes passed, and a white van slowed down as it approached the pub. Matt could see someone on the passenger side holding a large piece of paper; a map. He pointed to the pub sign. The van slowed down further and parked up outside. Two technicians got out of the van and met with Phoenix. They could not believe their luck, and they all walked off to the rear car park through the stone archway. The next few minutes, for Matt Baxter, were all about timing. He waited and waited. Bill came through to the bar.

"Them Porsche fellas got here then. That's not bad, you know, is it? But what do you expect when you pay that kind of money for a car?" said Bill.

"Do you think I should go outside and see if she needs anything else?" Matt said as he stood up and made his way to the exit door.

He stood by the doorway to the toilet and observed the situation. The car doors opened; no alarms sounded. The access control panel is a box, usually in the car's rear. To access this box meant they had to open the rear luggage area. Matt hoped it would reveal something; luggage—but whose luggage?

Here we go. Matt made his way over to the car.

"Hello, Phoenix. Is everything all right here? Do you need any help?" It was the first time Matt had addressed her as Phoenix; did she even recognise it?

"We are all right, thank you," she replied.

Matt made his way closer to the rear of the car. The technicians opened the rear tailgate, and Matt could see inside. There was a medium-sized black suitcase. His eyes lit up. The technician lifted it out and placed it by the side of the car. Matt twisted his neck to see if he could get more information, but there was none. No airline luggage label, no address label. He looked closer inside the rear of the car and there he saw something. A discarded airline luggage label, the three-letter airport code was half hidden by an old shoebox. Matt didn't want to reach in and move the box, so he tried to make out the three letters. The first letter was B; then E, but it could also have been a P or an R.

He moved closer, but if he moved too close, he would be in the way of the technicians and raise suspicions. Phoenix stood close by with her arms folded. She waited and watched every move the technicians made with one eye and every move Matt made with the other eye.

"Is that all the luggage you have, miss? That's not much for your stay, is it?" he said as he pointed to the black suitcase.

Phoenix rolled her eyes. She realised Matt was insinuating something. She crouched down and unzipped the bag.

"There, see for yourself," she said as she presented the contents for his examination.

Damn! Paintbrushes, tubes of paint, canvas materials, several fashion magazines. No ladies' or gentleman's business attire. After closing the cover, he stood up and walked to stand at the side of Phoenix. He also folded his arms, school principal fashion.

"There has been a murder in this village, miss; you are a stranger to this community, and I have a job to do. My offer of help, should you need any, is still there. I will be in the bar, finishing my lunch." Matt turned around and walked away.

Halfway to the entrance and he heard the engine roar as it started up. Matt turned around and observed a very lucky technician who got a lovely hug from the beautiful girl.

Back at the police station, the autopsy report arrived just a few minutes prior to Matt.

"Right, let's get you all up to speed. The forensics team will arrange DNA samples of Bill and Connie, the bar staff, and the guests," said Matt.

"I just received a phone call from Connie at the pub. The forensics team arrived there about ten minutes ago," interrupted Michelle.

Once again, after another review, the situation was still about the same. Matt revealed what he had discovered earlier at the petrol station. He mentioned nothing about the luggage tag he had seen earlier in the car. It didn't contribute anything at this stage.

"Push on, people," announced Matt. "We need something soon."

Ryan joined Matt in his office for a closed-door meeting. Ryan's effort and input so far on this case had impressed Matt. Before they knew it, they both recognised several people leaving the building. A glance at the wall clock supplied the reason. Almost six o'clock already.

Matt went home to spend some time with Penny and their son, Henry. He had joined them for dinner that evening and would stay over to help Bill and Connie at the pub the next day. Matt enjoyed having a few bottles of beer with his son on these occasions—sitting at home, not being disturbed by anyone or anything. An early evening spring shower of rain had dampened the grass on the rear porch. The cool evening was perfect for sitting around a barbeque as they caught up on family stories. A heady aroma filled the atmosphere—a unique mixture of vanilla, brandy, and blackberries with burning pork fat. Matt provided the more pleasant aromas from his Dunhill ruby bark white spot burning some Firedance flake, and Henry contributed as he flipped the sausages and burgers on the grill. The wind changed direction and forced the smoke trail over the fence.

Mick, the next-door neighbour, appeared over the wooden fence:

"What's that smell?" he asked. His wife, Pauline, appeared alongside him.

"It smells delicious," she said.

"Come on over, you two," shouted Matt.

"Throw another prawn on the barbie, Henry," said Matt, to tease him.

"Never mind, throw another prawn, throw me another stubbie. It gets hot standing over this grill," said Henry.

"I would love to come over, but we are off down to t'shoulder. Are you coming down later?" asked Mick.

"Happen not, mate; we will have to wait and see," Matt continued as he puffed away.

"Sounds like a good idea to me, Dad. I hear there's quite an attractive Italian woman staying at the pub these last few days," said Henry.

"Aye, there is . . . and she is a bit more than attractive, I don't mind saying," said Matt. He turned around to check on the whereabouts of his wife, "and not woman, mind. She's about your age."

"Are we having a stroll down there after dinner?" asked Henry as a broad smile appeared across his face. "It will be handy for me to see what Bill has got lined up for tomorrow's events."

"And for you to see if it's true about the girl . . . ?" Matt followed on.

The evening went on, and the Baxter family ended up with a visit to the local pub.

Bill's pub was never short of atmosphere. It was almost part of the furniture. A lot of the atmosphere actually comes from the people who use the bar rooms. The constant chatter inside conjures up a natural feeling of warmth and friendliness.

Phoenix stood near the bar as she talked to some local people. Unfortunately, they obscured Henry's view but he still managed to notice her, and he made it quite clear. Phoenix, likewise, noticed Henry. She stood opposite him as she sipped her cocktail; looked like a martini. It could have been a Gibson.

"Is that the one?" he asked his father.

Matt swivelled his head around from one side to the other as he looked around the room.

"What do you think?" asked Matt.

"Hey up, Jimbo; what time can you come in tomorrow?" asked Bill.

"It could be I stay here all night yet, Bill." He nudged Bill and nodded towards Phoenix.

"Hahaha," Bill laughed and said, "I can't understand it; we're not usually as busy as this on a Friday night."

"Must be because of the village festival tomorrow, mate," said Matt.

"Any news, Matt?" asked Bill.

"Bugger all; it's baffling. It's the weekend now, so knowing the lazy buggers over in Leeds, we won't get anything else until next week," said Matt.

"They got all the DNA they needed earlier this afternoon. You won't see the results from that until Wednesday at the earliest; it could even be Thursday," said Bill.

As Matt and Bill talked together, Henry noticed that the pretty girl glanced in his direction. Their eyes met several times. This forced a quick facial expression from both of them. The people she had been talking to moved away to find a seat, and he thought this was his opportunity.

"Hello, are they looking after you?" he asked.

"Hello," replied Phoenix. "They are such lovely people, friendly and helpful. I have found most people here to be that way."

"Is there anything I can help you with? Can I get you another drink?" asked Henry.

"Thank you, but I already have one," she said as she pointed to a fresh cocktail sitting on the bar. "Allow me to buy you one; you've almost finished that beer."

Henry accepted her offer and, whilst waiting, they introduced themselves.

"The gentleman was explaining to me how to reach Ingleton avoiding the horrible hill road. I drove over it on Wednesday evening, and it was quite scary," she said.

"Yes, there are two other ways. Whichever one you take adds about thirty to forty minutes. Quite a detour and can be quite busy, as many people avoid the hill road. If you get caught behind a tractor on the other two roads, it can take forever. Take my advice and take the hilltop road. Drive slowly, no rush," explained Henry. "If you went during the evening, it can be quite dangerous."

"Yes, it was an early evening when I went over on Wednesday and came back in the dark. That was even more scary. To make things worse, it was raining so heavy, you know, where the long straight road is on the top. When I got back here someone said something about some dogs and cats up there," said Phoenix.

Henry stared into her eyes; she stared back.

"I felt sorry for the poor things, getting caught out in that storm," continued Phoenix.

Henry was speechless, just for a few seconds, and then, with a smirk on his face, he asked, "When are you going to Ingleton next? I don't mind driving you there if it makes you feel more comfortable."

"That is so sweet of you, thank you," she said, and she moved to stand closer to Henry. "I will let you know . . . and why are you smiling at me so much?"

She provided Henry with a perfect opportunity to open up a topic of conversation, animal-related or otherwise, whilst the other occupants went about their own business.

Penny was already deep in conversation with Barbara, about why her husband had left her again or how it is such a struggle to keep the stray dogs' home functioning. Matt discussed with Bill about murder suspects or the next meeting at their lodge.

Matt Baxter frequently diverted his attention though. There's a lot one can learn from body language.

FOUR

Henry suggested a family breakfast at the pub. He claimed it was Bill's original idea so that he could start early in the day. But the mother knew her son only too well, and she realised that this was his excuse to meet up with the pretty girl again. Penny didn't mind, as it meant she didn't have to prepare breakfast. Plus, she had also promised Connie that she would help in preparation for the village event. That meant Matt would be alone, but he had plenty to keep him busy.

It was a delightful spring morning with clear blue skies and a crisp temperature. There were no signs or forecasts of rain for the day: perfect for the village festival. The Baxter family reached the pub.

"Good morning, Bill. Who was that bunch we saw leaving, mate?" asked Matt.

"Good morning, all, the anglers. I doubt they'll do anything today, mind. Too warm this morning for the fish to bite. Double egg on all, is it?" said Bill as he cleared a table.

"What's Connie got lined up for you, Mum?" asked Henry, trying to start a conversation away from his father's work.

Not long after, Bill returned with a pot of tea, two cups, and saucers. Like father, like son, as the saying goes, and a cup of brewed coffee for Penny.

"She said she needs a hand with the roly-poly, the spotted Dick, and the Eton mess," replied Penny.

"Listen to her, Matt," said Bill. "I thought Connie wanted help with the food preparation."

Matt and Bill's schoolboy laughter filled the room.

"Bugger, he gets worse," said Matt after his friend returned to the kitchen.

Matt realised that there wasn't much he could do on the murder case until they got the report on the weapons. However, he had to do some more investigating, and this meant a visit to the Royal Hotel in Ingleton to interview the staff.

Connie appeared with two plates loaded with food. Penny and Henry made a start, and Matt's bottom lip trembled until he saw Bill appear with a third plate.

With breakfast over, Matt set off and drove towards Shackleton Bottom to get to the hilltop road. Matt knew this road very well: the bends rise to a plateau, Mount Ashton, and the road then meanders again down to a valley. Small cottages with beautiful gardens lined both sides of the narrow road. The gardens appeared to be competing with each other for being the most beautiful and the displays of roses, carnations, and chrysanthemums were magnificent. These presentations of flora and fauna contribute to making some of Yorkshire's prettiest hamlets. The Royal Hotel stands in about twenty acres of beautiful, peaceful surroundings. It was an old family mansion, which had recently been completely renovated and transformed into a very comfortable boutique hotel.

A grand vestibule entrance was now the main feature with a winding staircase on each side. Matt looked around the entrance area, looking for the reception.

"Good morning, sir; how may I help you?" a very deep-toned voice spoke out.

"Good morning, mate. Can you tell me where the reception is, please?" asked Matt to the individual standing by a tall wooden lectern.

"Sir, The Royal doesn't use a reception desk or similar facility. Do you have a reservation with us?" asked the concierge. He switched on his computer screen.

"No," said Matt, and he showed his identity card. "I am here to check on one of your guests from a couple of days ago."

The concierge moved swiftly towards Matt:

"Please, sir. No need to display that here." He looked around, concerned others may recognize the ID card.

"How can I assist you, sir?" His voice lowered.

"You had a guest booked in here last Wednesday. David Illya was his name," said Matt.

The concierge remembered him.

"But how do you remember him? He never checked in," asked Matt, bewildered.

"Ah, yes, sir. He arrived at the hotel about four o'clock. I met him here at the entrance. Mr. Illya explained he was late for a meeting outside, and he had to dash off, so he asked me to keep his room for a late check-in. He said he would return later, in the evening," said the concierge. He looked at his screen.

"Did he give a time he would be back?" asked Matt.

"Yes, he did. It is on his record here. I remember as I was about to go off duty. Here it is, between nine p.m. and ten p.m., sir," said the concierge.

"Was he alone? Anyone waiting in his car?" asked Matt, routine questions.

"I noticed he was alone in his car. I had to ask him to park up, as we do not allow waiting at the entrance area; hotel policy," explained the concierge.

The concierge explained that the guest never returned on Wednesday evening but then he remembered something.

"Oh, there was one thing I found strange. He said he was running late, and yet after he parked his car, he went drinking at the terrace bar. The bartender remembers very well. When he gave the bill, he explained he couldn't sign the charges to his room, as he had not checked in yet. Mr. Illya was happy to pay cash and I understand he also tipped quite well."

"And one more thing, also strange. Mr. Illya asked if we could provide him with accommodation until Sunday if he found he needed to extend his stay. So, he added Friday and Saturday night," explained the concierge.

"Why would you think that is strange?" asked Matt. "This is a hotel."

"Because he had no luggage, sir," replied the concierge. "I offered to unload his vehicle, but he informed me he had no luggage."

"Just imagine, no clean clothes . . . for five days!" said the concierge.

"Has anyone phoned in about his intended stay here or why he never turned up? Perhaps a worried wife?" asked Matt.

"As far as I know, no one else contacted us. You would have to check with our telephone operator," explained the concierge.

"Mind if I have a quick look around the hotel and the terrace there?" asked Matt.

"Be my guest, sir," said the concierge as he lowered his head and took two steps backwards.

Matt walked through the beautiful building. An excellent renovation, losing none of the original charms. Two spacious rooms were on each side of the secondary entrance. One served as a restaurant, and the other room appeared to be a bar lounge and a more casual dining area.

Wait! Who is that he recognised in the lounge?

A very smart and stylish Phoenix Istaza was in there with two other people.

"What on earth is she doing here?" he said under his breath.

Matt walked through the lobby and out onto the terrace. He sat for a few minutes, enjoyed a very spectacular view, and breathed in the invigorating fresh air. He contemplated a nice pot of tea as the server approached him. He picked up the tabletop menu and promptly changed his mind when he saw the prices.

"Phu! That wouldn't look good on the exes," he said to himself.

"I'm waiting for someone," he said to the server as he left the table to return inside. He looked towards the lounge, where he had seen Phoenix a few minutes earlier, but she was no longer there.

There was nothing more here.

In the pub, Henry had prepared the lounge for the fabulous spread that was being prepared in the kitchen. As he worked, he heard the car park access door swing open and slam shut again. His curiosity aroused, he went through to the barroom to see what had caused the unexpected noise. Nothing. Then another door closed, and Phoenix was standing there, a few feet away from him. She did not look thrilled at all.

"Good morning, Henry; excuse me, please," she said as she moved forward and walked straight past him.

"Good morning, Phoenix," said Henry as he moved backwards. "Are you all right?"

"No, I am not. I will tell you later. First, I need to get out of these ridiculous clothes," said Phoenix, and off she went upstairs as she slammed more doors on her way.

"Hey up, has your old man been upsetting her again?" asked Bill as he appeared from the kitchen.

"Food will start coming out in fifteen minutes, lad. Are you all right? Here, I can help you with the rest of the tables and chairs," said Bill.

Henry asked Bill what he meant by the comment that Matt had been upsetting her.

"What do you mean, Bill, 'again'?" asked Henry.

"They had some words yesterday, I heard. But Miss Malta upstairs doesn't realise, or she doesn't know, that your dad is only doing his job. I have seen this before, mate; a lot of countries don't do examinations as we do over here. Don't let it worry you, but take my advice, lad, and don't mention it to the girl," said Bill.

Meanwhile, a van pulled up outside the pub and the rear doors opened to allow several people to alight.

"Oh, the band is here. I asked them to come early. I didn't expect them this early, though," said Bill. He left Henry and went over to meet them.

Within minutes, the band crew was hard at work, erecting a wooden stage. Upon this stage, they positioned their amplifiers, speakers, drum kit, and microphone stands.

Bill and Connie don't do things by halves, thought Henry.

Along Station Road, the village community had set up several wooden stalls. These stalls sold anything from local knitted handicrafts to delicious homemade pork pies. Throughout the day the villagers strolled amongst the stalls as they made their way for lunch. Until a few years ago, people considered the Cooper's Wood village festival as the start of spring. The surrounding villages would see it as an annual get-together for the entire region. Decorated floats would parade through the streets from nearby Ribblesdale, Shackleton Bottom, and further afield, Mount Ashton and Ingleton, and end up at the pub.

At the top of Stave Hill, near Oakwood Lodge cottage, there was always a free beer stall. Bill had yet to take his wooden trestle table and set it up with a complimentary cask of beer. The problem was, he had no one to occupy the stall, as they were short on staff for the day. It would be a waste to delegate Henry there.

Over at Cooper's Wood regional police station, Matt had met Myles. They discussed the two murder weapons and the coincidence of the name of the car driver. There was still nothing to link the abandoned car driver to the murder. The business cards appeared to provide some sort of link.

"One of our juniors has web searched most of them. They all seem to be legitimate companies," said Matt.

"The next step, Matt. On Monday, get someone to phone all these companies and make enquiries about this David guy."

"We have to get a lead somewhere. This is very odd," said Myles.

"The hotel in Ingleton also confirmed he never returned to check in to his room on Wednesday evening. They also said that a member of our team was up there yesterday morning to make some routine enquiries. It must have been after the briefing," Matt concluded.

"The manager at the hotel called me. We use their restaurant quite a lot when we have the big guns in town. He said they also reported the fact that the guest didn't turn up when they heard the news of a dead body in Cooper's Wood.

"Reported it to Leeds; no one picked up the phone at our station. Bloody government cutbacks!" said Myles.

"We need to have something by the middle of next week, Matt. Wednesday at the absolute latest," he said.

"There is something, sir. This foreign lady, young woman, mid-twenties, has turned up earlier this week. She has been staying at the Shoulder. It is very difficult to get any background information from her. She comes across as quite peculiar to me and she drives a brand-new top-of-the-range Porsche SUV. It must be a hundred grand worth of motor," said Matt.

"I was over at the old petrol station at Shackleton Bottom there yesterday and the old man there remembers a young lady, very similar on Wednesday afternoon. She filled up a posh German car, milky coffee colour."

"Unfortunately, they never found out where she came from or where she was going. But I can't help feeling she might be involved," said Matt.

"Then again, this young woman reached the village and fuelled up before parking her car up. I do it all the time. We need something more than that, Matt," Myles replied. "Anyway, keep on it, Matt."

Everything was ready for lunch, and a casually dressed Phoenix returned.

"Hi there," she said to Henry. "I notice you like to keep yourself busy."

"I said I would help Bill and Connie with the festival today. It will be a busy day for everyone. It's a pleasant event, though. It usually starts slowly and livens up later. Sorry, I must get on." Henry excused himself.

She took a seat on a high stool at the bar. Bill and Connie came out with more food.

"Anything I can do to help?" asked Phoenix.

"Yes, now I come to think about it. Do you have your passport with you?" asked Bill.

"No, it's up in my room. Why?" she asked.

"I didn't make a good enough copy for the cops the other day. They would like another better copy, a full copy, place of birth, and all that." Bill looked rather shy. "Don't bother yourself now, lass, but let me have it later on, love."

"Aye, awreet," she replied.

It was difficult to make out who blushed the most. Bill, upon hearing her first attempt at a Yorkshire accent, or Phoenix, for attempting it.

Just as Bill predicted, the pub quickly filled up when the lunch was ready. Bill and Connie ran an excellent pub and had a lot of respect from the village community.

Bill's other prediction from earlier in the day had also turned out correct, as it was discovered when the fishermen returned with not a single fish between them. Bill served a complimentary pint of beer to each of the anglers.

"Is the beer barrel set up already, Bill?" called out one angler, his moustache white with foam from the beer.

"Is it hell? I don't have anyone to serve it. It will be the first year we won't have the free beer barrel. The lads at the brewery tell me it's cracking good ale this year as well," he said.

"What's this?" asked Phoenix.

Bill explained the tradition of the beer barrel set up at the top of the hill. As the beer is free, it is intriguing to see how many people are ready to walk up Stave Hill to get a couple of pints.

"We record the time to see how long it takes to finish the barrel . . . if they finish the barrel," explained Bill.

"Nay beer barrel, Bill; that's not good, is it? What's the best time, anyway?" asked one customer.

"One hour and forty-seven minutes is the record time. From 2012 when I and a few of the lads knew how to sup ale," said Bill.

"I'll do it," announced Phoenix, as she almost stood to attention.

All the customers focused on her.

"Would you, lass? Would you? Do you mind?" Bill was ecstatic. "Do you know how to pull a pint of beer?"

"No, but I bet you can soon teach me, Bill," she said as she pushed him behind the bar and placed him in front of a beer pump. "Well, what are you waiting for?"

Bill pulled a pint of beer and then passed the girl an empty pint pot. She leaned forward, wrapped her fingers around the beer pump handle, and pulled her first pint. Not perfect, but nothing to be ashamed of either. She placed the full glass on the bar in front of several thirsty customers. Once again, she found herself as the centre of attraction, helped by the low V-neck Pigalle cotton blouse she wore rather than the beer pulling skills she had recently gained.

"Come on! My car's ready loaded up. Jimbo loaded it earlier this morning," said Bill.

Bill and Phoenix left to the rear car park and took off through the narrow village streets.

"Bill, may I ask, who or what is Jimbo?" asked Phoenix.

"Hahaha, Henry, the lad you've taken a shine to," said Bill. "His middle name is James, so his rugby name is Jimbo, or it was."

Bill looked at Phoenix from the corner of his eye.

"Ah, him, he's Jimbo, and what do you mean I have taken a shine to?" she asked, knowing exactly what Bill meant. She blushed.

———————

Matt deposited his briefcase inside Oakwood Lodge and made his way to the free beer stall. There is a small flat patch of land at the end of the narrow access lane leading from Matt's cottage. As he approached the beer stall, he could see Bill struggling with a cask of beer.

"That's a firkin lot of beer you got there, mate. Why don't you drink some first; it will be much easier to lift?" shouted Matt.

"Come and give me a hand here," Bill responded as Phoenix appeared from behind the car. "Hang on, love; you can't lift it; he'll give us a hand."

"Hello, Mr. Baxter," she said, turning on the charm.

Matt supported Bill as he started to fall backwards. Phoenix watched them with a lot of interest and a little concern. As they struggled, it became a little interest and a lot of concern. But somehow, they got the cask in position and it was ready to dispense beer.

"Who's on the tap?" Matt queried.

"I am if that means who is pulling the beer?" exclaimed Phoenix as she laid out the empty glasses.

"Right! Great, well-done, love, and good luck with that. Come on, let me start it off." Matt's voice and manner were completely different now. *Is that what "off duty" means?* Phoenix thought.

"Bill, why is Mr. Baxter swearing at you? He was using the f-word. I thought he was your friend?" whispered Phoenix.

"F-word? When?" replied Bill. "Oh, no, firkin. You mean firkin. That's not swearing. Nay, a firkin is a name for a small barrel of beer, or what we call a cask these days. It comes from an old Dutch dialect, and it means fourth, or as we would say, a quarter. Two firkins make a kilderkin, and two kilderkins make a barrel," explained Bill.

"So, you mean they come bigger than this?" asked Phoenix as she pointed down to the cask.

"Oh, yes, this is small. It holds nine gallons of beer," said Bill.

"Wow! You guys will drink all this beer today, this afternoon?" asked Phoenix.

"That's our intention, love. Do you fancy helping us out?" asked Matt as he offered her a clean glass.

"It is seventy-two pints, but we will only get about sixty pints out of this one, I guess. It doesn't help the beer moving it around so much," said Bill. "Mind, some of these buggers will sup owt if it is free."

Bill explained he was going back to the pub, but later on, he or someone would come over and collect her.

"Whatever you do, do not serve Tom, the lad from the petrol station. You will recognise him. He'll be alone, wearing headphones. Nobody talks to him; he's weird like—" were Bill's last words as he got in his car with Matt, and they set off back to the pub.

After about fifteen minutes, people left the pub and started trudging up the hill. They all stopped at the top to drink a glass of beer, considered by many as being a good glass of ale. Some rested a while as they took in the magnificent view across the valley and a free second pint, of course. As the afternoon went on, people made their way back to the village and Phoenix found herself alone. She didn't enjoy being alone. But as she looked down towards Station Road, she could see what looked like Bill's car coming towards her. The car got nearer and nearer, with a flash of the headlights. It was Henry. Her knight in shining armour.

"Come on, the party's started; let's get that in the back. Put the tray of glasses on the back seat," said Henry. He talked as he worked.

They both jumped in the car, and away they went. Henry went back through the village streets and parked up in the rear car park. He got out and saw the Porsche car parked on the side.

"Wow, nice outfit, that," he said. "I wonder who owns that beauty?"

"I do," she said as she opened the rear door of Bill's car.

Before Henry got his hands on the beer barrel, she took hold of him and started kissing him passionately.

"Mmm, maybe I will take you for a ride in it one day!" she said.

Henry was speechless. He recomposed himself, and together with Phoenix, they made their way back inside.

"Well done, lass," shouted out several villagers. *Such friendly people,* thought Phoenix.

"I did my best, Bill, but we couldn't beat your record," she said as she took a long drink from a gin and tonic, courtesy of a grateful landlord.

"You did grand, love," he said and winked at her.

Henry started behind the bar as Phoenix went outside to join some young locals and watched the entertainment; they were good. She felt she could now relax and enjoy the evening.

As the evening went on and the drinks flowed, Henry found himself always busy behind the bar. His mind, sometimes, on the brief encounter he had enjoyed earlier in the evening in the car park. An event that had been way too short for him. Phoenix sat outside the pub. The evening was chilly, but she had a double-ply cashmere wrap to keep her warm. She relaxed and enjoyed her wine, the company of the local village people, and even Penny joined her for a chat. The music continued, as did the drinks, courtesy of Bill and Henry, it seemed.

The evening wound down, and a lot of the village residents made their way back home. Phoenix stayed outside and listened to the music. The temperature dropped further. The band announced their last set. The slow set, where was Henry?

He came out to join her and they both sat down and enjoyed a glass of wine, or two, and cuddled up to each other to get warm. Bill and Connie stood on the doorstep at the main entrance. They also needed a rest, and they noticed the young couple getting closer. How happy they looked. Difficult to accept that they had only known each other for over twenty-four hours.

Matt and Penny bid goodnight to all and started their walk back home. Stave Hill looked quite steep after two bottles of wine.

FIVE

On a usual Sunday morning, the kitchen at Oakwood Lodge would be abuzz with activity. On this day of the week, Matt gave his beloved wife some time to herself. He usually prepared a splendid breakfast for them both. Today was an exception, as Matt felt he needed to recuperate from the stress of the last few days.

Yet, she still managed her weekly *lie in* and Penny walked into the kitchen, still tired, she yawned as she looked at the wall clock.

"What time did you get up? I never heard you," she asked.

"Not long; half an hour," Matt replied. "I have a pot of coffee on for you. Here, a slice of toast until later."

"What time did he get in?" she asked as she approached Henry's bedroom.

"I don't know. I was out, myself," said Matt.

Penny delicately tapped on the door, and before she heard a reply, she slowly opened the door. She didn't want the sight of a half-naked Maltese girl to startle her so early. But Henry had been a good boy and returned home alone last night. He needed some rest, as it had been a long day yesterday. She closed the door and returned to the kitchen.

"He's still fast asleep," she said.

They started a conversation about their son and his relationship with Phoenix. Or was it only going to be a bit of fun for him? For them both?

"We can only wait and see what develops. She is due to leave for London today. They might never hear from each other again," said Penny. "That's young ones today, Matt."

"You're right there," he said. "Well, I'll try to do a bit of work, do some research."

Matt turned on his laptop and searched for hits on the internet. He tried several entries and then had a thought as he recalled the address on the personal card:

Type: Illya, Sultan Suleiman Street

Hits: usual hits: Jerusalem Arabic name . . . Sultan Suleiman found dead in Beirut.

When was that? he thought. He immediately clicked on the link.

The article opened, and he read:

A well-known entrepreneur was found dead late last night in his hotel room in Beirut. He has been named Sultan Suleiman. The cause of death is unknown. A member of housekeeping found the body as they were doing their late-night service.

Matt clicked on the local TV network link. A new window opened.

Bloody hell! It was in Arabic.

The cameraman panned around the room and zoomed in on the white outline of where they found the victim. But wait a minute! Something else attracted Matt's attention to the screen and he wound the video back. The cameraman didn't zoom in. Why on earth should he? Matt tried to magnify the screen larger. He had identified two articles on a low-level coffee table. He recognised them as a builder's square and a wooden block level. He paused the play button and sat back in his chair. He stared at the screen, rewound the video, and played it again once, twice more.

Penny had gone back through to the bedroom, where she relaxed and watched the television news. Matt went into the bedroom and put himself down on the bed beside her. He pointed to the news article shown on his laptop screen.

"I searched for the address of that Tamara woman. Look at this, Penny; read that and then watch the video report," he said. He clicked the video play button, then paused it and put her television on mute.

She read the news report and clicked to restart the video.

"Matt, it's in a foreign language. Greek or something. I don't want to watch this rubbish," she cried.

"Wait, watch it," he insisted, "and it's Arabic, by the way."

Matt walked over to the wardrobe, reached the top shelf, and lifted down a small black briefcase. He put it at the foot of the bed and then opened the top so that his wife could not see the contents. He stopped the news clip at the scene with the two articles he had observed. He went back to the briefcase, stood behind it, and held up three small stainless-steel tools. Penny stared; what on earth was Matt doing?

"The mallet, the chisel, and the twenty-four-inch gauge," he said as he held them up.

"These implements, or tools, have a symbolic reference to the 'Boy Scouts for adults' as you call it," he said.

Penny rolled her eyes.

"That reference we needn't get into right now," said Matt.

"They are used in part of the ceremony for a first-degree Freemason," he said.

"And the guy murdered in the old brickyard had two wounds," said Matt. He held up two of the tools and described how they may have inflicted the wound.

"Now, look at the video," he said as he picked up the level and the square from the briefcase. He pointed to the level on the screen and then showed his level. He then pointed to the square, again on the screen, and then showed his square.

"Two of the three so-called working tools of a second-degree Freemason. The third one being a plumb rule," he said. He held up his plumb rule from his briefcase.

He now had his wife's attention.

"Go on, then," she said.

"If we assume that the victim here is the driver of the abandoned car, his name is David Illya. David, one of the most popular names in the world, of course. But what about this Suleiman guy in Lebanon? Suleiman is the adapted name of Sulayman. Which the Arab people have used for centuries for the name Solomon," said Matt.

"And King Solomon was the son of King David," said Penny.

Matt smiled.

"Now, let's put these two names aside for a moment," said Matt.

"This David guy hired the car in London. Now . . . there was a named driver in the rental agreement called Tamara Illya. This person could have been David's wife, his sister, who knows? But no one has seen this woman. The petrol station guys said no one was with the driver of the Audi when he filled up on Wednesday afternoon. The hotel also said he was alone when he went to inform them of his late check in. He only booked single occupancy at his hotel in Ingleton. So, she has also disappeared if she was ever here. Now, get this, there was no sign of luggage in the abandoned car or the hotel either. That's strange, don't you think?" he asked.

"Meanwhile, Phoenix Istaza arrived in the village a few days earlier," continued Matt.

"But she came here on Tuesday, Matt; she's been here for five days already," said Penny.

"Yes, I know. She intrigues me. I also got a look at her car on Friday, and nothing, also no luggage. There was a black case; she opened it. It had some painting materials and fashion magazines inside," said Matt.

"Do you think the girl did it?" she asked.

"I don't know," came Matt's standard inspector answer in these cases.

"Anyway, her luggage will be in her room at the pub, Matt. You only need to ask her if you can check in her room. She doesn't look like a girl who skimps on her clothing, from what we have seen of her. Every time we have seen her, she has been wearing a different outfit. They all cost a few quid; you can bet. Did you see the Pigalle blouse she—" said Penny.

"It's *his* luggage we are looking for!" interrupted Matt.

"Then, today's news and a dead body with the name Solomon has turned up in Beirut. And still no sign anywhere of the Tamara person," said Matt.

"Oh, I see. Now you are wondering if this Tamara woman is the murderer of both victims?" said Penny. "So, she did the guy in here and then hopped halfway around the world to do another one," she added.

"Not halfway, love; it's nearer than you think," said Matt as he closed his briefcase. Penny stopped him.

"And just out of interest, the third-degree?" she pointed to the briefcase and Matt placed it back on the bed. He flicked open the spring locks.

"The skirret, the pencil, and the compasses." He held them at arm's length.

"At least you don't have to worry about *murder by pencil* in the future," she laughed.

Matt put the tools back in the case and returned it back in the wardrobe. He went into the bathroom. A few seconds later, the bathroom door flew open.

"Get yourself ready; we're going to Lebanon!" He reached for his phone.

There was a sudden burst of activity as they got ready and headed towards the door.

"I need to meet Bill. I'd like to get him on board on this one. And I have to brief Myles as well. I need to get his approval to travel whilst this investigation is going on. That won't be easy. He wants something from me," said Matt. "Let's meet Bill first, and we plan from there."

Penny picked up a power bank from the countertop.

"Whenever we go out, Penny, you always remember to bring a power bank," said Matt.

"Only in case we need to charge the phones in an emergency," she replied as she scribbled a note for their son.

"I have a power outlet in the car," replied Matt.

"Didn't you hear me? In an emergency," Penny said to emphasise her point.

"So, why would some people carry two power banks, even when their car has a charging socket? If the driver of the hired car was the victim, where is his phone?" Matt said, more of a mumble, thinking out loud. "Or phones," he continued.

———————————

"Please, say nothing to Connie until I have finished with Bill," Matt whispered to his wife as they walked through the main doors.

"Bill, have you got a minute, mate?" said Matt as he beckoned to Bill to join him away from the bar area.

Matt explained his latest discovery to Bill.

Bill, also a Freemason, widened his eyes as Matt spun more and more of the tale to him. Bill immediately recognised the connections.

"Beirut, Lebanon," said Bill. "Blimey mate, it's dodgy over there right now, as you know."

"Bill, you're a forensic pathologist. I will be in uncharted waters; I will need someone with me I can work with, rely on, and trust. We cannot overlook the Masonic reference, Bill," said Matt. "Plus you've got the history and knowledge and other trivia stuff going on."

Bill looked at him.

"What do you mean, 'other trivia stuff'?" said Bill.

"Come on, and it will be a pleasant break for the girls. They can go off on tour to the holy lands and all that. Our Penny has always wanted to go there. It's going to be quiet here for the next week or two, I guess," said Matt.

"Do you think your lad can manage for us?" asked Bill.

"Will she still be around?" Matt said as he pointed upwards.

"She's supposed to be leaving today, going down south, I understand," said Bill.

"Bill, I know it's a lot to ask, but do you think you and Connie could be ready for a flight to Dubai this evening? I'll book us out of Manchester. We need to get there soon as possible," Matt said.

"I don't see why not? I will talk to Connie, and you talk to your lad," said Bill.

Somehow, while talking to Connie in the kitchen, Bill convinced her into going along on this trip.

"We'll be away a week at the very most," said Bill.

"Our lad is on board, Bill," shouted Matt as he gave the familiar thumbs-up sign. "He says he will be down here in about an hour."

Matt now found himself in a rather tricky situation. Myles had tried to join a Masonic lodge for years, with no success. Myles knew Matt was quite high in the Provincial Masonic hierarchy of the order. Hence, he knew Matt would be an ideal person to submit his name forward.

How can Matt go to Myles with his theory about the connection between the two victims and the weapons? Will his boss challenge him on the topic? It was different yesterday, as he only needed to explain the weapons and the name of the driver of the abandoned car. This recent development, if connected, could put it in a whole new perspective.

Matt imagined how the conversation would go:

"You know Matt; if I was a Mason and I was aware of these facts a little more. Of course, I would be in a much better position to support your actions."

Matt couldn't leave the country without the super's permission whilst a murder investigation was underway. He would return to the UK jobless, and he couldn't afford that yet. So, he went and met Myles to explain the situation and that he felt he was leaving the case in excellent hands with Ryan. As new to the group as he was, he had shown great initiative.

On his way to Myles' house, Matt dropped Penny at home so she could start packing for the evening flight.

"Don't say too much yet; I have also asked Bill and Connie to keep it between ourselves. We are only going to Dubai for a few days," said Matt as Penny got out of the car.

"I'll be back in forty-five minutes, and then we get some lunch when we drop Henry at the pub."

Matt met with Myles at his house, and the story was, once again, explained. He secured the approval to travel from Myles. The senior officer will also make the phone calls to alert the relevant Lebanese authorities. The next subject was as Matt expected, and he explained what had to be done.

"So that's all I must do, Matt?" said Myles.

"Yes, that's it," said Matt. "When I get back, I will take it forward; it's different from what a lot of folks think."

"And the case here," Myles continued. "If you're so confident about this Ryan chap handling the case from here on, then it should be okay. Of course, I am here to help him where I can. A quick result is always good for them upstairs, but I see the point you are making. In fairness, you've never had much to go on here."

Myles walked Matt to his front door to bid farewell and bon voyage.

Next, back to the cottage to book the tickets and hotel. Matt booked a good package deal with return flights to Beirut via Dubai, and a very nice-looking hotel. They will stay at the Phoenician Gold Coast Hotel, north of Beirut. It looked very picturesque with spectacular views over Zaitunay Bay.

Shortly after, the Baxter family were all in the car as they headed back to The Shoulder of Mutton. The pub had filled with Sunday lunch customers, and who should they see behind the bar as they entered?

"Good afternoon, and welcome to The Shoulder and Mutton," said Phoenix.

"No, love," said Connie. "The Shoulder of Mutton."

"Ah, sorry. Welcome to The Shoulder of Mutton," Phoenix repeated.

"All this time, I have been calling it the wrong name," Phoenix whispered to Henry. "How are you today?"

"I am fine; thank you. I had to sleep late; exhausted. What about you?" asked Henry.

"Yes, same here, lad. But a few pints o' best beer in Yorkshire and tha' be reet'," she said. She emphasised her recently adopted Yorkshire accent.

Henry went to find Bill. Matt and Penny sat down and browsed the menu, usual stuff.

Seafood all next week, Matt thought. *Roast pork for me*. Bill joined them.

"Right," he said and clapped his hands. "All done!"

"Our flight leaves Manchester at nine forty-five, so we have to be there by eight o'clock, latest," said Matt.

"Let's get Terry's Taxis to pick us up from here at six o'clock. That gives us two hours on a Sunday evening. We should be fine," said Bill.

"Bill, send me a photo of your passports, please. We can check in online now, so then we can drop the luggage at the check-in counter," explained Matt.

Lunch arrived.

"See you back here later," said Bill.

Matt's phone rang out.

"Hello, hello . . . hello?" Not connected, and then a faint voice that sounded quite distressed.

"Hello, Mr. Matthew, how are you? I am Inspector Harold Othman; call me Harry. I work with the Beirut Police Department. I understand you will come to Beirut tomorrow. I want to let you know, you are most welcome to our country," said the voice on the other end of the call.

"Hello, Harry. I was expecting your call but thought it would be later in the day," Matt replied.

"Your office already contacted our headquarters. Mr. Matthew, please let me know your flight and arrival time. It will be my pleasure to receive you at Beirut airport," came the response down the line.

"We arrive from Dubai at around noon tomorrow. We will be four people altogether," Matt said.

"Our case must be important to you if you are sending four people," he replied. "I wish you an enjoyable journey and look forward to seeing you tomorrow. We will wait for you at gate number three. Bye-bye." The line closed.

———————

A glance at the weight indicator as Matt and Bill stood at the check-in counter at Manchester airport. The bags were on the conveyor, already tagged and labelled, and boarding passes printed. The two wives discussed their plans for their upcoming adventure. Phoenix had informed them, before they left the pub, that she now intended to stay on for a few more days.

Bill and Connie were well pleased about this, and Matt considered she was up to something. He was still suspicious of her. Henry, of course, was more pleased than any of them.

Matt took back the passports and boarding passes and heard the words, "Have a pleasant flight."

The conveyor motor fired up, and the bags moved forward.

Matt froze.

"Hang on, stop! Can you bring the bags back, please?" he asked.

She reversed the conveyor belt, and the bags came back to the start of the conveyor.

"Bloody hell, Matt. Have you packed a power bank inside your bag?" asked Penny.

Matt leaned over and took hold of the white paper loop luggage tag wrapped through the suitcase handle. He read the bold black letters.

"B E Y, DXB/BEY. BEY is the airport code for Beirut," he said. No one understood.

Seeing this immediately took his mind back to what he had seen in the rear compartment of Phoenix's car.

"It's okay. Thank you very much," he said to the girl.

They made their way through immigration, enjoyed a drink at the bar, and boarded the aeroplane. The plane departed on time, and they were on their way to Dubai.

SIX

It was difficult to take Bill's attention away from the video screen. The two individuals at the front of the aisle had more success. One faced Bill and the other faced backwards. Bill leaned over and whispered, "Why don't they start the bar service from the rear of the plane?"

Glasses filled, they discussed the scenarios of the Cooper's Wood murder. They did not overlook the abandoned car, but it didn't seem so significant now.

"The news had named the second victim as Suleiman or Solomon. We both know that Solomon means 'man of peace,' but most people make a mistake and think it means 'man of wisdom.' This is because, in one thousand BC, King Solomon was said to be the wisest man who ever lived," explained Bill.

He continued. "It was because of his reputation as a peaceful man that he stepped down as head of his own army. He appointed his elder half-brother, Adonijah. The same guy who had claimed the throne from his father, David, even before he had died.

"Here is another fascinating fact that many people are not aware of. After Solomon took the throne, Adonijah became very close to Solomon's mother, Bathsheba. He convinced Bathsheba to talk to Solomon to allow his marriage to a woman called Abishag.

"Bathsheba talked to Solomon and tried to convince him to let this marriage go ahead. Solomon declared, 'You might as well ask me to give him my kingdom,'" continued Bill. "King Solomon considered what Adonijah had planned was treason and later the same day, King Solomon ordered his military commander, Benaiah, quite literally to 'go and kill Adonijah,' and he did so.

"By the way, Abishag was the same beautiful young girl that, years before, King David summoned to be with him in his bed. As King David grew older, he found he could not get his body warm, so he used this young girl for this purpose. There was never any intimacy at all between King David and Abishag," explained Bill.

"So, if Adonijah claimed the throne as the eldest and so-called heir-apparent, how come he didn't become king? Solomon succeeded David, correct?" said Matt.

"Years ago, and in this Holy Land region, they didn't always follow the heir-apparent procedure. Things were very different, as we all know, compared to today. But to answer your question, God could also declare who the next king would be. The prophets have also appointed kings, doing so by passing on God's wishes," explained Bill.

Bill's knowledge of history, in particular the Old Testament, was exceptional. He might run a good boozer, but for his pastime, he reads book after book about the ancient history of the region. Bill's history lesson was perfect for getting them through the flight to Dubai. After a meal and an attempt to watch a movie, which caused a short sleep for them, they descended to the Dubai airport.

A short connection time in Dubai. Then a flight to Beirut. It was around 21°C in Beirut and this climate would be perfect for either working or sightseeing.

Upon leaving the immigration area, several individuals surrounded the four travellers. They offered various services, from a mundane taxi to the hotel to tours of the Holy Land. There were also several shouts of "the best dollar rate in Beirut!" The visitors kept their heads down and made their way to the pre-arranged meeting point. There, standing, almost to attention, were several well-armed police officers.

"Welcome to Beirut, Mr. Baxter," announced a short, stocky individual. He rubbed a string of prayer beads in his left hand as he extended his right hand. "Our transport is waiting to take you to your hotel."

Harold assured the two ladies that there were many attractions to visit in and around Beirut. A trip to the Holy Land, if it was even possible, or safe, would need two days.

Penny and Connie preferred to go to the hotel, get checked in, and unpack their bags. The usual stuff. Bill joined them. Matt accompanied Harold Othman to the police station to start the investigation.

"Bill is an old friend of mine, Harry, an ex-copper himself and he was due a break, so he joined us for a few days with his wife." Matt wanted to keep Bill out of the case until he had made an initial examination. He also masqueraded Bill as ex-police rather than ex-forensics. An approach to the case they had discussed and agreed on during the flight over.

They entered Harold's office; it was exactly as Matt imagined it. Very modest in size, the equipment, and the decoration. The walls featured a photograph of someone who resembled Harold Othman. But the character in the photo was standing astride the gun barrel on a tank.

"Kuwait," said Harold. "I was with the Kuwait Police after I graduated. That was just after the Iraqi invasion in 1990. We assisted with gathering all the Iraqi tanks left behind on the streets."

A small, window-type air-conditioning unit sounded as though it was about to stop completely. Then it resurged back to life, then it died again, and then back to life again. The paint on the inside of the window frames was the same since the building had opened. On the floor laid a well-trodden rug. It looked like a cheap one, made to look like a Persian by featuring Islamic patterns. There was one other chair in the entire office. It creaked under Matt's weight as he carefully positioned himself. A small wooden table was next to the chair.

"May I offer you a cup of tea, Mr. Matthew? It is the afternoon, after all. We should take one, as I find it most invigorating," said Harold.

A young male clerk placed a small cup with no handle, not much bigger than an egg cup, on the small table. The tea was piping hot. Sadly though, tea leaves floated on top.

"Mr. Matthew, may I ask, what is your approach to this case; what would you like to see; whom do you wish to interview? Do you wish to meet our investigation team before we proceed?" asked Harold, as he tried to be very accommodating.

"Please." Harold beckoned for Matt to drink his tea.

Matt shuddered and resisted.

"The first thing we need to do, of course, is to go to the scene of the crime. Then a visit to the medical examiner. And finally, go over the profile of the victim with you and your officers. I understand that Mr. Sultan was very wealthy. He had many business interests, here and overseas," said Matt.

"He was a successful entrepreneur. His principal business was property development and investments. He and his family are very wealthy, but he also squandered a lot of his fortune. By the way, Sultan wasn't his actual name. No, he inherited that from his father as a nickname or family name. Family and friends called him Sultan . . . or Solly," explained Harold as he passed a piece of paper over to Matt.

"Suleiman had one weakness, which, as everyone who knew him will tell you, was beautiful women. He had one wife, who I understand now lives in Dubai. This provided him with the opportunity for his philandering lifestyle. But I can assure you, he was also a very generous and kind person," explained Harold.

Matt stared at the paper that he had received. His eyes were wide open with disbelief. He preferred to keep quiet at this stage about what he had read on the paper.

"Many times, we have heard stories of his donations to the poor people in Jordan, Syria, and also here in Lebanon. My staff will provide you with more information about Mr. Suleiman that you feel you may need. I understand this latest project was facing some issues with the local authorities. We should go," explained Harold.

Tea, reluctantly finished, there was one mouthful.

The afternoon temperature seemed to have increased a lot in the short time they had been inside. The constant blaring of car and motorbike horns annoyed Matt, as it did many others. He wondered if the alarm was being used to warn of a possible collision or only to say "hi there" to someone. Added to this were the sirens from the outriders and even the car they were riding in. Matt wondered if this fiasco was for his benefit, or if this was normal.

The motorcade slowed and came to a stop outside an oriental, palatial-looking building—the aptly named Beirut Qasr Hotel. The exterior of the building had deteriorated over the years. The brilliance of the paint had mellowed. Yet somehow it still kept a certain amount of its mystic charm. It was still referred to by many of its regular guests as simply "The Palace." Staff from the reception scurried down the steps to open the car doors for Matt and inspector Othman. The hotel staff almost marched the entourage through the lobby. Within seconds they were in the elevator and up to the fourteenth floor—the top floor, the exclusive level.

Prints by Monet, Seurat, Delacroix, and Renoir decorated the corridor walls. The velvet-finish wallpaper and serene lights provided an atmosphere conjuring up days gone by of French colonialism. A large wicker laundry basket stood outside of a room. *How odd*, Matt thought. *The laundry basket is almost as wide as the corridor itself.*

The rooms were spacious suites, and the furniture was first class.

Harold explained that the manager of the hotel was not in Beirut at the moment, as he had made a prior appointment at the hotel's new property in Tripoli. The hotel security officer would join them, but he was nowhere to be seen. Matt had difficulty accepting this, but he kept quiet.

As soon as they entered the room, there was a short corridor, almost ten feet long. The inside of the outer wall of the building was on the left-hand side, and behind the right-hand wall was the bathroom. At the end of the short corridor, there was a lounge area, and the bed was set back, on the right-hand side, next to the bathroom.

"Where was the body found?" Matt asked. They showed him.

"Has anyone removed or disturbed anything from this room, other than the body?" asked Matt.

"No. We received instructions not to do anything until you arrived," said one of the plain-clothed officers.

"But you have done the routine? Dusted for prints, checked for blood splatter, searched for the murder weapon? Who removed the body?" Matt asked relatively mundane questions but never received a single answer, positive or negative. The local police officers looked around at each other's blank expressions. Matt stared at Harold Othman, who never moved.

Matt walked around the room. "Where are the instruments that were here on the table? There were some wooden tools here. Where are they?" he asked.

"Wooden tools? No one has moved anything. Our instructions were not to move anything from this room," said one policeman.

Matt retraced his steps to the entrance to mimic a person entering the room. Again, something here didn't add up. Something attracted his attention. There was an area of scratched wallpaper on the wall. He crouched down, Sherlockian style, and examined it close-up.

"Has anyone reported this damage to the hotel? Was it done before the murder?" Matt asked as he eased the damaged wallpaper with a pencil. Once again, blank stares.

Something else drew his attention. There was a stain on the carpet about six feet forward from where he was standing. It was outside the white body line. He crouched down again. All that was missing was a magnifying glass and the deerstalker headwear.

"Blood!" He turned around. Again, only to see the police officers and the detective, still with totally blank faces.

"It's the pattern, sir. It's a Persian," said one officer.

"Mate, I don't care if it's Persian, Indian, or Martian. It's blood, and it is not the carpet pattern. Has the forensics team seen this?" asked Matt.

"No, sir. Detective Othman informed us," said the officer.

"Okay," said Matt. "But even waiting for my arrival, the forensics team still needed to examine the area as soon as possible. Get the forensics squad in here now, and I mean in the next fifteen minutes." Matt raised his voice.

He took out his phone and pressed the keypad. Bill's phone rang.

"Hey up mate . . . what, what? Sitting by the pool with the girls . . . Getaway, shocking. Aye, all right, hotel what? Beirut Qasr. What's that, you say? Okay, explain more when I get there. I can jump in a cab." He ended the call and put his phone back in his shirt pocket.

"Matt asked me to join him at the hotel straight away," he said, standing up from his sun lounger. "He said that they haven't even started doing forensics at the crime scene yet. Hahaha, I don't know. We'll be back later. Anyone fancy seafood for dinner?" he said as he pointed at the sea.

Bill changed into suitable attire and went to the hotel lobby. Harold Othman arranged for a driver to collect Bill from his hotel. He didn't get the escort, but it was easier than taking a taxi.

Bill entered the room:

"What do you mean they haven't done forensics?" asked Bill.

"It might be a blessing in disguise, mate," replied Matt. "I will tell you later."

Matt pointed to the white line illustrating the position of the victim. It was easy to align the bloodstain and it appeared the victim struck a small glass-topped table as he fell. Matt then showed the damaged wallpaper at the entrance side of the doorway. Bill immediately looked at the light switch. Very odd.

"You said something about a square and a level," Bill whispered to Matt.

"They've gone," declared Matt.

Bill walked around the suite. He entered the bathroom and examined behind the shower curtain. He opened the bathroom wall cabinet: nothing in there. At the washbasin, there was nothing unusual, only the usual personal amenities.

"Make sure forensics bag all this," said Bill to the officers. They nodded their heads.

He pointed up at the removable ceiling tiles in the bathroom.

"Has anyone been in here?" he asked. "It looks like someone has moved a tile."

They all shook their heads. The local officers followed Bill around, very much as sheep follow the shepherd. The occupant had not even slept in the bed and there were wrinkles as if he had laid down and taken a nap. He pulled back the bedsheets; nothing. In the lounge area of the suite, there were several heavy pieces of regal-looking furniture. Bill looked behind the curtains and liners. Again, nothing. In the corner of the room, there was a wooden door, which accessed an adjoining room.

Bill made his way to the door and tried to open it. His side opened. The second door was locked from the other side, as they always are.

"Vacant?" Bill asked as he pointed at the door.

"Yes," replied Harold.

"What about on the night of the murder? Do you know who was staying in there?" asked Matt.

"The hotel has provided us with the details. We informed the hotel housekeeping to keep both rooms untouched until you came over. I will get 1403 opened for you now," said Harold Othman.

He turned and gave the instructions in Arabic to an officer, who promptly left the room.

"Excuse me, gentlemen," said Harold, as he followed a few seconds after the officer. "I will locate the hotel security officer and send him to you."

Bill turned to Matt and spoke in a lowered voice. "You said a square and a level were present, but now they have disappeared. Any sign of a plumb rule?"

"No sign of a plumb rule either," said Matt.

"Come over here a minute, mate," said Bill.

They both walked over to the entrance. Bill closed the door shut and stood with his back against the closed door.

"How tall was the victim?" asked Bill.

"They say about one point six or seven, so that's about five feet, six inches," Matt replied.

"Build?" asked Bill.

"Medium," replied Matt.

"So not very tall, and not a big guy, either. But how to overcome him? Now think about a plumb rule. How long is a builder's plumb rule? Forget what we see at the lodge." Bill was on to something here. And yet Matt is the detective!

"I would say about five feet long, could be a bit more," Matt said. He parted his hands to show the same distance.

"So, look how narrow the entrance to the room is here, and, for some strange reason, the light switch is at the end of the wall. Look," said Bill. He pointed to the switch.

"Now, what if the attacker wedged a builder's wooden plumb rule across the corridor here? One end on the skirting board, there." He pointed to some scratched paint.

"The width of the entrance here is about four feet. And using a five-feet plumb rule means the other end would be there. About three feet from the top of the skirting board on the opposite wall," demonstrated Bill. He showed his estimation with the damaged wallpaper.

"How do you know that?" asked Matt.

"Come on, mate; have you forgotten the forty-seventh problem of Euclid already? Or the Pythagorean Theorem, as it is better known," said Bill.

"Now, we open the door," said Bill as he pretended to open it.

He then positioned Matt so that they both could see the scenario that Bill tried to illustrate.

"Imagine, as soon as someone entered the room, he could not use his own forward movement to remove a wedged barrier he was totally unaware of. Yes, his calves would hit the tool. Remember, it is pitch dark in here, as he hadn't reached the light switch yet. Also, he will not have expected a barrier in his way," said Bill as he showed where the barrier would be.

"Besides, he's also had a few glasses of bubbly, and down he goes. As he went down, he has dislodged the barrier and that action provided damage to the wallpaper and the paintwork.

"This wouldn't kill him, though, surely," Matt chipped in.

"I doubt very much that it was intended to kill him, and that is why we now need to see the body and see how the death occurred," said Bill.

"The tools you saw on the video; were they proper builder's tools?" Bill asked.

"Yes, proper builder's tools; that's how I could recognise them. The level looked like an old wooden block level, and the square was a builder's wooden square. They were both there on that table," said Matt.

One last look around. Bill bent down and focused on the corner of a low-level table. He combed the carpet fabric with his fingers and picked up some small particles of wood.

"Look, splinters of wood," he said. Bill was back to forensics.

"We had better hang around and make sure the forensics guys get everything. There's something fishy here, mate," said Bill as the forensics team arrived. They got to work straight away.

The connecting door opened from the adjoining room, 1403, and Matt and Bill went through. The room was similar in the layout of furniture and décor. Matt and Bill both recognised the consequence that this room did not feature the short corridor upon entering like in the previous room. Everything had been left as when the guest departed. At the windows, the curtains were still closed; bedsheets were still in the same state. A bath towel hung over the back of an armchair and the writing bureau had been used at some stage. Sheets of disregarded hotel notepaper laid on the bureau top. Bill examined the wastepaper basket, where he found a screwed-up hotel message envelope with the letters 4M8001625. Was it a booking reference for a hotel or car hire? It could have been anything.

"He must have left something behind," said Matt. "I always leave something behind in hotel rooms; everybody does."

Bill entered the bathroom to continue their examination and found a hotel bathrobe on the rear of the door.

"Haha! Look at this!" exclaimed Bill.

"He hung the bathrobe over it and missed it when he left," said Bill.

He held out a necktie, dark green. There was a crest embroidered and above the crest were the initials AMBIC.

"Golfer?" asked Matt.

"It could mean anything, couldn't it?" said Bill. "Let me see."

He looked closer at the crest.

"Odd motif, that is. Looks like a seahorse on one side and a lizard on the other side," said Bill.

"Amphibian Beirut International Conference, who knows?" said Matt as he rolled up the tie and put it in his jacket pocket.

Bill stood motionless.

"Are you okay, mate?" asked Matt.

Bill hesitated for a moment.

"Yes, fine, thanks. Something leapt to mind, but it's gone now," said Bill.

"It can't have been that important then, Bill," Matt said. He heard a knock on the door. "Who's there?" he shouted out, but no reply.

"Hey, don't go removing any evidence, Matt. Forensics will need that necktie." Bill made a point as he opened the door. A large-framed Arabic man stood there motionless. He appeared to perspire heavily, which Bill found quite odd as a strong aroma of gentleman's cologne and its wearer entered the hotel room without invitation.

"Hello, how are you? My name is Wasim. How can I help you?"

Matt asked Wasim if the door locks on the rooms featured time tracking. He ended up having to explain to the security officer what time tracking meant. In doing this, Matt concluded he had answered his own question.

"Do you have the name of the guest who was staying here? A copy of his passport or anything from when he checked in," said Matt.

Wasim handed a piece of paper to Matt, a photocopy of an identity card. He read aloud:

"Amin Sadiq Al Bunuk."

"No passport? You don't take a photocopy of your visitor's passports?" asked Bill.

"Unnecessary. If a visitor is from local, we can use ID card," explained Wasim.

"He comes here quite many times," said the security officer. "Sometimes alone, sometimes with a lady. Last week, no lady, alone only."

"Can you tell us when he arrived and departed, and do you have his permanent address on file, please?" asked Bill.

"Yes, he check-in on Saturday morning and he check-out on Monday morning. See, it is here on the paper. Address and phone, we cannot give out, hotel policy. Talk to the hotel manager," he said.

"Does your staff have any record of him leaving early? There is a possibility that he may have left the hotel before his booking states. It could even have been very early on Sunday morning," asked Bill.

"I can check, but it is no problem. He paid until Monday," said the security officer.

"The amount he paid isn't the point here. The point is that the morning after a dead body was discovered in the next room, you allow the guest in the adjoining room to leave the hotel. Before any police interview or anything. Correct?" Matt asked, astonished.

With some humiliation, the security officer nodded his head. His throat moved with a heavy swallow.

"He paid until Monday. For us, it is okay," the security officer tried to explain again.

They made one last survey of the room and returned to the adjoining room.

"Label this room 1403, please," said Matt to one of the forensic team and he passed the rolled-up necktie. "Check for prints, yeh."

Matt had doubts about the information that he received from the local police. He knew some items had disappeared from the victim's room. It was a question of who had removed them and when. Matt and Bill stayed to gather any more evidence that they considered important.

———————

Downstairs, Harold was in the lounge, a cup of tea in one hand while he ran prayer beads through his fingers with the other. He talked with a member of the hotel staff, who walked away as he offered a seat to Matt and Bill.

"I guess you have a copy of this already," said Matt as he passed a copy of the ID card.

Harold shrugged his shoulders and smirked. Matt looked at Bill.

"Irony, Mr. Matthew?" said Harold.

"Sorry, I am not with you there," said Matt.

"Amin Sadiq . . . faithful friend . . . Amin Sadiq is Arabic for a faithful friend," explained Harold.

"Is there any connection with that?" asked Bill.

"I don't know. To me, it is just a name," replied Harold.

Matt stared at Harold. Harold's words reminded Matt of the comment from his young assistant back in the retail car park a few days ago. This time Matt thought it better not to make the same statement to the Lebanese detective.

"And the family name, Al Bunuk, any clue there?" asked Bill.

"I am afraid not. I am not familiar with this name, but it does not appear to be a local name. It could be Saudi origin or UAE—yes, possibly UAE. He registered with a Dubai address, I recall," said Harold.

"But he registered with a Lebanese ID card," said Matt.

"That means nothing, mate. This is Beirut. I bet you can buy an ID card down in Badaro and get it whilst you wait for your drinks to be served," said Bill.

"You know Beirut very well, Mr. Bill," said Harold.

"But how can a guest in a hotel use an overseas registration address and present a local ID card? Surely this is not the regular security protocols of hotels in Beirut," said Matt.

"Or anywhere," added Bill.

A message alert on Othman's phone.

"Ah, they are ready for you. So, gentlemen. Let us see what time you finish at the coroner's office. Then we decide if we should meet again later this afternoon. Is that okay with you, gentlemen?" asked Harold.

"It sounds a good idea to me," said Matt.

Harold explained he could not go with them, as his superiors had summoned him to a meeting upstairs.

A digital temperature indicator on the Beirut Bank building showed 25 degrees. The humidity made it feel much more. Fortunately, the car provided them with suitable air conditioning.

"Here, look at this, mate. I didn't want to say anything back there," said Matt.

He passed Bill the photocopy he collected in Harold's office.

"What the bloody hell, Matt?" Bill exclaimed when he read the paper.

"Illya, come on, Bill. What do you know about the name Illya?" asked Matt.

"Illya was the Arabic name for Jerusalem after the seventh-century siege of the city. It is the Arabic pronunciation of the first part of the name Aelia Capitolina; Jerusalem. The Romans changed the name of Jerusalem to Aelia Capitolina after the siege in 70CE." Bill continued looking over the document. "Aelia was the Roman route name of Hadrian and Capitolin is one of the seven hills of Rome. Some believe it was the location of the Temple of Jupiter," explained Bill.

"Well, let's look at it like this, until two hours ago, we still didn't know the identity of the victim back in Yorkshire," said Matt, "but with this . . . don't you think we are on to something here, mate?"

"David Illya and Solomon Illya, both murdered using some of the working tools of a Freemason. An order that has its roots in the history of the construction of the most famous building in Jerusalem. I think we are onto something . . . and I think we are onto something big!" said Matt.

The car came to a stop and as soon as they got out, Bill's spectacles fogged over.

"Bloody humidity," said Bill, "I'm fed up with this already."

As they entered the medical examiner's building, the temperature changed little. A police officer accompanied them to the examination room. No white suits here. They went straight into where the victim was on a cotton-covered examination trolley.

Bill, being courteous, requested permission to study the corpse for an initial review. On the front of the calves, he noticed a slight bruise, but not much skin damage. As suspected, nothing strange there. Not much on any other parts of the body, maybe some superficial bruising. Finally, on to the neck and the head region. There was a wound on the side of the forehead. This was where the victim must have hit the small glass-topped table and hence the bloodstain. The neck was an absolute mess. There were several wounds that went all the way around the neck and cut into the throat area. Bill leaned forward to take a closer examination.

"There is this," said the coroner.

He turned the victim's head in one direction and pointed to an indentation that had created a wound. Then after a couple of seconds, he rotated the head in the other direction, and again, he showed a similar injury.

A sharp blow could have made the wound to the left-hand side of the head. The other looked as though a dull, more heavy strike could have made it. Bill finished his examination and stood straight up, supporting his back as he did so.

"Matt, are you familiar with the French term *la loupe*?" he asked.

"No, not at all," came the reply.

"Okay, *la loupe* was a rather grotesque method of garrotting people. The French Foreign Legion developed this method. It consisted of two thin strands—piano wire or other powerful line attached to a wooden baton or stick. The two strands are then wrapped around the victim's neck in a particular pattern and secured by the wooden baton. This method is very effective. If the victim tries to free himself by pulling on one wire, the other wire will tighten itself round his own neck. History tells us that garrotting was a popular way of executing criminals, in particular, throughout the Spanish colonies of South America," Bill explained as he used his knowledge of old execution methods.

Bill ushered Matt outside, where they could talk between themselves.

"Here's what could have happened. The victim came in, tripped over the plumb rule, fell to the floor. The attacker knew of his height and size and knew what they would need for getting his victim down on the ground. When the body hit the floor, the attacker jumped on him and hit him twice in the back of the head. First, on the left, the indention suggests a blow with a sharp object. A ninety-degree angle, a wooden square? Yes, sure, why not? The blow to the right was with a heavier object, a builder's wooden level. Again, it is quite possible; there is no reason why not. The victim is now, very likely, unconscious," explained Bill.

"So, the attacker picked up the plumb rule, modified as a garrotting weapon, looped the wire around the neck, and within, what, twenty seconds…" continued Bill as he made a cutting motion across his own throat.

"Where are the weapons, especially the plumb rule or garrotting weapon?" asked Matt.

"Well, we both know it's always difficult to say how villains react at the crime scene. I suspect that in his haste, the attacker completely forgot about the square and the level. He, or she, focused on getting away with the murder weapon itself," replied Bill.

Bill was more than a forensic pathologist—much more.

They left the coroner's building to face what looked like a car park. Car after car after car crawled along the streets of downtown Beirut. The police vehicle waited for them, and they decided they had done enough for the time being. A nice relaxing beer on the hotel terrace would be the perfect round-off for the day. The driver set off to their hotel, and he telephoned the information to Harold Othman.

"Inspector Othman is not ready with hotel information yet, he said. Tomorrow morning is better for him and the hotel," said the driver. They returned to their hotel.

Monday was always a quiet day in The Shoulder and Mutton. Henry sat waiting for customers, or at least one, to enter and break the monotony. *How dull life had become*, he thought. But at least Phoenix had stayed on for a few more days. It pleased Henry, as he found he had to rely on her help last night, as the pub was quite busy. Earlier in the day, she had shared lunch with Henry and then enjoyed a relaxing afternoon in her room.

It was as she lay on her bed on that Sunday afternoon that she came to realise she was with a group of friendly people. Phoenix had experienced an unusual upbringing. As a teenager, she attended a private school for young ladies in the suburbs of Paris. Imagine living in Paris as a teenager and not being allowed to go out and experience the culture. For an artist, this must have been some sort of torture.

Henry had insisted that he stay in one of the guest rooms at the pub for the duration of his relief manager spell. Obviously, he hoped this might work out to provide him with a bonus. How fortunate Henry was, as his wish came true sooner than he expected. After closing on Sunday night, Henry lay on his bed watching the late sports news. He heard a gentle tapping noise on his bedroom door. As he slowly opened the door, he saw Phoenix standing there. She wore very little, only her underwear and a light, flimsy nightdress. In her left hand, she held a bottle of wine, and in her right hand, she held two glasses.

"Fancy a nightcap?" she asked.

She shoved him into his room and closed the door behind her with her foot.

Phoenix poured two glasses of wine and they sat on the edge of the bed, talking as if they had known each other for years. After a few minutes, Phoenix reached over and kissed Henry. She placed her hand above Henry's knee and, with her thumb on one side and her fingers on the other side of his thigh, she squeezed. It surprised him where she got her strength from. As her grip tightened, he looked into her eyes. At first, he wasn't sure, but it seemed that some type of telepathy had happened. He now knew exactly what Phoenix wanted. Phoenix looked into Henry's eyes, and she recognised Henry knew exactly what she wanted.

But that was last night, and today was Monday, and so far, a very mundane Monday. The shelves were well-stocked; the place was spotlessly clean. They sorted the cellar out for the delivery the next day. All that they needed now were some customers.

Henry wondered how his father and Bill were occupying themselves.

————————————

Matt and Bill immediately made their way to the terrace that overlooked the eastern Mediterranean Sea. The temperature and humidity had dropped, and it was quite comfortable now. Just right for the boys to enjoy a cold beer and the ladies to join them with a gin and tonic. The wives were ahead of them and showed their enthusiasm as they shook their empty glasses in the direction of Matt and Bill as they walked on the terrace, aptly named "Montmartre."

"Well, we are on holiday, Connie," said Penny.

Lebanon still showed strong French colonial connections. The terrace itself had been adequately constructed and resembled an old, cobbled street of the famous Paris suburb. Chanson music played in the background. The aroma of freshly baked French bread wafted along in the gentle evening breeze. Above the bar a red windmill rotated to break and scatter soft lights across the terrace.

Springtime in Paris meant one thing to Matt and Bill: *bière de printemps* and the sign on the bar said it was served deliciously ice cold.

Matt smiled to himself. He observed several people smoking hookahs, or Hubbly Bubblies. He had no hesitation in taking out his Savinelli Alligator, already bowled up with some plum pudding.

Earlier that afternoon, the two ladies had ventured outside and into the Beirut souks.

"Mate, they were there for one hour, and now we need to buy extra luggage for the stuff they purchased," said Bill.

These market traders are very smart at what they do.

Matt took out his phone and moved over to the edge of the terrace, his wife not far behind him. He pressed CONTACTS/HENRY/MOB; after a few seconds, it rang.

"Hello Henry, are you all right, mate? Yes, everything's fine, we are all fine. It's a tad warmer here than there. Well, I guess that is normal for a Monday, don't worry. I will let Bill know. He says to remind you that the draymen will come tomorrow. They don't have a certain time. It will be first thing in the morning or more toward lunchtime. Okay, mate, and you, just be careful. Bye," said Matt. "Hang on, Mum wants a word," and he passed the phone to Penny, who said a few brief words and hung up.

"That lad of ours has definitely taken to this Phoenix girl. She had something she simply had to attend to in Paris today when I was talking to her last week. Mind you, we could all see him eyeing her up the other night in the pub. Did you notice them?" said Matt.

Connie chipped in: "Notice them? I don't know about him taking to her, probably the other way around, Matt. She was doing her fair share of eyeing him up as well. She couldn't take her eyes off him on Saturday night. You should have seen the two of them after you both went home."

"Henry says the pub is dead, mate," said Matt.

"Ahh, only three o'clock there. It's still early; it'll pick up later, but Mondays are always quiet. I wonder if she got a job offer from that interview she went to at the hotel in Ingleton the other day. The managers there like that posh lady on their staff," Bill said.

"Ah, that's why she was there. I saw her on Saturday morning when I went over to see them about this David character. She was there when I went to have a look around the outside terrace, but she had gone when I went back inside. I can't have been outside for five minutes," Matt said.

"I still can't handle her," said Matt. "She seems to be a very confident and pleasant young lady, Bill, but there is something nagging at me. What do you think?" asked Matt.

"I say she is the shyest person you will ever meet in your entire life . . . for the first five minutes," said Bill.

"And after the first five minutes?" A rhetorical question from Penny.

"She will talk to you like she has known you all her life," said Bill.

"You men," Penny said as she shook her head. "You'll never understand it, will you?"

"By the way, I remembered to get this for you. Ryan asked me to get a better copy with date and place of birth," said Bill.

Matt unfolded the piece of paper Bill passed to him and read aloud: "Family name: Istaza; given name: Phoenix; place of birth: it says here, Caesarea; born: 14 JUNE 1995."

He looked up at Bill.

"Well, I never . . . sounds Italian. Why would an Italian need a Maltese passport?" said Matt.

"It sounds Italian, but it's not Italian. Matt, I can tell you, we may be dealing with extremely wealthy and very powerful people here, my friend. Caesarea is a town on the coast of Israel, north of Tel Aviv and halfway to Haifa. It is the only privately managed development council in the country. And the chair of that council is none other than Baron Rothschild."

"What did I tell you all? There's something about that girl," said Matt as he raised his glass and turned around to the two wives.

"Of course, Matt, she's a Gemini . . . and you won't find a better example of the twins anywhere, from what I have seen and heard from her," said Connie.

"Cheers!"

Matt and Bill discussed more and agreed on a schedule for the next day.

"Now, who's for one more before we freshen up for that seafood dinner Bill is going to treat us to?" said Matt.

"Only if you put that bloody pipe away!" exclaimed Penny.

SEVEN

The next morning, Matt and Bill arrived at police headquarters, courtesy of Harold's driver.

"Good morning, Harry. How are you? Have you got your station Wi-Fi password, please? I have something interesting to show you here," said Matt as he set up his laptop.

Harold shouted out a command in Arabic, and a young man walked in and attended to Matt's computer. He then took Matt's phone, pressed a few buttons, and handed it back with a polite smile.

"Here, look. I can zoom in. Look here, Harry," said Matt as he pointed to his computer screen.

He played the video of the TV broadcast for Harold. Bill had already seen it several times.

The two tools, which Matt had claimed all along were present in the bedroom, were there on the screen for all to see. Bill leaned in to look closer. He could see that the size and type of the tools could easily inflict wounds on the victim. Matt explained to Harry that they needed to find these two objects.

"As we said yesterday, the television crew may have picked them up by mistake," said Matt.

Harold suggested, "You must go to the television crew immediately. I recognise the broadcaster in the video. We know them. I will make the arrangements and send you over there as soon as possible."

"Can we visit the Beirut Qasr Hotel on the way to the television studio, please? We need the information we asked for yesterday," asked Matt.

"Yes, of course, we will go there now, and then you can continue to the television studios alone," said Harold.

Another motorcade to the hotel and a repeat of the drama from the day before to guide them to the lobby lounge.

"Gentlemen, we have a few minutes spare, so I have asked the hotel manager to meet us," he said as he showed them to help themselves to tea.

"Harry," started Matt, "I must ask you something. Has your team made a thorough search of the hotel, inside and outside, for any murder weapons? We are not saying that the two items on the video are the murder weapons. Our concern is that they may provide some evidence or leads. Have they searched the immediate vicinity, around the hotel premises?"

"My team has searched in and around the hotel grounds since the evening of the murder. So far, we found nothing," replied Harold. "As far as we can determine, no one removed anything. We stopped the forensics people from entering the room when we heard that Scotland Yard was sending some people over."

"You flatter us, Harry," said Matt, "but that wouldn't stop someone from walking away with crucial evidence."

"Harold, can you explain why the news reporters were in there to do a report so soon after the discovery of the victim?" asked Bill.

"Ah, I expected this question, yes. A dead body, a potential murder, found in the Qasr Hotel in Beirut. This is big news here. The station broadcasts all over the Levant and even to Europe," explained Harold.

"Where is the information we requested? It is taking a long time to get such relatively simple information," Matt said, showing his frustration.

Bill repeatedly tapped the top of Matt's knee to show him to *calm down*.

"Harold, coming back to the deceased. What can you tell us about him? Did he have any enemies? An angry husband or two?" asked Bill.

Harold started his explanation, sitting back in the armchair. "Mr. Matthew, Mr. Bill, about Mr. Suleiman's behaviour towards women. Yes, he was a bit of a rogue. Yet, as far as I know, he never associated himself in any relationship with any married lady—never. He was only interested in single ladies. I have never known him, or heard of him, to be adulterous," said Harold.

"As far as business goes, he was very shrewd; he may have made a few enemies over the years. I understand he was facing some issues over this current project he was working on," said Harold.

"What else can you tell us about this project he was working on, please, Harry? Is it near Beirut; is it worthwhile we visit it?" asked Matt.

"It isn't here in Beirut or even here in Lebanon. It is a construction project in Jordan. If you go southwest from Amman towards the Dead Sea, there is an area known as the Ma'in Hot Springs. This region is where he is building the project. It started as a health spa, and later it will include restaurants, bars, nightclubs, and even a casino. Three of the top brands of hotels have already signed up their premises," Harold continued.

"Indeed, Suleiman had a dream about this magnificent project in Jordan. But some people, the conservatives, were against the entire project," said Harold.

"But surely such a project will benefit many people. Provide hundreds of jobs, bring in tourists, spend thousands of dollars," said Matt.

"The authorities objected to the name he wanted to use for the resort," said Harold. "It was causing issues with some of the more conservative councilmembers."

"Go on." Matt and Bill exchanged glances with each other.

"He wanted to name it The Magnificent Ma'in," Harold said, with an amazed look on his face.

Again, Matt and Bill glanced at each other.

"Suleiman the Magnificent!" Harold said.

Bill jumped from his seat, striking the armrests. "Good God!" he shouted.

Matt stared at Bill, puzzled. Harold, stunned, poured himself a glass of water.

Bill paced up and down the lounge area where they were sitting and after a few seconds, he started, "Suleiman the Magnificent was the most successful ruler of the Ottoman Empire. During Suleiman's reign, he conquered several Christian countries. He started in the Levant region and moved north into Europe and south into Arabia to spread Islam.

"He was personally responsible for changing many of the Ottoman laws, so he also became known as Suleiman the Lawgiver. The people also referred to this period of rule as the Transformation of the Ottoman Empire.

"He had many sons. They all died except for two. One of these two sons, Sehzade Bayezid, refused to follow the orders of his father. He formed his own small army together with his own sons. This army attempted a rebellion and suffered several defeats in the Ottoman and Persian regions. Bayezid's army fled from the region we now know as southeast Turkey. They took refuge in northwest Persia. But they were not safe there, and the Shah imprisoned them under orders from Suleiman. Over the next few years, Suleiman tried many times to have them executed. Finally, he succeeded. After financial compensation to the Shah, they were all executed. And the method of execution was . . . garrotting."

Matt's face drained.

"My goodness," Matt said to himself, "good old Bill Cooper."

Harold looked at his phone. "Well, the TV studio can meet you whenever you are ready. My driver will take you there, and then we decide on the next step," said Harold.

"But I thought we were waiting for the hotel manager to join us here first," said Bill.

Harold summoned the receptionist, and she spoke to Harold in Arabic.

"Very well; thank you, miss. The manager sends his apologies, as there is a delay and he will meet with us later on," explained Harold.

Soon, Matt and Bill made their way to the television company that made the report. Upon arrival, several of the staff escorted Matt and Bill through the lobby and into a meeting room. A very drab, cold meeting room. Matt immediately compared it to Harold's office; it wasn't much better. The air conditioning was central, built into the structure of the building, as opposed to a noisy box rattling away inside a windowpane. It also meant it worked.

It wasn't long before a very lean local guy came in, accompanied by a rather attractive female. The lady, her name was Zaiton, was to act as an interpreter, or so it seemed.

Matt asked about what the film crew did after they finished filming. He asked if they knew if any of their crew picked up any items, by mistake, from the hotel room last Saturday night. Despite both of them appearing to understand the question, they took it upon themselves to discuss further in Arabic.

Matt interjected immediately and said, "Excuse me. This is a murder investigation. If you wish to communicate separately with each other, I must end this interview until we can arrange for our interpreter to be present."

Both of the staff looked at each other, astonished, and then swapped glances with Matt and Bill. They agreed to carry on the interview in the English language. They explained they would need to contact the crew who had attended the scene. Also, they will check their storage space where they might keep any such articles.

"We realise it will not be a five-minute job, but we must recover all the evidence from the crime scene as soon as possible."

Matt did not mention any items in particular and asked another question. "Does your station send a different report to the other news channels? I mean, using a different reporter speaking Hebrew, Turkish, or English?"

"We work with several television companies in the Near and Middle East," said Zaiton. "Usually, for these items we would use one report in Arabic and subbies."

"Subbies?" asked Matt.

"Subtitles," she answered. "It is the most economical way. A thirty-second clip and add the subtitles."

"With international news, it is quite different, of course," she added.

"We may need to interview the reporter who covered this item and any other crew members who entered the hotel room at any time before or during the broadcast itself," said Matt.

"It shouldn't be a problem. Have you talked to Inspector Othman? We can only cooperate with his approval," she said.

Zaiton agreed she would find the information and send it to Harold Othman.

Then a question from Bill. "How did you hear so soon about the murder and mobilise a reporting team so fast to the hotel? You made your broadcast within one hour from when the body was removed," he asked. A similar question to the one he had posed to Harold Othman.

"Oh yes, I remember. There was an international conference at a nearby hotel, the Phoenicia. We had some spare crew there," said Zaiton. She was very helpful.

"Conference," asked Matt. "Can you recall what the conference was about?"

"Yes, it was about medicine and biomedical development. The principals of the association did an interview here yesterday. They left Beirut this morning, I understand—why? Is it important to your investigation?" asked Zaiton.

"Everything is important in a murder investigation," said Matt.

They were back in the car and on their way to the Qasr Hotel to pick up where they left off earlier.

"Something I have noticed about the pattern of all these places we visit, Bill," said Matt.

"I think I know what you mean, go on," said Bill.

"Every location we visit, it is almost as if they have rehearsed our visit," said Matt.

"And it is always so difficult to get information. Everything needs a rubber stamp from Othman," added Bill, also getting frustrated.

"That and the local police don't provide much help," said Matt. "We could chase our tail around for days here if we are not careful."

"I am thinking of doing a bit of private detective work tomorrow," Matt said as he winked at Bill.

Matt tapped the driver on the shoulder and asked to go to the Qasr Hotel. The driver immediately made a telephone call, presumably to Harold.

"What about this medicine and biomedical conference, Bill? Any thoughts on that?" asked Matt.

"I will be honest, mate. I have thought little about that."

"If 1403 was here for a conference, we need much more details on his movements during his stay," said Bill. "But that tie, that bloody tie, there is something in the back of my mind about that tie," said Bill.

"I don't believe he was here for any conference; he was here for one thing and one thing only," added Matt.

When they reached the hotel, this time, it seemed their arrival was not expected. They made their way through to the bar and sat down and ordered a pot of tea, English tea, not the Arabic version. Not long after, the hotel manager passed by the bar and he came in to greet them. He sat down.

"Good afternoon, gentlemen. My name is Michel Haddad. How can I assist you further? May I offer you something?" said the manager.

They opened the conversation about the handling of the investigation so far.

Matt asked a very routine question to start: to whom did the hotel pass on the staff details? But Michel's response amazed Matt and Bill.

"The local police never asked for a list of our staff on duty that or any other night," said Michel Haddad.

"Is there any possibility that you can provide us with such a list, please?" asked Matt.

The hotel manager insisted he could only surrender this information to the Beirut police.

Another question, what did he know about this Mr. Amin Sadiq Al Bunuk?

"I only met him once; the first time was last week," he said.

"But your security officer informed us yesterday that this Mr. Amin was a regular guest at this hotel. In such a hotel like this, I would have thought you would know your regular guests," Matt said.

Bill followed on. "Sometimes alone, sometimes with a woman. This time, he was alone. Check-in Saturday morning, check-out Monday morning, but we suspect he may have left the hotel early on Sunday morning. It seems he walked through the reception and left with no luggage."

A light bulb lit up in Matt's head when he heard the two words: *no luggage*.

The manager shook his head; he looked rather embarrassed.

"Gentlemen, as far as our records show, the guest last Saturday in 1403 has never used this hotel before. I only met him last week because he was arguing with one of our staff, Ahmad, in the hotel bar on Saturday afternoon. Someone complained about a disturbance in the bar, and we do not accept such behaviour here in the Beirut Qasr. He was disrespectful to one of our servers, but we cleared everything up. It turned out that the server was the nephew of the guest," said the manager.

"Very odd," said Bill.

"He had put his nephew through school when he was younger, and they haven't seen each other in a long time. Nevertheless, on that day there was some disagreement between the two of them."

"By the way, may we please interview your security officer again? The one we met yesterday. I have forgotten his name," said Matt.

"Our regular security officer was not on duty yesterday; we used a replacement supplied by the agency," said Michel.

"Excuse me, do your guest room door locks have a time trace installed?" asked Bill.

"Of course, we are a *five*-star hotel!" the manager barked.

The manager excused himself and went to collect the information they had requested. He also agreed to provide a copy of the key activity logs for rooms 1401 and 1403.

"This Haddad chap seems to know how to run his hotel, mate. But how did they allow the guest in 1403 to leave as they did? How do we know if the police even know about this Al Bunuk guy, let alone have spoken to him?" asked Bill.

"Really, what a mess here," Matt said, again with a tone of frustration.

Matt and Bill sat back to finish their tea and waited for the manager to return.

Tuesday morning at the Shoulder of Mutton is drayman's day, beer delivery day. Depending on the time of day, they expect either a full English or a good healthy serving of shepherd's pie. With this in mind, stand-in manager Henry Baxter is out of bed and downstairs in the kitchen. The old stagecoach stop-off place can be eerie when it is like this. The stone walls and floors keep the internal temperature way down. Even on these spring days, it can still be quite invigorating until after mid-morning.

Henry waited around and he switched the television on in the bar area to catch up on the football results. He looked at the clock, five minutes after he had looked last time. He understood there would always be so many things to do at the pub. But now, when you got around to it, what was there to do? He can only sit around and wait for the draymen to arrive. Henry wondered if it was worth disturbing Phoenix so early. He was in a mischievous mood. He thought about how he could spend some time under the duvet with her, or on top of it if it came to that. There was still a lot he needed to find out about this girl. He decided he would try to start a conversation about her past.

"Rain and windy, especially on the high ground," announced the television broadcaster.

"Great," said Henry. "It will be very quiet the next few days."

The aroma of fresh coffee drifted through the building, and it brought Phoenix downstairs. She had dressed in a white V-neck t-shirt, a skimpy pair of knickers, and her favourite pair of old slippers.

"Ooh, I can smell coffee. I love the smell of fresh-brewed coffee," she said.

"Help yourself. If the draymen come, please go back upstairs. If they try to roll the barrels down the cellar with you dressed like that, they will probably smash the barrels open," laughed Henry.

Phoenix moved closer to him and looked for some warmth. She put her bare arms inside his woollen sweater and hugged him. Her semi-tanned legs changed colour to a rather blueish tint.

"You're like toast," she said.

"Come on with you, get back upstairs," he said.

"Only if you come with me," she said as she walked backwards and pulled him along.

"The Draymen are due. They might be here in ten minutes," he said.

"What I want to do won't take ten minutes." She kissed him.

She led him back to the bottom of the stairs to the guest rooms and opened the door. A very agile girl, she held a cup of coffee in one hand and guided Henry along with the other while she kept lips to lips contact.

"Let's hope they go to the Rainbow first," said Henry, giving in to her persuasion.

Was this another opportunity for sex, or had these two youngsters developed deeper feelings for each other?

Henry was happy, especially since it lasted more than ten minutes.

"I bet you are ready for your full English now?" she teased him.

Phoenix got dressed, this time into something that could provide some warmth, and she joined Henry downstairs. Henry had prepared breakfast for either the draymen or the couple in room 5, depending on who got there first.

"None of that fried fatty stuff for me, thank you," she said as she opened a carton of yoghurt.

"Henry, may I ask you?" asked Phoenix. "Tell me, what's it like having a police officer as a father?"

"Difficult . . . it was much worse when I was younger, of course. If anything went wrong at my school, there was always a full investigation. It could be quite embarrassing," Henry replied.

"I can understand that. It was quite difficult when he interviewed me about that dead body," she said. "He asked me a lot of questions, most of them nothing to do with the murder."

"Don't say it like that. You're not the only one. He's interviewed loads of others. They have a method of asking questions that you least expect, and then they analyse your response. It's science. But it's his job." Henry came closer to her. "And anyway, who said it was a murder?"

"Now you sound like him!" she screamed. "Maybe it's because it was the first time that I have been in that situation. It just felt odd, that's all," she tried to explain.

"So, you mean it's the first time you have had an interview as a murder suspect! Great; can't wait to tell my mates from uni. Their girlfriends get interviewed for murder two or three times every week," he said, teasing her.

"Don't be sarcastic, and who says I am your girlfriend?" Her expression changed. "Are you still at university? You're a bit old for uni, aren't you?"

"Nah, finished a few years back, but we still keep in touch, old mates and all that. Me and two others did some travelling, Southeast Asia, Australia, you know, gap year stuff," he said.

"What year?" Phoenix hadn't heard this term before.

"Gap year; where've you been for the last ten years?"

"Australia, Singapore, Dubai," she said.

"Uh, Australia, eh? I loved it there. I could stay there if I had a chance," Henry said.

"My father's company is building a hotel resort complex over in New South Wales in a place called Lake Macquarie. I forget the exact address now, Pelican or something. It's near Belmont. I have been twice. It's wonderful, the lake on one side and the ocean on the other," said Phoenix.

"You're a very fortunate girl," said Henry. "What's that smell?"

"Hahaha; see, this is healthier for you," she said, pointing to the yoghurt and fresh fruit.

"Somebody is knocking at the front door. Would you like me to answer it?" she raised her voice.

She didn't wait for an answer and walked over to the front door.

"Good morning," she announced cheerfully to two well-set males wearing brown dungarees.

"Blimey, Dan. What do we 'ave 'ere?" said one, removing his cap and wiping his brow.

"Allow me to introduce myself. My name is Holly, and this is my husband Paul, but I call him Fred as he resembles my brother," said Phoenix, doing her Audrey Hepburn impression.

Speechless, the draymen set about restocking the beer cellar. After a couple of minutes, one drayman came back into the pub; he held up a car key.

"Aye up. Do any of your guests drive a Porsche? Somebody must have lost this. We found it on the cellar door support ledge when we opened the doors," he said.

He left the key down on the corner of the bar counter and went back outside.

"So, that's where it got to!" said Phoenix, as she picked up the key. "How on earth did it get there?"

"It doesn't matter," said Henry. "What's important is that you have got it back. Mind you; it's no good now they have issued you with a new one, anyway."

Meanwhile, the two overnight guests had come down from the guest quarters:

"Good morning. Two for full English breakfast, please, when you are ready," said Mr. Hartley, the guest from room 5.

The manager of the hotel now realised that he had put himself in a difficult position. The reputation of the hotel could be in jeopardy. He knew he had to supply all information about the case through the local police. But the hotel had also slipped up on cooperating with pertinent information so Haddad knew he had to find a compromise. He provided Matt and Bill with as much information as possible and still tried to keep to the local police protocol. He gave them a copy of the key logs.

"Please read this in your hotel. Thank you," said Michel.

Michel then continued and disclosed that there were no records of transactions for room service, bars, or restaurants for 1403 for that evening. The housekeeping department recalls a DO NOT DISTURB sign was on the door handle all day on Sunday. He could only check with the night shift housekeeper later in the day.

"I am afraid that is all the information we have on file, gentlemen. Thank you and have a good day. Oh, by the way, here is my card," and he handed over an elegant satin-finished business card.

Matt stuffed it into his shirt pocket, and they made their way outside.

"Coffee shop over there, Bill. Let's take a few minutes," suggested Matt.

Matt had to dig deep in his memory now and think about the business cards that they collected from the abandoned car last week. He was sure there was something about the post box numbers on the cards, 8844 or 4488.

He reached into his shirt pocket for some cash. "Hey, look at this, mate," said Matt.

He noticed the handwriting on the reverse side of the manager's card.

1403
Sun 4/7 - DXB/Sydney
EX412 dep 1415

"So, whoever he is, or was, it looks as though he is in Australia now. What day is it today, Bill?"

"Let's get back. Harold has invited us all for dinner this evening; we can have a few scoops before we meet him," said Matt.

A short taxi ride back to their hotel, and Harold Othman was waiting at the reception. He was sitting in an old Georgian, low-back style arm-chair, hands placed on his knees. His face was very stern. However, as they approached him, he smiled.

"Good afternoon, gentlemen. I am sorry to inform you that your services are no longer needed here in Beirut." He came straight to the point. "Our executive director of internal affairs has informed me this afternoon you are to return to England as soon as possible. It is now the job of our local police to handle this case.

"Your presence has been very worthwhile, and we thank you," Harold continued. "Headquarters now believe the time has come for our person-nel to fulfil the outcome of the case."

This news did not surprise Matt and Bill. Not surprised one bit. There was something very odd about this whole scenario here in Beirut.

"We understand, Harry, and we would like to thank you for your warm hospitality during our stay here. I am not sure about our return tickets, but, of course, we respect the wishes of your superior officers. We will change our departure date and let you know shortly." Matt was very complimentary.

"I extended my invitation to you and your good ladies for dinner with my good lady and myself this evening. Of course, my invitation still stands. Work is work. It would be impolite of me to cancel," said Harold. "So, please, change your booking for tomorrow. Amelia and I look forward to the pleasure of your company this evening. I promise you an exquisite meal in superb surroundings."

"That's wonderful; thank you, Harry." Matt took his hand and shook it rather emphatically. "Dinner this evening. What time?" he asked.

"My driver will collect you at seven. Please dress formally. The restaurant requires a jacket and tie, and I look forward to your company," Harold said. He bowed to both and departed.

Matt and Bill walked through the reception area of their hotel.

"Bill, have you ever seen the movie *Casablanca*, the Bogart and Bergman classic?" asked Matt.

"Of course, Captain Louis Renault," laughed Bill.

Back to work. Matt set up his laptop in his room. No sign of the girls as they had booked a sightseeing tour since nine o'clock and were due back around four, so no drama there.

"Right, Bill. Now where's that list of key access times?" said Matt.

Bill unfolded the paper and smoothed it on the writing bureau top. Matt picked up a pencil and wrote the details according to the time printed on the left.

Bill examined the list of key entries:

"Look here," started Bill. "1401, there is a tiny digit there in the top corner '3' but here in 1403, in the same place, it is '2.'"

"The small number usually indicates that three separate door key cards were issued for 1401 and so only two keys for room 1403," submitted Matt. "The key cards are issued by the check-in system, so it records the information."

"But the guest in 1401 was alone. Why would they issue three separate door keys?" asked Bill.

"That is a question we should put to the hotel," said Matt. "But I imagine it is routine to issue two cards. Most hotels have one of those power-saving slots these days and a second key means the guest can leave the room with the power still on to run the air conditioning."

"So, three cards . . . unusual," said Bill.

"Yes, it means there is a good chance that the attacker and his accomplice did not rely upon the hotel housekeeping for access to the victim's room at any time," Matt explained.

RM 1401*
ENT 1427 primary key – checking in (master switch)
RM 1401²
ENT 1542 Return to room after lunch
ENT 1717 return after walk - maybe??
ENT 2103 return after dinner – early??
RM 1401³
ENT 2049 14 mins before Key 2 @ 2103
ENT 0258 next morning 3 am???

RM 1403²
ENT 1152 checking in
ENT 1403 after lunch & drinks in the bar (met someone?)
ENT 2033 what for??
ENT 0315 next morning – why?

"So, looking at this, Bill, it is quite easy for us to work out the sequence, isn't it? Unfortunately, we only get the entry times and no exit times," said Matt.

"But where did Suleiman go after he checked in?" asked Bill.

"My theory is this. This Amin Sadiq knew what time Suleiman would check in to the hotel. He made sure he had his lunch well before Suleiman arrived. What does that suggest, Bill?" asked Matt.

"They knew each other," Bill replied.

"Absolutely," said Matt.

"During his lunch in the bar, Sadiq met his nephew, Ahmad. There was some kind of complaint about a disturbance between the two of them," continued Matt.

"Consider the nephew may have objected to something he was being pressed into doing by his uncle. Have you thought about that scenario, mate?" asked Bill.

"And the key log for 1403 shows another time, 2033. What was that for, I wonder?" said Matt.

"Let's go through those key times again, Matt. There's still something missing."

"The key log shows the first time that the Sadiq guy entered the room. The time after that was when he returned after his lunch," said Bill. "Then he went somewhere after Suleiman had gone down for his dinner."

"Let's now suppose Suleiman went for dinner around seven o'clock. While he was away, Sadiq left his room again, possibly to meet with his accomplice to ensure the arrangements were in place. Having done so, he got back to his room just after half-past eight."

"Now, a few minutes later, 2049, someone used the third key to enter 1401. It must have been to open the adjoining door from that side."

"Suleiman returns to his room at nine o'clock. Don't you find that odd, Bill? I find it very odd."

"It must have been to collect something to use during his meeting," said Matt.

"We need to know where Suleiman had dinner and if he had any company. That will help us," said Bill.

"Hang on, at three the next morning, look at the activity between the two rooms," said Bill as he looked down the list again.

"Could this have been when he went back into the victim's room to remove the weapons he left behind?" asked Matt.

"Possibly; there's another entry time there seventeen minutes after someone entered 1401 again. But seventeen minutes sounds like a hell of a long time for someone to remove the two articles you say disappeared. Don't you think so, mate? Remember, once inside 1401, 1403 can be accessed if both adjoining doors are open," said Bill.

"Mmmm, yes; they can't risk leaving the door ajar as a lot of these hotels have an alarm if the door is open for a pre-set time, say thirty seconds," explained Matt.

"Another thing. How do you get rid of a five-foot-long piece of wood into a deluxe hotel? Walk through the reception with that under your arm and a few heads will turn. This is a five-star hotel, not Butlins," said Bill.

"But we are not part of the local mafia here, Bill, and that means so much in these parts. If you want something done, somebody somewhere will know someone who will do it," added Matt. "There's always that person who can fix almost anything."

"Ferrari!" exclaimed Bill; he clicked his fingers. He still had *Casablanca* on his mind.

"Anyway," said Matt, acknowledging Bill's point, "Sadiq leaves the hotel the next morning, quite early. Who knows, maybe he just walked straight out of the hotel. He doesn't need to check out and we don't even know what time he left."

"So, Bill, again. Why did Suleiman leave his dinner and return to his room so early? Just after nine o'clock. It doesn't add up."

"I was thinking the same myself. Let's establish why he went back to his room in the first place, shall we? We need to go back to the Qasr?" said Bill.

"Come on." Matt jumped up, and they rushed out of the door.

The time passed as they crawled in the traffic. They didn't want to run short of time and make themselves late for their dinner appointment with Harold and Amelia Othman. Matt had an idea. He telephoned the manager to meet him at the rear of the hotel. Upon arrival, Matt asked the taxi driver to wait for ten minutes.

From the rear entrance, they first passed through the laundry department and then on towards the kitchen. It was dinner preparation time. A faint aroma of mirepoix filled the kitchen and accompanied the almost constant sound of pots, pans, and other iron utensils being put to use. One chef delicately pressed the surface of a beef tenderloin and another looked close up into the eyes of a large kingfish. Proper preparation is crucial.

Organised chaos, thought Matt as he looked around.

The general manager led them to a small staff meeting room away from prying eyes. Matt explained they were short of time and requested the manager's cooperation to determine the movements of Suleiman and with whom he dined on Saturday evening.

"Oh, monsieur, our limousine always collects Mr. Suleiman from the airport. Of course, he doesn't always arrive directly at the hotel, in case he has a place to visit first. I do, however, recall that last Saturday, he checked in to the hotel. Shortly afterwards, he requested our vehicle to take him to collect two parcels that had come in from Europe. He wouldn't have them delivered as he said the contents were very fragile.

"When he returned, he contacted me to say he was going to rest for a short time before he freshened up, and he asked me to join him around six-thirty in the cocktail bar for a black rose. Monsieur, the local blackberries are in season; they are exquisite—mmmhuah!" said the hotel manager.

"Can you recall what Mr. Suleiman did for dinner on Saturday evening?" asked Bill.

"Yes, he had dinner with Sir Rupert Chapman," added the hotel manager.

"Who is this Sir Rupert guy? Why are we only just getting this information now?" said Matt, again using a frustrated tone of voice.

"He lives here in Beirut. He has lived here for many years. I understand he is some type of consultant, or investor, an Englishman."

"Sir Rupert, yes, he'll be English all right," said Bill.

"They have been doing some work together on the Suleiman project in Jordan. They had dinner in Les Fleur des Jardin, our French restaurant. Drank quite a lot of wine, as usual, before and during dinner. I have already given this information to the police," said Michel Haddad.

"I thought you said the police had not interviewed the hotel staff?" asked Bill.

"The staff, no, but I am the manager. They *must* interview me," he said, almost standing to attention.

"Do you know why Suleiman returned to his room so early, seems to be halfway through their dinner . . . strange?" asked Bill.

"No, I didn't ask this question of Sir Rupert. More than that, I am afraid I cannot help you. But if Mr. Suleiman was up to his habit to go to a club, he could have gone to his room to get something for Sir Rupert before he departed for his club—quite possible.

"I recall the wine server informed me that Mr. Suleiman ordered a bottle of the '65 Chateau Dubois. A very nice wine. As Suleiman left the restaurant, he told the wine server he would be back in about twelve minutes. 'Open it now and it will be perfect by the time I get back,' were his exact words," explained the manager.

"Thank you very much, indeed. You have been a tremendous help. Now we must hurry. We have a dinner appointment with Harold Othman this evening," Matt said as he left the room.

"Ahh, okay, I have already provided this information to Inspector Othman. If you ask him, I am sure he will provide you with all the details," shouted the manager as Matt and Bill departed.

"What a method for us to secure vital pieces of information. What is this Harold Othman up to?" asked Bill as their car drove away to return them to their hotel.

"It is indeed a strange method of investigating they use here," said Matt. "Speaking of which, let's see what our friend Ryan is up to," said Matt as he dialled on his phone.

The loudspeaker rang out. Ryan answered.

"Hello, Ryan, it's Matt."

"Yeah, I know. I see your caller ID," Ryan replied.

"I need to be quick. Have you got those business cards we found in the abandoned car last week?"

"Yes, and the ones we found on the victim," replied Ryan.

"Look, instead of reading them all out here, can you make a photocopy of them all and email it to me? Keep it as two lots if you can—the ones from the car and the ones we found on the body," Matt explained.

"We are expecting the DNA results back later today, latest tomorrow. By the way, that Maltese girl is still here," said Ryan.

"We heard," said Matt.

"How's it going over there?" Ryan asked.

"It hasn't been easy, mate, and you thought Billericay was difficult!" said Matt.

EIGHT

The party of six took their places on the corniche terrace of the Bayt Al Parisienne Restaurant. Harold had brought along his wife, Amelia. Their table caught the evening sea breeze perfectly as it blew across the terrace. The menus illustrated a variety of excellent dishes, especially seafood, and two bottles of champagne sat on the table. After popping the champagne corks, their evening began. Matt already had a list of topics in his mind that he would use to control the flow of conversation. None of them related to work. The usual opener: where did Harold and Amelia first meet?

Harold told the story of how their long-distance romance blossomed over several years, as Amelia travelled a lot. A few years ago, she set up her own interior design company in Beirut. Her company does a lot of work in hotels and restaurants. Even the one they were sitting in. Amelia mentioned she had recently returned from Jordan. She had been working on a large project, which was unfortunately now on hold. Harold stared at her over his spectacles as he read the menu.

Not long into the story, plate after plate of food arrived at the table. Each time the server put a plate down, he would reposition several others to provide enough room. After a few minutes, another server arrived with a large breadbasket on his shoulder.

"My friends. Lebanese Mezza, the best in the world, welcome to Beirut," said Harold as he rose to his feet, holding a glass of champagne.

Penny continued with their story and Connie finished with her and Bill's saga as they battled their way through the traditional Lebanese starter.

Meanwhile, Matt started on the other topics he had already set in his mind. Hobbies, pastimes, sporting activities, historical connections of the country, and the area itself. The subjects would flow, one after the other, without touching politics or religion, something that both Matt and Bill were familiar with because of their lodge meetings.

Connie asked Harold about the taxi system that operates in Beirut. "Penny and I had to wait for ages for a taxi to come back from the stairs place. When we caught one, the driver stopped twice to pick up two other passengers. We have never seen this before. We got quite worried, and it took us ages to get back."

"We know this as 'service' in Beirut. A shared taxi service. You need to be careful, as the drivers can go wherever they want," explained Harold. "My advice: arrange transport with your hotel."

The name Suleiman cropped up in conversation. Bill made a comment to compare the victim's habit with a similar one of Solomon. So, Harold gave them a story about King Solomon's reputation from a unique perspective.

"Yes, King Solomon was also famous for his womanising. He had over seven hundred wives and three hundred concubines. But he had one favourite wife, and it was not, as many believe, the queen of Sheba or the pharaoh's daughter.

"Solomon took a wife from Memphis, Egypt. Her name was Moti Maris. One day her father travelled to Jerusalem, and he brought many gifts. But his real reason was an attempt to overthrow Solomon and take Jerusalem on behalf of the king of Egypt. After a few weeks, the father of Moti Maris asked her to arrange a meeting with Solomon. He also poisoned the wine she would serve during the meeting. After Moti Maris poured wine for her father and husband, she noticed her father didn't pick up his cup. As Solomon was about to drink his wine, she snatched the cup and drank the wine herself. The father fled immediately, and Moti Maris died in the arms of King Solomon.

"So much was Solomon's grief that he buried her underneath the temple. Archaeologists have recently discovered and unearthed her tomb. They say that the treasures in the tomb exceed those found in the tomb of Tutankhamen." Harold told a wonderful story.

"Fascinating," said Bill. "And one I haven't heard or read about."

Matt shook his head, in disbelief, upon hearing this.

"So, who was the queen of Sheba then?" asked Connie.

"She was, some say, the queen of a region in Eastern Africa, which may even have crossed over into Yemen or southern Arabia. She heard of Solomon's wisdom and wealth from one of her trading agents, and she insisted on travelling to Jerusalem to see for herself.

"They never married, but she fell in love with Solomon; however, the time came for the queen to return to her native land. King Solomon threw a lavish party for her and at the end of the party, he requested the queen to spend one night with him.

"She agreed, but only on the condition that King Solomon would not take anything from her during the night. King Solomon agreed, only with the same condition on her.

"People often said King Solomon was wise; however, on this occasion, perhaps cunning was a better word. That evening he made sure that the food would be more spicy than usual. During the night, the queen woke up with a severe thirst. She went to the king's pantry and helped herself to a glass of water. King Solomon, of course, waited for this to happen and he declared she had broken their agreement. To compensate, she must now allow the king to take something from her.

"On her way back to her homeland, the queen gave birth to a son, and she named him Menelik. It means *the son of a wise man*. Some historians say that the dynasty created by Menelik continued to rule Ethiopia until the overthrow of Haile Selassie in 1973."

Another interesting tale from Harold.

The dinner went on, and the mood was very gracious. The pace of the food was timed to perfection, and dinner ended with a serving of excellent French cognac. Harold announced the end of the evening, and the three ladies each received a red rose.

"*Merci beaucoup*," said Harold as he rose from the table.

Matt, Bill, and their wives were on the way to their hotel when Matt suggested a nightcap in the bar. They all sat in the corner, and the server approached them. Matt kicked Bill's foot and mouthed towards the server, pointing to his jacket breast pocket.

The server's name badge said: AHMAD.

They ordered drinks. Bill leaned over to Matt and, in a half-whisper, said, "Matt, this is the Middle East. Ahmad is like the name Peter in Yorkshire!"

"Oh, yeah! Well, how many Peters do you know in Yorkshire then?" said Matt.

Matt started a casual conversation with Ahmad. How long he had worked at the hotel? Where did he do his training? Which school did he go to? Which country is he from? The server replied, but he was very nervous. Matt needed more time to develop this relationship; time they didn't have.

A message alert on Matt's phone from Myles:

> News just come in, murder in Newcastle.

"That's news?" said Matt.

"There must be one a day," said Bill.

Message alert on Matt's phone:

> Sorry, Newcastle, Australia, body found in Masonic lodge building

Matt sat upright, startled, and passed his phone to Bill. His smile turned to a frown within a few seconds, and he looked back at Matt.

"Don't we know of someone who recently travelled to Australia?" asked Matt.

"Oh no," replied Bill. "We haven't got visas, anyway!"

The next morning, Wednesday, Matt and Bill met with the assistant to the vice-consul at the British embassy in Beirut.

"They use the e-visa system these days, so we should have them issued within the next twenty to thirty minutes. Now, we will hook you up with our consular representative down there. I will get you his name before you leave. No doubt the local police there will work with you on this one. The vice-consul would like to meet you before you jet off. Let me check if he is free," said the clerk.

"This way, chaps," he announced.

Matt and Bill walked through into another office, more like a lounge. They chatted about the case in Beirut; not much to elaborate on except to mention the connection to the murder back in Yorkshire. The vice-consul knew of the victim, Sultan Suleiman, and knew of his success in business. Other than that, he could not say any more.

"I say, I understand you chaps are going to overnight in Dubai. I can put you in touch with our man there if you need anything," he said.

"Actually, we only have one lead to follow up on while we are there. We will get in late tonight, around midnight, do our work early tomorrow morning, and then leave for Sydney," explained Matt.

The phone rang.

"I say, splendid work, bring them in. Here are your visas now," announced the vice-consul.

The door opened, and a clerk, bespectacled, in a pink cardigan and knee-high plaid skirt, brought in the four passports.

Matt and Bill stood up, and she passed the passports to Matt. "All done," she said with a very sweet smile.

"Well, chaps, I wish you jolly good luck over there," said the vice-consul.

There was another round of shaking hands, and Matt and Bill departed.

"Ryan said he would have the copies of the business cards for me before noon today, Bill. They broke the bloody photocopier machine yesterday. The dozy bugger could have taken photos on his phone," said Matt as they were leaving.

"What else do we have to deal with here before we leave? Still no murder weapons," exclaimed Matt.

"Hey, we can't leave until we track down this Sir Rupert character. We must meet him before we go. He was probably the last person who saw this Suleiman guy alive," said Bill.

"You're quite right there. Isn't it funny how Othman has never even mentioned this guy?" said Matt. "Hang on, I know; let's go back in here."

Matt stopped, spun around, and went back inside the embassy. He approached the secretary.

"Excuse me. Do you think you could help us with the contact number for Sir Rupert Chapman, please?" asked Matt.

"Oh, I'm frightfully sorry, but we cannot give out such information. But, as you are on official business, I can contact Sir Rupert's secretary and ask them to arrange for him to contact you. Are your details on the registration form? Ah, yes, Phoenician Gold Coast, very good. I will send a message to his secretary's office to pass on to him," she said.

"Very efficient lady," said Matt. "She'll never be short of work here, I bet."

"So, no need for the Beirut Qasr, and we keep away from the police from now on. Low-profile time, Bill. Come on, back to our hotel," Matt said.

As they entered the hotel lobby, a message alert appeared on Matt's phone: "An update from Ryan here, mate. He has emailed copies of cards; great timing. I'll get my laptop started up and we will have a look," Matt said, the lift doors closing.

"Can you ask Ryan to please get something on the DNA results?" asked Bill.

In the room, Penny had packed. She mumbled something about last-minute arrangements. What about getting back home? How will the pub continue? Will Henry be all right?

No need to worry about Henry, Penny. He's having a great time.

"Hey, Phoenix, a message from Mum on my phone here. Something has developed with the case that Dad is working on, and they have to go to Australia. They set off for Sydney later today, overnight in Dubai—that's a bit of luck for them," said Henry. He read from his phone as he nibbled on a slice of rye bread. Phoenix's wonderful influence was already working. Gone were the days of all that fried, fatty rubbish for breakfast.

"I didn't know they were on a case. I thought they went for a vacation," said Phoenix.

Then Henry remembered. He was never to discuss his father's position or work with anyone else, no matter who that other person may be. He changed the subject.

"They're flying from Dubai tomorrow morning. I took that flight when I was over there a couple of years ago, stopped off in Bangkok for a few days first," he said.

"You can see some stunning ladies over in Bangkok," she said. She laughed as she made the speech mark sign with her fingers when she said the word *ladies*.

Henry approached her and put his arms around her.

"Not as stunning as you!" he said with a quick kiss.

"Your dad comes across as being rather secretive to me," she said.

"What do you expect from a Mason?" said Henry, rereading the message in case he had missed any details.

"What? Your dad is a Mason, a Freemason? Temple of Jerusalem, secret handshakes, and all that other stuff?" said Phoenix. Her voice increased in volume, and her face took on a vacant stare. "Anyway, never mind that. Where else did you go after Bangkok?"

"We took a train to Malaysia. That was fun; overnight train, sixty or seventy people sleeping in the carriages. There's a restaurant car—unbelievable how they cook food in there," said Henry.

"I would love to do that someday. Where else?" she asked.

"Then, we went by train to Kuala Lumpur and a few nights there, then a short flight to Singapore, about thirty minutes, maybe less," he said. "From there, we went to Australia, and I started doing some work: farms, bars, restaurants. I loved it. You used to live in Australia, lucky you." He had successfully changed the subject.

"I miss Australia," she sighed and rested her chin on her knees as she sat squat like on the high-backed dining chair.

"Me too," added Henry.

Phoenix stared, her eyes wide open.

"Do you fancy going?" she asked.

"When? I have to look after the pub." Henry spoke with a disappointed tone.

"No, you don't." She jumped down. "You have to look after me. Come on, upstairs."

Henry's eyes lit up. These morning sex sessions were getting to be a part of the daily routine these days, which he didn't mind a bit.

In her room, she opened her laptop and typed in her browser search bar:

Air-tickets from London to Melbourne, Newcastle; enter:

In a few seconds, hundreds of hits.

"Newcastle?" alarmed Henry.

"Yes, I always prefer to fly to Melbourne and get a connection to Newcastle, north of Sydney. Arriving at Sydney and then messing around with land transport is a headache." Phoenix spoke as a well-experienced world traveller.

"Try Manchester, better. Only a couple of hours' drive away. I can take you over in my dad's car if you don't want to leave your car at the airport. It will be safer here," said Henry.

"Here we are," she said. "A flight tomorrow morning, out of Manchester. Change in Dubai and reach Melbourne on Friday afternoon. Thursday night on the plane." She smiled at Henry.

"We get the six o'clock to Newcastle and be in the resort by eight. Perfect. Oh, hang on, though. I hate Dubai; it brings back some terrible memories," said Phoenix.

"Pass me your passport, please. Is your visa still valid?" she said. "I will book the seats."

"Phoenix, stop. I cannot go to Australia. I have this!" He held out his arms to illustrate the pub and building around him.

"Yours, is it?" she said as she changed her approach and went and stood in front of Henry. "Henry, do you like me?"

"That's a silly question. Of course, I do. I knew it the first day I saw you, last week." Henry was blushing up.

"Well, I like you. And I have lost other men in the past, or men have left me, and I am not ready for it to happen again," she said. "Not with you, anyway."

"Why would anyone want to leave you? You're wonderful," he said in his most compassionate voice. "We met just a few days ago but I feel like we have known each other a lifetime."

"I feel the same way about you, Henry, but there is a lot you don't know about me; one day, I will tell you, maybe on the plane." She kissed him.

"But Bill has entrusted me to look after his pub whilst he is away, Phoenix," said Henry. "It wouldn't be right."

"And things have changed since he left. Get the staff together and tell them. I am sure they will all understand. Now give me your passport!" said Phoenix.

Sod it, said Henry to himself. *I am going.* He took his passport from his wallet, checked the visa. Yes, it was still valid, and he gave it to Phoenix.

"I need to call the staff together," and he went back downstairs.

"Management meeting," teased Phoenix.

"If you need anything from your car, better get it now and then I will lock the key in the safe in Bill's room," said Henry as he left the room. "Bugger!" he exclaimed in a soft voice as he flicked the dishcloth. Not so much as he thought of surrendering the responsibility entrusted to him, but he didn't get his leg over!

―――――――――

Back in the hotel, Matt had changed their flights: six o'clock departure from Beirut. Penny and Connie had gone out to pick up a few things. It was Autumn in Australia so they should have something decent for when they arrived there.

"But Autumn in Australia is not the same as Autumn in Yorkshire," stated Bill.

Anyway, it got them out of the hotel room.

"Here it is now, Bill; the email from Ryan," said Matt as he worked on his laptop. The file downloaded, and Matt opened it.

There, in full view: two pages, one headed FROM CAR, the other headed FROM BODY, just as Matt had requested.

FROM CAR: From the business cards of the MESOL branches, it would be difficult for anyone to guess what business they are in. Each card had the same basic design. It featured an old wooden ladder image, which spread from the bottom left corner to the top right corner.

Bill studied the cards. He looked puzzled; *painting and decorating,* he thought, and kept quiet. Only the location address details were different on each card. Dubai, Jeddah, and Bahrain.

The one that Matt's and Bill's eyes both fell together on was:

MESOL
PO Box 8844, Deira, Dubai,
United Arab Emirates

FROM BODY: Several cards from oil companies, construction companies, banks, the usual stuff. Amongst them, another one, satin beige:

Tamara Illya
3rd Floor, Balat Al-Rashed Building,
Sultan Suleiman Street,
Musrara

"Where is Musrara, Bill?" asked Matt. "Somebody back home said it was in Abu Dhabi."

"That's Musaffah, the rig support area over the bridge," replied Bill. "Google it."

A few seconds later, on the screen:

Renovation project, Sultan Suleiman Street, Jerusalem

"Ahh, yes. I've seen this before over the years," said Bill. "Many people who live there deliberately leave Israel off their card. And I have seen the German GSM telephone number dodge used a few times as well."

Matt threw himself back in the chair. "It has to be the same person for both murders!" he announced. "I knew it. I've had this hunch all along.

That's the Dubai address this Amin Sadiq guy used when he registered at the hotel in Beirut."

"I am not with you here," said Bill. "Why would the murderer here use the same address as the one on the cards that you found back in the car?"

"Look at the address on Suleiman's registration card, printed by the hotel. If the first thing the police checked were the addresses of 1403 and 1401, which are the same, they would assume they were travelling together; it's reasonable enough. This would have been enough to keep the local police away from Sadiq overnight. Then he can make his escape early the next morning," explained Matt.

"Long shot that mate, awfully long shot," replied Bill.

"But one very important thing the murderer here didn't think of, Bill. He or she never expected the coppers from the case in England would be the same ones to investigate the case in Beirut," said Matt.

"And Tamara—are we to assume his wife or daughter?" asked Bill.

"Of whom?" asked Matt. "The mother of David and wife of Suleiman, or vice-versa?"

"We need more information on Suleiman—whatever it is, address. When I first saw the name Suleiman last Sunday morning, I said to Penny I had seen the name somewhere else recently. It never connected. Too much of that rather nice Beaujolais we had at your place on Saturday," said Matt.

Just then, the phone in the room rang out. Matt picked up the receiver, and a voice announced that Sir Rupert Chapman was in the hotel reception and wished to meet with Mr. Baxter.

"Oh, let him know we will be down in a few minutes," replied Matt.

No, the operator said that he wanted to come to the room of Mr. Baxter, and so Matt informed the operator to send him up. The operator informed Matt that sending an unaccompanied guest to a hotel room was against hotel policy. This statement completely baffled Matt so he decided on his own action.

As the elevator slowed to a stop on the ground level, the doors opened, and there in front stood a fine, very well-groomed gentleman. He entered the lift without saying a word. The doors closed.

"Good afternoon, detective chief inspector. I am Sir Rupert Chapman. I am pleased to meet you," and they shook hands.

They made their way to Matt's room; the door had been left ajar on the swing-over door latch. Bill had gone.

Matt offered a seat to Sir Rupert, followed by an offer of refreshments.

"I cannot offer you a cup of tea? Unfortunately, there is no teapot in the room, and I refuse to make tea in a cup," Matt explained one of his peculiar habits.

"It is all right, young man; I understand you are here to investigate the death of Mr. Suleiman. May I offer you any help that you feel you may need during your stay here?" he said.

Matt described a brief background of the other case in England and how it may be connected to the one in Beirut.

Bill returned, carrying a tray with a teapot, cups, and saucers.

"Good afternoon," Bill said as he entered the room. "I had them send it to my room instead."

Matt introduced him to their guest.

Matt asked what the purpose of their meeting at dinner on Saturday was about, which Sir Rupert answered. He gave the same story as Michel Haddad explained.

"How was Mr. Suleiman? Was he feeling all right during your dinner?" Matt asked.

"Yes, he is always all right, that chap. Strong as an ox," replied Sir Rupert. "I remember he had lined himself up with a trip to the oriental nightclub. One of his favourite places where he can pick up girls, no strings attached if you know what I mean."

"Did he leave the restaurant at any time?" asked Matt.

"Yes, he did. He mentioned he had brought birthday gifts for our daughters; we have twin girls. It would be their birthday the next day. He thought it better to get the gifts from his room as he was going out after I left him for the evening. I rather think he had someone lined up already," said Sir Rupert. He winked. "We invited him to come along the next day, but he refused. With this Jordan project, he simply never knows if he is here or there, from one day to another. I do not know where he used to get the stamina from," explained Sir Rupert. "Good show, I said, and off he went, never to come back to the dinner table. I wondered what happened to him as I had gone through almost half another bottle of red before Michel, the manager, requested to have a quiet word with me. Good God, man, he was dead! You could have knocked me over with a feather," said Sir Rupert.

"So, your daughters missed their birthday gifts. Such a shame," Matt added.

"Oh, good gracious, no, not at all. Around five o'clock the next day, a police officer brought them over. He explained they confiscated them, but the police can now release them," Sir Rupert added.

"What were the gifts, sir?" asked Bill.

"Porcelain dolls. He buys the twins a porcelain doll each and every year for their birthday," said Sir Rupert.

"Twin girls, they must be a handful. Do you have any other children, Sir Rupert?" asked Matt.

"No, only our lovely twins, and yes, they can be a handful," said Sir Rupert. "We had them quite late on, you know; they wear me out, I can tell you."

"Thank you, sir; this has been most helpful. Also, if you can recollect, at what time did Mr. Suleiman go to his room to fetch the gifts, give or take fifteen minutes?"

"No need to give or take! I can tell you exactly; it was just before nine o'clock. I must take medicine at the same time every evening, at nine o'clock. I have a reminder set up on my phone here," said Sir Rupert as he held up his phone.

"Sir. Can you remember the name of your server? Was it Ahmad? He usually works in that restaurant, we understand," asked Matt.

"This, I could not say. Unfortunately, I am not very good with names. Sorry about that," said Sir Rupert.

"What about the time you met Mr. Suleiman on that evening?"

"It was around seven-thirty, a little after. He was enjoying himself in the cocktail bar when I arrived," said Sir Rupert.

Matt thanked their guest and explained they had to leave soon for the airport.

"Well, I better get out of your way. Going to Dubai, you say? Dubai is not what it used to be. Give my regards to your wives, and I wish you a safe trip. Oh, let me send my driver over to take you to the airport," said Sir Rupert.

Matt refused.

"I insist. You can't rely on the local taxis here at that time of day. Going to a pastry shop is one thing; catching a plane, completely different. I assume you are on the six o'clock flight. I will send my driver over about three to three-fifteen," he said as he left the room.

Penny and Connie arrived back, and this left them with just enough time to get prepared. They had thought ahead and had brought some food back to the hotel as a snack to eat before they left for the airport. By the time they had eaten, finalised packing, and freshened up, they were downstairs in the lobby.

Three o'clock, five past three, ten past three—the clock almost reached quarter past three. The hotel concierge beckoned Matt and Bill to come forward.

As they reached the exit, a beautiful white Rolls-Royce pulled up, and the driver got out.

"Mr. Baxter," he asked, and he took the luggage from the cart and placed it in the boot.

"Who ordered this?" asked Connie.

"Sir Rupert sent his car to take us to the airport," said Bill.

They climbed inside and off they went to Beirut airport.

Unknown to any of them, a police officer watched their every move from opposite the hotel. He ran his fingertip across the screen of his phone and tapped the keypad:

"Hello, yes, sir; they have gone from the hotel," said the officer.

There was also a packing frenzy going on upstairs in The Shoulder of Mutton. Meanwhile, downstairs, Henry had called the staff together and explained to them he had to go overseas urgently to join his mother and father. Bill and Connie were due back on Friday, so they would have to get through the next few days between themselves.

"The weather is pretty rotten right now, so we expect the next few days will be quiet. Anyway, we have arranged for two more staff to come in until Sunday.

"The draymen delivered yesterday, and there is enough wine and spirits in stock. If you need to order anything, the suppliers' names and contacts are on the board in the kitchen," explained Henry.

Thus, the pub staff had the rest of the day to get prepared and sort stuff out. It was no big issue, or so it seemed, in the manner that Henry delivered it to the staff. Charlie had agreed to stay overnight at the pub until Bill returned.

Henry displayed the makings of a future politician.

Phoenix had already booked them on a flight departing from Manchester late that evening via Doha. She had sorted her outfits on the bed when Henry entered the room.

Why did this girl have so many clothes? She looked stunning in a sleeveless vest and denim shorts.

"It's a good job you were able to get this big room," said Henry. "Look at all your stuff!"

"I am only taking two suitcases, but I am tight on space," she said. "May I ask you to do me a favour if you have room for this bag? It's used for a foldaway easel, but it's handy for carrying other stuff," Phoenix said as she held up a scruffy-looking canvas bag. "Have a look inside if you want; I don't like to put in with my clothes in case anything gets stained," she added. "I just took it from my car; here's the key for the safe."

"It's only some special artist's tools that I use and a few bits and pieces I said I would take back for my father. He's so tight, you know, never throws anything away," she said.

Henry glanced inside the bag, out of curiosity more than anything.

"I can squeeze it in my suitcase, no problem," said Henry.

"I will let Mum and Dad know about our travel plans. I hope we can meet up in Australia," said Henry as he looked around the room.

"Yes, you better have. It's true what they say, Henry; Australia is a vast country, but they have aeroplanes. It's easy enough to get around. Do you know which part they will be in?" replied Phoenix.

"Dad's message said Sydney. I have booked us a taxi for seven," said Henry.

"Ladies and gentlemen, please return to your seats, fasten your seat belts, and prepare for landing," announced the captain's voice over the PA as they descended to land in Dubai.

It had been quite a short flight from Beirut to Dubai, about three hours. Just enough time for a decent meal and a good movie, as Matt always joked. The descent continued; the cabin crew continued with their preparation for landing. Cabin lights were dimmed, and the engine sound was almost unheard. It was springtime in the gulf, with hardly any atmospheric changes, a very smooth descent.

"Dubai at night," said Bill to Penny and Connie as they stared out of the aircraft porthole window.

Over the dry docks, bright lights illuminated the night sky over the entire city. Skyscrapers stretched away into the distance. Farther inland, a column of flashing bright white lights. Burj Al Khalifa, the tallest building in the world. Then coming up on the right-hand side, toward the creek, water taxis, known as *abras*, were still taking passengers across the narrow stretch of water. The quays of the creek were also well lit up. These were lights installed to permit the loading of cargo onto the wooden vessels, *dhows*.

Once the plane was below two hundred feet, it appeared to touch the roofs of the warehouses below. A few more seconds and the aircraft landed. The silence turned to a tremendous noise as the engines threw out reverse thrust. The fuselage vibrated, just for a few seconds, until the aircraft slowed right down.

For anyone flying for the first time, surely the landing of such an immense piece of mechanical and engineering wonders is a marvel in itself.

"Ladies and gentlemen, welcome to Dubai, where it is ten-twenty in the evening. The outside temperature is twenty-seven degrees centigrade," came the announcement.

After making their way through immigration and the sprawling atrium of the Dubai airport, they headed to the taxi queue. Once again, as they exited the airport, the humidity hit them. It is never so hot in Dubai, like its dessert neighbours, but the humidity can be brutal.

The travellers had the foresight to check their luggage through to Sydney. Everything they needed for an overnight stay was in their carry-on luggage. This also provided Matt and Bill with as much free time as possible the next morning.

The sad fact was that, like many before them, they only had a PO box number and a telephone number to work with. This method has been the same for many business visitors to this region for years. Businesses in this part of the world seldom use a street address on their name cards.

Matt's experience suggested that they might be lucky, as he had noticed "Deira" on the card. Deira is the zone around the creek and the commercial or souk region. Al Nasr square is at the centre of Deira and their hotel is located on the creek, just in front of Al Nasr square.

So, they had to make a telephone call early in the morning to determine the MESOL office location. Before all that, a good night's sleep in their hotel.

Next morning, Thursday. "It's ringing." Matt held his upright finger to his lips.

"Hello, yes; good morning. This is Falcon Logistics calling from Sharjah. We have a parcel for you coming in from Amman, Jordan, and your address is not in our driver's hand-held device. Where is your location, please?" said Matt.

"Albift Tower, sixteenth floor, 1605, thank you." He hung up.

"We're in luck; less than five minutes of a walk. Come on," said Matt. *A good result*, he thought.

They reached Albift Tower; it was indeed only a few minutes of a walk along the creek road. The wooden plaque on the wall at the side of the office door said:

> *M E S O L*
> *PO Box 8844*
> *Deira, Dubai, UAE*
> *BRANCHES*
> *BAHRAIN – JEDDAH – PARIS*

Nothing else. Matt pressed the intercom button.

"Can I help you?" a voice came from the speaker on the wall.

"Good morning. We are here to meet with Mr. David Illya, please," Matt stated.

"I am sorry. Mr. David is not here right now. Come back later," replied the voice.

"Okay; what about Ms. Tamara?" said Matt.

"Also not here now. Come back later."

"Can we come in and leave our catalogues for Mr. David, please? We met him last week in London, and he asked us to drop by." Matt raised his shoulders and screwed his bottom lip.

Bizzzzzzzzzzzzzp!

The door latch sprung open. They entered the office and found a tastefully decorated reception area that led to several individual offices or meeting rooms. It looked like a hotel suite except that there were no beds. A petite, well-dressed female figure appeared from around the corner; she appeared to be Asian.

"Good morning, sir. You said you met with Mr. David last week." The "r" on sir was over-pronounced.

"Yes, we did. We met him last week in the UK. Please, tell me, what do you do here?" Matt asked.

"I am the secretary, sir," she replied.

"Sorry, I meant what does the company do, in these very nice offices," Matt explained.

"We are part of a large group, sir. We have offices in Jeddah and Bahrain, and we also have companies in Beirut and Paris, sir," she said.

"And in Manila," chipped in Bill.

"Sadly no, sir. Do you have the brochures you wish to leave for Mr.

David?" She looked at Matt and held out her hand.

Matt looked into his laptop bag, which doubled as his briefcase.

"How about that, we must have left them on the back seat of the car. How did we do that? Look, miss, I can see you are busy right now, so rather than disturb you again, we will leave them in an envelope with the security downstairs," said Matt.

"Sir, please attach your business card to the envelope." She mimicked the use of a stapler.

"Yes, okay. Do you mind if I also take one of your cards?" asked Matt.

They both had another quick look around. No clues whatsoever. The secretary handed him the card, which was the same as the other one they already had.

"Thank you for your help. Goodbye," Matt and Bill said, and they left.

"Not much there, mate; not much at all," said Bill.

"What do you expect on anything to do with these cases so far?" replied Matt with a tone of frustration in his voice.

They had a brisk walk back to the hotel, up to their rooms, a quick turnaround, and back downstairs. Dubai airport is almost downtown. So, it is a quick taxi ride to the airport.

At the airport, they went straight through immigration and to the departure gate. Fantastic timing, and just a few minutes later, they were boarded.

"This is a big one!" said Connie. "How on earth do these things even take off?"

As they sat down in their seats and prepared for take-off, about 235 miles due northwest, Henry and Phoenix had just landed in Doha.

"Dad said he was going to contact me last night when they reached Dubai. There's nothing on my phone yet," said Henry.

"We won't have a network connection yet," said Phoenix. "Wait until we reach the terminal."

Henry was anxious, and to make matters worse, there was some repair work to the apron area. Their plane will have to taxi the full length of the runway to make the turnaround to get to the terminal.

Doha is a long runway—a very long runway.

NINE

Henry sat back. His mind was in turmoil right now, aware of what he had left behind, and not knowing where his parents were or how they were. He had got himself involved with a wealthy young woman, and she must be wealthy. That or receiving a very generous allowance from her parents. Two tickets from Manchester to Australia aren't cheap, especially if you are sitting in the front. He turned his phone on. No connection. After they parked at the terminal, Henry was at the front of the queue to get off. He was away and inside the terminal as he searched for somewhere to get a connection on his phone.

Phoenix followed him.

"Come on; we will get Wi-Fi in the lounge," she said.

Henry made a hasty march. Phoenix was a little slower. It was still early for her. Even with the delay, they still had almost two hours before their next flight. Henry connected to the Wi-Fi network in the lounge and a few seconds later, some message alerts from his phone:

"'Arrived Dubai just after ten pm….. - just leaving hotel in Dubai, try U later - at DXB, delayed one hour.' He is also asking, 'where are you?' What should I tell him? I haven't told Bill I have left yet!" said Henry.

"That was not such a good idea, was it? Why didn't you send a message to Bill?" asked Phoenix.

"I will send one now," said Henry.

"Hang on, slow down. It might be better if you send a message to your father and ask him to pass the news on to Bill. Tell him to wait until they are at 35,000 feet, though," laughed Phoenix.

"You find this funny, eh?" frowned Henry.

"Come on, Jimbo," said Phoenix. Henry stared at her. "It's not the end of the world. You have your own life to live. Bill asked you to cover for him for a few days, which you have done. He will understand. We will talk when we reach Australia if we meet up with them."

Henry started a reply message:

> Dad, I need to ask you a favour...

After a few minutes, another message alert, this time Henry decided not to read it aloud:

> Are you crazy? I will talk to you later. We reach Sydney around 0900 then 2 hours' drive. Closing doors here, switching off. Take care, love U

"They're just setting off for Sydney. Great, we can meet up with them some time," said Henry, relieved and excited.

"I don't know if your dad will approve of that," said Phoenix.

"Let's get there and then I'll send him the details of where we are, and we can go from there. He said they have to drive two hours from Sydney," said Henry.

He picked up a newspaper, and he took a drink of fresh orange juice.

"Two hours' drive from Sydney could put them five or six hours away from us, easy," said Phoenix.

"Ha! Coincidence." He showed the newspaper to Phoenix. It was the *Sydney Morning Herald*, yesterday's edition.

As Henry was reading the major headlines, Phoenix tapped him on the arm and pointed to a story at the bottom of the page:

MAN FOUND DEAD IN NEWCASTLE MASONIC LODGE.

"Seen this story?" She pointed again.

Henry turned his attention to it and read it aloud. Phoenix looked around and placed her forefinger in front of her lips. "Keep your voice down," she said.

"A dead body has been found in a Masonic Lodge on the outskirts of Newcastle yesterday evening. The police do not suspect foul play. A spokesperson would not give any further comment. At the time of going to press, the police had not released the name of the deceased," whispered Henry.

"I bet that's why my dad got called over to Australia," said Henry.

"Why would your dad get involved in something that happened halfway around the world? Because he's a Mason? I don't think so, Henry; come on. That's rather extreme, don't you think?" suggested Phoenix.

"I wonder what the latest news is?" he asked.

"Google it," came Phoenix's suggestion.

He did and hit after hit listed on the phone screen, all much the same story.

"'The police now believe that an ulterior motive may mean they have to declare it as a murder investigation ... victim's name still not released ... the body is at the medical examiner's, waiting for an autopsy. The police are waiting for clarification by a forensic specialist before proceeding.'"

"That will be Bill, the forensic specialist," said Henry.

Phoenix stared at him and looked puzzled.

"Bill was one of the most well-known forensic pathologists in the UK, perhaps Europe, about twenty years ago," said Henry.

"Bill, Bill, as in Bill, the pub landlord? Are you winding me a joke?" Phoenix's command of the northern England language was getting better but still had a few flaws.

"You should see his photo albums. Newspaper clippings, photos with Maggie Thatcher, Queen Elizabeth. Lady Di is there, the Dalai Lama." He was winding her a joke this time.

"Let's have a few bubbles whilst we are here, shall we?" said Henry as he jumped up. It seemed the news article was not so important, after all.

They both sat back and relaxed until they heard an announcement over the PA: "Flight to Melbourne will board in approximately thirty minutes."

Enough time for another round of champagne. As they finished, a very well-dressed, uniformed lady approached them. "Miss Istaza, Mr. Baxter, may I see your boarding passes, please? Your flight to Melbourne is ready for boarding. Come this way, please," she said, and she led them to a mobile passenger carrier.

"Hop on. I will take you to the gate. There has been a change to your seats from the original ones when you first checked in yesterday," she said.

Once onboard, the cabin crew escorted them to their seats. They were in an area of two or three rows of seats. It is sometimes between first class and the more extensive business class section. The flight attendant approached and knelt in front of Phoenix.

"Would you like a drink before we take off, Miss Istaza?" she asked.

"Yes, please. I would like a glass of water, and will we be the only ones in this part of the cabin?" asked Phoenix.

"Yes, I believe so, Miss Istaza. We are not very full today, so the purser has spaced our guests out a bit more. Water for Mr. Baxter also?" said the flight attendant as she stood straight up again.

"Hear that, Henry? We are all alone in this compartment. How cosy. Have you ever done it on an aeroplane before? I haven't," said Phoenix, excited by the thought.

Henry shook his head. He was speechless.

———————————

Somewhere over the south of India, Penny and Connie had settled down in their seats. They had enjoyed a lovely lunch of smoked salmon starter, followed by a nice tangy prawn and mango curry. A couple of glasses of white wine washed it down nicely, and that was the first of three meals ticked off the list. Both women flicked through the movie channels. Matt's money was on *Dirty Dancing*, one of Penny's favourites, and Bill's money was on *Mary Poppins*. Connie was a fan of Julie Andrews, not Dick Van Dyke.

"So come on, Matt; the pressure is off. Jack is here to join us. What have we got? Let's go through it all again. We have some spare time now," said Bill, pointing to his miniature bottle of Jack Daniels whiskey.

They topped their glasses and once again exchanged plausible scenarios and theories. Bill was getting concerned about the time he had so far spent away from his livelihood. He expressed his concern to Matt, who chose this time to inform Bill about Henry and Phoenix leaving for Australia.

"We've got a pub to run, and to make matters worse, my relief manager has fallen in love with one of the guests and done a runner!" said Bill.

However, he soon focused back on the murder cases.

"There are still too many unanswered questions from the first crime, let alone the one we just left," said Bill.

"Yes, mate. And our job is to get those unanswered questions answered," Matt replied. "God knows what we will find when we reach the land down under."

"It all seems to me we are missing one piece of information to bring it all together. I emailed the details of this Suleiman guy through to Myles, and he is going to do some digging. The vice-consul couldn't help much yesterday, could he?" explained Matt.

"Surely they were related. Such an unusual name, but how? Father and son; could even have been brothers," said Bill.

"Could be father and son; why not? But my money is on brothers. It was difficult to judge the age of the victim back home because of the wounds," said Matt.

"Not having any ID, so we couldn't determine his date of birth," explained Bill. "How come he didn't have any passport or driver's license on him?"

"We need the DNA results ASAP," he said.

"Where's that flight attendant? I need a top-up," said Matt, ready to relax.

Matt put his headphones on and pressed the command buttons on the seatback video. Bill couldn't settle, and he stood up to retrieve his backpack from the overhead compartment. He took out a small blue book and a single white sheet, folded in half, which he placed on his seat. Matt picked up the little blue book and the white paper as Bill returned the backpack.

As Bill sat back down, Matt said, "You still don't know it all by heart yet?" pointing to the blue book.

Matt looked at the single sheet of paper. It was a Masonic Lodge summons. He froze.

"Bloody hell, Matt; it looks like you have just seen a ghost!" said Bill.

"Bugger me, Bill. I've screwed up, proper," Matt exclaimed as he turned the paper over and pointed to it.

"The summons. The paper they found on the dead body in the factory last week. I never gave it a second thought and just left it in an evidence bag. I must have still been half asleep. It was an A4 paper folded over, just like this one. But I remember now; it was inside out. I never looked at it. The inside just looked like a local tour guide. On the back, there were some lines of print, row after row, like this one. Sod it!" Some of the other passengers turned around and looked at him.

Matt pressed the call button. The steward arrived. He hoped for the tall, lean, blonde flight attendant. Never mind, disappointed, he asked, "Do you have a Wi-Fi connection on board, please?"

The steward attempted to explain something about a few minutes free or "giga-somethings" free, and then it would be chargeable. He had to send one message right now. Soon, Matt was online, for the free service, of course, and opened his message editor. He found Ryan in his contact list and started a message.

ENROUTE TO SYDNEY. RE BODY IN FACTORY. EMAIL ME FULL COPY OF SHEET OF PAPER FROM VICTIMS COAT. ALSO F/U ON DNA.

He turned off the phone, nodded to Bill, took another drink, and then returned to his movie.

On the flight from Doha to Melbourne, somewhere over the southern tip of India, Henry and Phoenix had settled down and tried to stay awake during the movie after they had enjoyed a pleasant lunch. Henry's mind was on other things as he looked around the cabin section they were in, all alone. The cabin was very comfortable as the shades blocked the bright sunshine. They had no one on either side of them. No one in front or behind. It made it a very cosy and intimate setting for the inside of an aeroplane, he thought.

"These seats are uncomfortable, don't you think? Rather awkward," he started a conversation.

"Awkward for what, sitting and watching rubbish movies for twelve or thirteen hours? I was looking for a flight that goes through Singapore. At least we can get off and stretch our legs, break the monotony for an hour. On the other hand, once you set off, it may be better to arrive as soon as possible," she replied.

"What time do we land?" asked Henry.

"Your mum warned me about you." She laughed. "Are we there yet? If we are on time, we should arrive about half-past nine tomorrow morning."

"What time is it now?" He looked at the screen in front. "Says four thirty-three where we are now and three minutes past ten in Melbourne. That can't be right," he said.

"Yeah, isn't India one of them funny places where they add half an hour?" said Phoenix, a very well-travelled lady.

Phoenix stood up and reached up into the overhead compartment. She pulled down a gym bag, and off she went toward the toilet. A few minutes later, she returned, wearing different clothes. She wore a long plain t-shirt, like a nightdress.

"Henry, can you help me here, please, and put this back up there?" Henry jumped up. He wondered why she couldn't do it for herself. Phoenix dropped herself into the seat, and Henry straddled across her. As he was right over her, she tapped his arm and pointed to him to look down. She raised the bottom of her t-shirt and revealed the reason she couldn't reach up to the overhead bins. Her naked body showed Henry what she had in mind.

She knew from her own flying experiences that this would be their best opportunity. The cabin crew would now eat and try to rest for a few hours. The days of two crews for the long-haul flights were over. Well, certainly for mid-haul, as this flight was. After Henry sat back in his seat, Phoenix stood by her seat as she pressed and held a button on the arm-rest. Then several whirring noises emanated from her seat. The backrest disengaged itself into two parts, and the seat extended in length. The footrest raised and positioned itself to act as a support. The width of this bed would be quite adequate for what she had in mind.

Phoenix was of medium height with slender legs. Her key attribute was her shape, as everything was exactly in the right proportion. Henry was not a hunk, but not a weed either.

She leaned over and whispered in Henry's ear, "Switch off your screen. Take down your jeans, don't take them off, move over here and put this blanket over your body," she said.

Henry followed her instructions. He nervously glanced over his shoulder. Phoenix switched off her own seatback screen. It was almost complete darkness. It was certainly dark enough, she thought.

"Put this on. If you hear something, just pretend you are sleeping. Lay down behind me, don't move and don't make any noise," she said as she passed him an eyeshade.

Henry positioned himself as close as possible towards the centre of the two seats and faced towards the aisle. She placed blankets around the two of them, and she then settled herself down in front of Henry.

"Two spoons," he whispered in her ear.

She twisted around, uncomfortably, just long enough to whisper, "Lie still; you don't move—it's known as *pompoir*."

Sounds French, thought Henry. He wondered what else they may have taught her in her school in Paris.

Henry returned to his own seat, and he repeated the routine to prepare his own bed.

"I thought you said that you had never made love on a plane before," he said.

"I haven't," she replied. Henry looked as if he didn't believe her, and she recognised it in his expression.

"I promise," she said as she put her right hand across her heart.

———————

Eight hours had passed; Matt, Bill, and their wives were over Barrow Island. They would soon meet landfall and start the five-and-a-half-hour trek across the largest island on earth. During the flight, strong head-winds over the Indonesian archipelago had slowed them down. It made little difference, as they all enjoyed a well-earned, restful sleep.

Penny was the first to switch on her seatback screen. Two o'clock in the morning, time for dinner. Some of the window lights slowly came on to bring back some illumination to the cabin. The cabin crew started another service. Connie woke up next, and she turned sideways to her friend.

"Sleep well?" whispered Connie.

"Not bad. I rarely sleep on planes. The last few days must have worn me out," replied Penny.

They both looked at their husbands. The tray table between their seats was still down. They had enjoyed the company of two others during the evening—two others by the names of Johnnie Walker and Jack Daniels.

"What about your lad then, Penny? Do you think there's anything between him and this Italian girl?" asked Connie.

"Italian?" asked Penny.

"Whatever she is. I heard someone say she's Italian," said Connie.

"She's Maltese," said Penny.

"No, she isn't," a quiet voice chipped in from the other side of the aisle. Bill had woken up. He still had both eyes closed. "We don't know what she is; it depends on how you judge it," he said. He slowly opened his eyes.

"We know she was born in Israel in 1994. Why she is travelling on a Maltese passport, we don't know, but Matt here is intent on finding out," said Bill.

Matt also woke up.

"Rise and shine, Matt. Hey, I don't know why we haven't thought about this before, but have you ever considered the Golden Passport scheme they used to have in Malta?" said Bill.

"Hang on, Bill. Let me get myself sorted first," said Matt. He quickly disappeared.

On land, on sea, or in the air, Matt had his habits. He returned a few minutes later. "Now, what were you saying? Golden Passports, what's that all about?"

"A few years back in Malta, they had a passport scheme. Anyone wealthy enough could buy a Maltese passport. You donated half a million quid to the Malta National Development Fund. Also invested a hundred and fifty thousand in the Maltese stock market. And bought a house for three hundred thousand. It cost the investor about a million quid. Still, it provided them with European resident status," Bill explained.

Matt raised his eyebrows. *It's certainly a possibility*, he thought.

"Our Henry has taken to her anyway," said Penny.

"Hardly surprising, is it? Penny, she's lovely," said Connie. "Have you seen some of the clothes she wears?"

"I have, but do you know something, Connie, I bet you could give that girl ten quid and she would go to the market and buy herself a beautiful outfit and get a six-pack of beer, a bottle of wine, and a pound of cheese from the change," said Penny.

"Phew! Why so much cheese?" said Bill sarcastically.

"I don't trust her," said Matt.

"I wonder if he's joined the *mile-high* club with her yet?" said Bill.

"B-ii-lll," said Penny, as she stretched his name over three syllables.

The cabin crew served the next meal.

———

After about nine hours, Henry and Phoenix were just over Barrow Island. They also would soon meet landfall and start the five-hour trek across the largest island on earth. The same winds had slowed them down and the screen showed they were twenty minutes behind schedule. The young couple had fallen asleep almost as soon as they started their chosen movies.

A low illumination came on in their compartment, and the service started. Phoenix ordered a glass of champagne and a Caesar salad with some fresh fruit. This confused Henry as he wondered, *how do we get to order what food we want?* Anyway, a glass of champagne sounded like an excellent idea. Henry ordered a seafood pasta dish.

A glass in each of their hands, "They say the best time to drink champagne is immediately after making love," she said.

"I have heard it is even better after a few hours of sleep. Cheers!" he replied.

"And now, it's time for that promise you made," said Henry. Phoenix pretended she didn't know what he referred to. She looked at him from over what would be the top of her spectacles if she had been wearing any.

"What promise? I never actually made any promise," she said. "You don't want to hear all that boring nonsense. You'll find out soon enough." She still wasn't ready.

"Okay, do you mind if I ask you a few questions and if you don't want to answer, just say no comment. Pretend it's a police interview," laughed Henry.

She laughed and agreed.

"Where were you born?"

"I was born in a small town called Caesarea."

"Where's that? It sounds Italian, Julius Caesar. He was from Rome, wasn't he?"

"*Et tu, Brute?* Cheers!"

"Are your parents still alive?"

"Yes, both of them."

"Do you still see or talk to them?"

"Yes, of course, I try to talk to both of them at least twice a week, and I love them dearly."

"Excuse me, here; are they still together?"

"No, no need to excuse yourself, Henry."

"Again, apologies, but were they ever together-together?"

"Only for a short period, of which I am the result."

"Will I meet your father on this trip?"

"I doubt it very much; he lives in the Middle East. But who knows? He travels a lot, so he may come over on a business trip."

"Will I meet your mother on this trip?"

"Certainly not. My mama doesn't travel very well at all."

He looked around the cabin, gesturing with his hands held up.

"Who's paying for all of . . . *this*?"

"My father."

"What does your father do for his business? He seems to be quite wealthy—your car, this flight, hotel development in Australia."

"No comment. You will find out, all in good time."

"What?" gasped Henry.

"Sorry; enough now, Henry, please." She held her head down and pretended to be close to tears.

"Okay, okay, that's enough. One last question, not family-related at all."

"What is it?" she looked up.

"Have you ever been in love before?"

"I don't know. Can I have some time to think about my answer?"

Henry smiled as he held out his glass of champagne.

———————

Thirteen hours and ten minutes after leaving Dubai, breakfast had finished. Penny and Connie placed a "DO NOT DISTURB - No Breakfast" sign on their seats.

Then, a sudden low voice over the PA. "Good morning, ladies and gentlemen, boys and girls. We hope you have enjoyed your flight with us so far. In a few minutes, we will start our descent for landing at Kingsford Smith airport. It's a beautiful, sunny morning in Sydney. Clear blue skies and a temperature of twenty degrees. Those on the left-hand side of the aircraft, keep your eyes open for a beautiful view of Sydney Harbour Bridge and the famous Opera House. Thank you for choosing to fly with us," announced the captain.

The two girls immediately, perhaps even instinctively, got busy and tidied up the seating area. They stuffed bags, wrappers, and empty plastic cups into the seat pocket in front of them. They rolled up the used blankets and stuffed them back into the bags. Now it was time for them both to use the toilet, and they went and stood in the queue.

Matt and Bill didn't move much at all as they watched the end of the movie. It was only when their wives returned and gave them a gentle nudge that they made any effort and prepared for arrival. After all, they had to put their shoes back on.

"Here we are then, mate; long flight but pleasant enough," said Bill. "What's the address where we have to go? Myles mentioned it in that email he sent to you."

"Well, the crime scene is at a place called Belmont, south of Newcastle. Near Lake Macquarie."

"Yesterday I got another email from Myles, and he said someone would meet us at Kingsford Smith. The local force has arranged a hotel for us out that way. It's supposed to be quite a pleasant spot," said Matt.

"Belmont is where the old airport used to be. They closed it down a few years back when the iron ore industry died down over there," added Bill. His trivia knowledge did not surprise Matt. They should start pub quizzes at the Shoulder; Bill has all the questions and answers already in his head!

———————

A few minutes short of fourteen hours, after they left Doha, Henry and Phoenix had also enjoyed a nice sleep, as they had consumed several glasses of champagne with their dinner.

Over the PA: "Good morning, ladies and gentlemen, boys and girls. We hope you have had a pleasant flight. We have begun our descent from our cruising altitude of thirty-eight thousand feet. We expect to be landing at Melbourne International Airport in approximately twenty-five minutes. A bit of good news: we picked up some tailwind once we got over land and we have made up some time."

Henry reached over and shook Phoenix. She insisted on sleeping a little longer.

"Come on, Phoenix; we are going to land soon." A bold statement from Henry. They were still twenty-four minutes away, and sleep is a precious commodity for goddesses. He tidied up and went to freshen up.

Henry's absence provided Phoenix with the opportunity she needed to wake herself up at her own pace. Not being a morning person, she yawned and opened her handbag to check the time of the connection of their flight to Newcastle. An eleven o'clock departure, perfect. There, a driver will meet them and take them about twenty-five kilometres to the resort.

Henry came back and Phoenix left to the bathroom.

Right on schedule, they disembarked with thanks to the cabin crew. Through the immigration formalities, a quick cup of coffee, and before they knew it, they were airborne again.

"It's rather crowded in here. Not used to this, are we?" Henry joked to Phoenix.

One and a half hours and they landed in Newcastle. Luggage reclaimed, Phoenix knew exactly where to go, and she approached a smart-looking driver.

"Good morning, Miss Istaza. May I help you?" said the driver.

He took the luggage trolley and pushed it outside to where a white family van waited for them.

"Come on, Henry," she said as she got in the vehicle.

Luggage loaded, they set off.

"Henry," she held his hand and started, "do you know, you are the first person who has ever treated me like a normal human being in a very long time? Do you remember last Saturday morning? I returned to the pub, and I was furious, and I said I would let you know the reason later? Well, since then, you have never even asked me what the reason was. I recognise things like that, Henry. There are reasons I do not tell you everything about my life at this stage. I want there to be a right time and place for everything and I hope you can understand me: you will see why soon."

"It's fine, really. I understand, but by the way, why were you pissed last Saturday morning when you came back?" said Henry.

"Oh, no, I hadn't been drinking," said Phoenix.

Henry had to explain the dual meaning of the word "pissed" in England and some other countries. For some reason, she was unaware.

"I had come from that posh hotel in Ingleton, where I had been for an interview for a job. That is why I asked for your advice the evening before in the pub," she explained.

"I guess you didn't get the job," said Henry.

"I don't want it. It was as a guest relations executive. The way the manageress and supervisor talked to me was as if I was like an alien. When they talked to me, they never even looked at me. They were more interested in checking out my outfit, and how my arse looked in my suit. One of them even asked me what perfume I was wearing—bitch!"

Henry smiled at her.

She continued, "You won't believe this, but I was praying for you to come and collect me from that silly beer stall. I only volunteered, thinking you would be around that stall, anyway. I was *pissed* when I had to stand there all alone." Again, a very charming smile as she emphasised the new word she had learned.

"Thank you, Henry, and one day you will know more about me and my life, I promise you," she said.

"Is there anything I need to know now?" asked Henry. "What about this hotel we are staying at?"

"The Valide, it's built along the riverbank; well, not a riverbank, as it overlooks a lake," explained Phoenix.

"Oh, a lake bank?" suggested Henry.

Phoenix gave a lovely description, and on arriving at the hotel, it turned out to be quite an accurate one.

Not far away, in Belmont, the Baxters and the Coopers had also checked into their hotel. It was another lovely property called The Kuringai Beach Resort.

TEN

L ocated south of Newcastle, Lake Macquarie is the largest coastal saltwater lake in Australia. It is a popular area, of course, for water sports enthusiasts. As they drove in, Matt and Bill could see a lot of recent development. There were many new buildings under construction in the area. It was clear to see that there had been, and still was, considerable investment in this region.

"They are waiting for us downstairs, Bill. Let's make the most of it and, at least, go and see the crime scene. Are you okay? Not too tired?" asked Matt after checking in and freshening up.

"I'm good, Matt. That Jack Daniels sang me a lullaby or two on the plane last night; bless him," said Bill.

"Give me two minutes. I want to check my email," said Matt as he switched on his laptop.

Matt fingered down the list of emails.

Copy of paper from victim in factory.

"Ah, here it is," said Matt. "The one about the paper removed from the victim's body in Cooper's Wood."

He opened the image on the screen.

Lodge of Illya
A travelling Lodge

SUMMONS
Meeting odd months throughout the year
Thursday 28th March 2019
Tapton Hall, Shore Lane, Sheffield S10 3BU, England
Tyling at 6.30 pm
by invitation only

Matt pointed to the screen. "Well, will you look at that? The Lodge of Illya, a travelling lodge, had an invitation-only meeting in Sheffield a couple of weeks ago. And the name of the guy who hired the car in London was David Illya. This is the summons I was telling you about, found on the first victim."

"Still proves nothing, Matt," said Bill.

"Yes, I know. Let's look at the back; usually, there is a list of officers."

Triumphant Worshipful Master Suleiman Illya
Triumphant Senior Warden David Illya
Triumphant Junior Warden Saul Illya

The list went on.

"There's the email with the DNA results as well. We will come back to these after we have been to this crime scene with the local bobbies," said Matt as he closed the laptop and they left the room.

"What's all this 'triumphant' about, Bill?" asked Matt. "I've been in the craft for over thirty years now, and I have never seen that before."

"Let me think about that, Matt. I need a couple of hours to readjust if you know what I mean," replied Bill.

The two plain-clothed officers, Mitch and Louise, waited for them outside. They all got in the car and set off for the crime scene. They arrived at a fairly old-looking building when compared to the newer developments they had observed around the region. The caretaker waited for their arrival. He was with his wife, who invited them for a cup of tea, which sounded like an excellent idea, and off she went to brew up.

The caretaker led the way. Matt, Bill, and the police officers walked up a few steps positioned between two ornate concrete pillars. They entered the building through two magnificent old oak doors that creaked as they slowly opened.

"The temple is upstairs," said the caretaker. They ascended a stone staircase.

Before entering any Masonic temple there is a *robing area*. Here the members put on their aprons, sashes, etc.—whatever they need for the upcoming ceremony.

"This is where I found him, laid out," said the caretaker, pointing at a broad white line.

Matt and Bill strolled around the area. Bill pointed to a few scratches on the wooden floor. A pair of shoes, heel down, dragged across the floor could have made these marks.

"Have you got the name of the victim yet?" Matt asked Mitch.

"Shamir, Saul Shamir; many people just called him Shamir," said the caretaker before Mitch answered Matt's question.

"Yes, but that's not his actual name. Lou, pass him that photocopy, please," said Mitch.

"Not a local, then? It certainly doesn't sound like a local name. Any other details?" said Matt.

Just then, the penny dropped, and Matt looked across at Bill. But Bill had been focused on Matt since he had heard the word "Saul."

Matt received a copy of a passport and read aloud: "Saul Illya, born in Jerusalem in 1971." His mouth remained open, showing disbelief.

"So, where does the Shamir come from?" asked Matt.

"Something to do with dark green eyes. They said it was unusual for people from his country. He had a habit of staring at people. He would hold his eyes wide open and stare for ages. His other brothers used to make a joke out of it and said it was like he could burn through stones with his eyes," the caretaker explained.

"Ha, there's a story there," said Bill.

"Did you know him, sir?" asked Mitch.

Matt shook his head. "No, mate. But it certainly feels like I did. Do we know how he died?"

"The coroner says most likely poisoned, sir," said Mitch.

"How? What with?" asked Bill.

"They're still working on that, sir. We can go there when we have finished here. It's in Newcastle, about half an hour away," offered Louise.

Matt didn't respond to the offer but went on: "Have you found any weapons or any odd-looking instruments lying around? Either inside or outside, anything you might consider odd. Try to remember anything. Anything at all. It may seem strange to you, but it could be vital to the case." Matt aimed his question at all three, but none of them gave any response.

"You were quite familiar with him by the sound of it, mate. Can you tell us a bit more about him please . . . sorry . . . what's your name?" said Bill.

"I'm Basil, sir. Saul, or Shamir, has been coming to this lodge for the last two years or more. He joined when they started work on that Macquarie hotel that his company took over. You couldn't wish to meet nicer people—him or his brothers. I haven't seen his brothers in a year, could be more, but it seems they are all like Saul and spend half their lives on a plane. They sometimes come here to attend meetings. It's nice when all three are in town, as they invite all the members back to their hotel for supper after the meetings. We hear some funny stories about the goings-on there," said the caretaker.

"Can you both make another thorough search of this room around here, please, Mitch?" said Matt. "I want you to look for something that you would normally not consider as unusual."

Matt and Bill entered the temple next to the robing room, and Bill looked around.

The walls almost gleamed with spectacular white paint. Long, narrow double windows stretched up from waist-high to meet the ceiling. The roof was a high dome which would create an echo inside. Long dark blue drapes, not curtains, were tied back at the sides of the windows. No doubt they are never used or drawn but could well assist in reducing the echo inside the temple itself. There were two rows of wooden chairs positioned on two opposite sides of the room. Each row on both sides had a large wooden desk halfway down, so there were four seating areas. At each end of the room stood another large wooden block table with a large, heavy, ornate chair. At one end of the room, a two-step platform elevated the table and chair—the chair of King Solomon, *in the east*. On both sides of this block table, there were three rows of chairs.

This table, and two of the other three, had an artificial candlestick on one corner at the front of the table. A carved twenty-inch-high wooden column was lying down at the opposite corner. Medieval wall lights with

LED bulbs added to the decorations. Altogether it conjured up a surreal atmosphere of ancient mystery.

Bill walked to the table without a column and candlestick. Two small wooden boxes were on the surface. He opened both; he was familiar with the contents and found nothing to cause any concern. The contents of the drawers didn't provide any clues. But inside the cupboard was a large polished wooden box with a square and compasses on the lid. Bill lifted the lid. Inside were the builder's tools or implements known as The Working Tools of a Freemason.

"Hey up, look here," he said as he held up one particular tool.

It was a wooden mechanism about eight inches long; it looked quite old. The top looked like a cotton bob, made of thin pieces of wood joined at both ends. It was like an angler's hand reel. The top rotated around the shaft. It was a skirret, an old builder's tool used to mark out straight lines for long runs, possibly a wall, on a building site. There should have been a yarn wound around the top, but the yarn was missing.

"Very interesting," said Matt. "Let's check outside in the robing room. We might spot something that the local coppers have missed."

"Have you found anything here?" Matt asked Mitch and Louise. Both shook their heads, and Matt and Bill joined in the search.

After a few minutes, "Matt, look at this," said Bill as he lifted down a small cardboard carton.

"TimTams? What the bloody hell are TimTams?" asked Matt.

Bill delicately loosened a piece of string that was wrapped around the carton. Some old books and pamphlets were inside the carton.

"What about this, then?" asked Bill. "Go on, look inside the cupboards."

"They are all open; only the flaps crossed over. This is the only one wrapped with string," commented Matt.

"Louise, can you get this over to forensics ASAP, please?" said Bill as he passed her the small carton.

"Leave all the stuff inside; it's important not to disturb anything, especially the string," said Bill.

"Mmm, ChocMint, my favourite," she said as she licked her lips.

"Better take the car, Lou. We can get a ride back to the hotel if you're not back in time," suggested Mitch.

"Tell me something, Basil. Have any strangers been around here over the last few days?" asked Matt. "Any unusual visitors or deliveries of any kind?"

"Actually, yes, come to think about it. A few days ago, our security guard at the gate shouted over to me about a delivery van that wanted to come in. The man in the van said it was some special regalia. I thought it was strange at the time as if we get any deliveries, one of the lodge members will usually let us know beforehand," said Basil.

"Why did you think it was strange? Because no one had informed you about it?" asked Bill.

"Two lodges have their meetings here. One is an English group, and the other is a Scottish group, and it was only last year that they all got new regalia. I remember it because they held a joint meeting and had a celebration evening for the fiftieth anniversary of this building. They wanted to raise some funds for the local orphanage. Saul supplied brand-new special aprons he had made for all the members of both lodges. Smashing evening, it was, and we raised a few dollars for the orphanage," said Basil.

"Did you get the name of the driver who made this delivery?"

"There were two of them, a man and a woman; she was driving. I remember that, and they will have signed in at the guardhouse at the entrance," said Basil as they walked toward the guardhouse. Basil took the book from the security guard and ran his finger down one side of the book.

"Mmm, Tuesday, Tuesday, Tuesday. Yes, here it is."

9/4 1422 J. RIBERA ID… blank vehicle reg: 831 ZQA Tel: unreadable

"Your security doesn't take a phone number for anyone coming in?" asked Bill.

"Yes, normally they do. There it is," said Basil, pointing to the column in the logbook. Recognising it was unreadable, he scolded the security guard.

"No copy of passport, driver's license, or ID card is taken, then?" asked Matt.

"No, sorry; this is our normal procedure. We just write the details and telephone number," explained Basil.

"Can you have a go at describing any of them for us, Basil?" asked Bill. "Take your time, mate."

"They were in the car most of the time, and the windows were up. But I remember thinking to myself that the woman looked Spanish or Italian. She could have been from over west, Perth side—a lot of Italians over there," explained Basil.

"West, Perth side, around here, west of Newcastle?" asked Matt.

"Aye, Matt, about five hours west by plane. Perth is in Western Australia," explained Bill.

"Were you there the whole time that they unloaded their delivery?" asked Bill.

"I had to open the main doors for them and show them upstairs where to put the boxes," said Basil, looking a little anxious.

"Don't worry, mate," reassured Bill. "Take your time. Did the man and woman follow you upstairs when you showed them where to put the boxes?"

"Well, hang on; let me explain. At first, I told them that I could only allow them to leave the boxes at the main entrance. But the bloke said that Saul insisted they take them upstairs, as they would need them for a meeting that evening. As they met at seven, they wouldn't have much time to arrange it later. Then I showed him upstairs, where the best place to store them would be." Basil grew increasingly anxious.

He continued, "When they mentioned Saul's name, I assumed it was okay. I wish I had phoned him now."

"Basil, again, did the man and the woman both follow you upstairs and unload the cartons from the van?" asked Bill.

"No, only the man. She sat in the van the whole time. She never got out," replied Basil.

"Basil, one more question, and then we can have a nice cup of tea. The van, did it have an access door on the side?" asked Bill.

"Yes, it did; behind the passenger's door," came the reply. "This is where they unloaded the cartons from."

"Which way did she park the van?"

"Oh, I remember that. The woman driver went all the way over the grass there. Almost going through my rhododendron beds. So that she was facing the security gate when she parked up. I had a go at her as I had been tidying them beds up all morning," said Basil.

"So, if only the man unloaded, how long did it take him?" asked Bill.

"I never saw her get out at all. On her phone all the time, from what I remember. The boxes they brought in weren't so heavy. Maybe three trips upstairs were all it needed—not long, ten minutes," said Basil.

"Where were you while they were unloading?" asked Matt.

"After a couple of minutes, our security guard at the gate called me over to his hut there. The electric company had phoned to make an appointment about a new electrical connection, and they insisted on talking to me. By the time I walked over to the guardhouse, they had hung up. Buggers!" exclaimed Basil.

"So, altogether, the vehicle waited, say, ten, fifteen minutes, give or take?" asked Bill.

"Max," he said, "here look in the book; see, out at 1434."

"Basil, you have been a tremendous help, mate. Where's that cup of tea?" said Bill.

A wrought-iron table and chairs stood outside the entrance to the building, upon which Basil's wife kindly placed some tea and biscuits. Matt immediately noticed the brand on the packet of biscuits and indicated such to Bill.

"They're very popular here," said Bill. "It's a shame Louise had to go to forensics; they're her favourites."

They discussed lodge meetings, the recent developments in the town. Australian Rules football came up in the conversation. Basil invited Matt and Bill to the local game on Sunday.

"That would be nice, mate. We will see if we are free. Tomorrow is Saturday, Mitch. May we continue with the investigation tomorrow morning? The time difference seems to have crept up on me. I could fall asleep right here, right now," explained Matt.

"Me too, mate," said Bill.

The local police now had to trace the vehicle registration and the name J. Ribera. The scribbled telephone number had caused more problems, but the team was on it.

But one question remained in the minds of both Matt and Bill; were there more than two people in that delivery van?

Matt and Bill returned to their hotel and intended to rest up with their wives.

"Have you forgotten about our son?" called out Penny.

"I bet he is like us: tired." Matt immediately had an excuse!

Matt took out his phone and tried to send a message.

"Call him," said Bill. "You haven't seen him all week. We've all travelled to the other side of the world and you want to text your son? Use that messenger app you downloaded. Before you do that, save me that summons to a thumb drive. I'll get us a couple of copies printed."

Matt did so, passed it to Bill, and off he went, leaving Matt to make his call.

"Hello, Henry; hello, son; are you all right? Yes, we are fine, thanks. Mum, she's here, mate. Do you want to have a word? We are at the Kuringai Beach Hotel. What? He's asking that Italian lass." Matt smirked.

"What's that? Get away! Well, I never . . . really? In that case, we will see you in a couple of hours then. Okay, see you then. Bye." He closed the line.

"Would you believe it? He's in a hotel, not ten minutes from here. Unbelievable, isn't it? We travel to the other side of the world and can't get away from the lad. He asked if we would like to meet them later for a drink. They're staying in that fancy new resort, Validay or something; the copper was telling us about on the way in." Matt showed his excitement.

Bill returned, and he gave the thumb drive and a copy of the paper to Matt, keeping a copy for himself.

"Bill, let's have a look at that summons again before we go any further. Let's see if we can get any more information about this 'Triumphant Lodge' thing. I've booted up the laptop. Type it in, will you, please, Bill?" said Matt. "Lodge of Illya, that's it."

Matt was giving out the instructions without realising Bill was way ahead of him already.

The screen filled up with several hits. There was nothing on the first page of any interest, but on the next page, there was a hit that caught their eye.

Illya Lodge embarks on a trip around the world.

Bill clicked on the link and opened the news article:

> *The relatively unknown Masonic order, The Lodge of Illya, known as a travelling lodge, has set off on their annual world tour. They will hold their first meeting in New Orleans in January, followed by a meeting in March in Sheffield, England. After which, they will be in Lisbon, Portugal, and two months later, they will be at the historic building on Coleman Street in Singapore. Tokyo will be their penultimate meeting before a final meeting in Newcastle, Australia.*
>
> *The order dates back to Jerusalem in the 10th century. The caretakers or supervisors for security created an association of artisans. Over the centuries, Masonic rituals have influenced the practice in their own ceremonies. It takes the name Illya from the first word of the old Roman name for Jerusalem, Aelia Capitolina. Some historians have traced the family of the original founders back to the siege of the 7th century.*
>
> *The Lodge of Illya, being an independent order, cannot be an associate or affiliate with any so-called Grand Lodge.*
>
> *The Lodge of Illya uses a unique Masonic ritual during their meeting. Each meeting or ceremony includes all three degrees of Freemasonry. Each degree, includes a unique and somewhat elaborate presentation of what Freemasons know as "The Working Tools."*
>
> *Attendance at these meetings is by invitation only.*
>
> *Source, MESOL Publications, Cologne*

"Well, that throws some light on it, but we had an idea about the history anyway," said Bill.

"Yes, but look at the news source, mate. Our friends at MESOL again," said Matt.

Bill started an explanation: "I was thinking earlier in the car when you asked me about the 'triumphant' thing. We all know from school that on Palm Sunday, Jesus entered Jerusalem riding a donkey. He intended it as, we could say, a publicity stunt. So, the citizens may recognise a king entering the great city in such a humble manner.

"He wasn't the first to do this, actually, as King Solomon did the same when his father David appointed him to the throne."

"Solomon's brother, Adonijah, was having a lavish party to celebrate his appointment as the next king. Bathsheba brought this to the attention of her husband, King David, as he lay on his bed, dying. David gave his own mule to Solomon and ordered that he ride it into Jerusalem. He did so, but only after Nathan the prophet had proclaimed Solomon as king. The crowd cheered when they saw King Solomon ride into town on the back of a donkey. The cheers and jubilation were so loud that they drowned out the noise from Adonijah's party.

"The Bible and other historical recordings state both these events as triumphant."

Matt examined the photocopies of the victims' passports.

"Bill, don't you find it odd how people in this region use different names. Sometimes entirely different from their proper name? I mean I get Bill comes from William; Betty comes from Elizabeth," said Matt.

"The bit about the changing of the names doesn't surprise me at all. This habit has happened for years. It's quite common practice around the Middle East and Asia," said Bill.

"Let's see what else it says in the summons. Open it up," Matt said.

The double-page spread of the summons was a write-up about the history of the order, pretty much the same as the news article.

"Any previous ruling masters?" asked Bill. He read through the document further.

"That's odd; the same three people for the last nine years, just rotate the three principal officers, look."

Saul, David, Suleiman
David, Suleiman, Saul
Suleiman, Saul, David

"And each time the senior and junior wardens are the other two that have not taken the chair for that term. Talk about 'best kept in the family,'" said Matt.

"What about other current officers?" said Matt as he turned to the back page.

"Senior Deacon, Mustafa Omar; Junior Deacon, Ravi Kumar; Inner Guard, I can't even pronounce that; most look to be regional or local names," said Bill.

"All except the D of C; look," said Bill. "Edward Chapman is the director of ceremonies."

"Here's the DNA information we have been after," said Matt as the next email appeared on the screen.

The report gave some very startling news. The DNA taken from Phoenix Istaza showed a match to the victim.

"Wait a minute; am I reading this right?" Matt asked. "It says here, some of the hair samples found at the crime scene also prove a match to the victim. It doesn't clarify if they are hair samples belonging to Phoenix or different. We need that clarified as soon as possible."

"Let's not jump the gun here, Matt. You need the exact percentage to draw any real conclusion. You need the makeup and if they allowed the ethnicity factor. But, I admit, it's a start." Bill educated Matt with his forensic experience.

"What do we need to do now, Bill?" asked Matt.

"I need to speak with the DNA analysis guy. We need to narrow the match criteria and see if they have started a cross-reference on the ethnicity. That will give us a much clearer line to work from. What's their phone number?"

"It's the last chance we will get before the weekend, bloody government cutbacks. You never know if these departments still work the weekend or not. Not like that in my day. Pass me your phone, please, Matt," said Bill.

"You might have to give it an hour, mate; we are nine hours ahead here. British summertime just kicked in a couple of weeks ago," explained Matt.

"Come on. I need a drink," he said.

They joined their wives in the Kuringai Resort lobby and they all proceeded to the hotel where Henry and Phoenix stayed.

The Valide at Little Pelican was a new resort-style development. It has revitalised Swan Bay on the southeast part of Lake Macquarie. The resort is an upmarket facility that provides deluxe accommodation. It has promised to bring wealthy tourists from near and far, as explained by the police officer earlier.

They all met in the hotel lobby. Hugs and kisses all around for Henry and his family. Phoenix stood cross-legged, a few feet away from the Baxter family greeting. She appeared very well presented, as usual. The situation was awkward for Matt; the others seemed okay and relaxed.

They all shook hands; Penny and Phoenix kissed each other's cheeks. Connie and Phoenix did likewise.

"My best stand-in beer puller in many a year is this lass," said Bill as he hugged Phoenix.

"It's wonderful to see you again, love," said Connie, "but who is looking after our pub? He can't sleep at night." She pointed to Bill.

"And it's lovely to see you all again," said Phoenix. "This time in my home."

They all moved through into the bar area on the terrace, with its lovely view of Lake Macquarie. The first question was about the hotel in which they were staying.

"There are two villas down over there," she said as she pointed to the end of the principal building, "away from the hotel itself. Four rooms in each villa. Henry and I are in one villa, and someone else from my family is occupying the other villa."

"Why stay here?" asked Matt as he rubbed two fingers and a thumb together.

"Because we own it," said Phoenix. She shrugged her shoulders.

Matt stared at Penny, who stared at Connie, who stared at Bill, who stared at Matt. "I need a beer; anyone else?" he said.

Matt ordered drinks. He took a long swallow of his first Australian beer, and the broad smile on his face showed his appreciation.

"May I?" asked Matt as he took out a Butz Choquin Cobra and a tin of Frog Morton on the Bayou.

"Sorry, we are a completely smoke-free premises, I am afraid," she said as she shook her head slowly.

"But we are outside," said Bill.

"Good," spouted Penny. "Filthy habit. I keep telling him to pack it in."

"It's therapeutic, and in this job, sometimes we need a bit of a therapution—Is that actually a word, Bill?" said Matt light-heartedly.

"Tell us some more about the property, love; it's fascinating," said Penny.

"The corporation started development about two years ago. There is still a lot to do; there could be another five years of work. They also had plans to reopen Belmont airport for tourist traffic. That will be an enormous project alone. Henry says he would like a job here," Phoenix explained.

"How many months of the year are you out here, love?" asked Connie.

"It depends on what I want to do, where I want to do it and with whom I want to do it. At the moment, I am happy right now. I have found a friend on my last trip, so Copper's Wood is also a very special place for me," she said as she winked across at Matt.

Without having the knowledge of English humour, she was unaware of what she had just said. And what it may mean, especially when followed up with the wink of an eye, to the father of her boyfriend, a father who also happens to be a copper.

Matt was speechless for a few seconds, but she appeared completely relaxed.

"Miss Istaza, may I ask you a personal question?" said Matt.

"Not as personal as the third degree your son gave me on the plane, I hope." She laughed.

"I don't know about that. Does the family name Illya mean anything to you?" asked Matt, emphasising the name itself.

"Yes, of course." She immediately appeared surprised and didn't know which direction to look. Luckily, she noticed the general manager of the hotel as he waved at her from near the lobby.

"Oh, Marcus is waving. He wants me over there. He said there is something important he has to tell me. Excuse me, please," she said as she got up and walked away.

Matt turned to Henry. "Now, listen here, Henry. You better follow your girlfriend and be by her side. Don't ask why; go on, off you go," said Matt.

Henry joined up with Phoenix as Marcus started to talk to her.

"What's going on, Matt?" asked Penny.

Suddenly they heard a piercing, drawn-out scream from the lobby area. They all turned to see Henry holding Phoenix in his arms. Marcus rushed to put a chair behind her.

It was now down to Matt, with the help of Bill, to tell their wives about what they had discovered over the last few days. They thought it better to return to their own hotel to do so, and they excused themselves to Henry.

"Henry, it's better if we leave you here with Phoenix. We know she has received some shocking news," said Matt.

"How do you know, Dad?" asked Henry.

"Tomorrow, son, we will talk tomorrow," said Matt as he turned away.

As they walked to the exit, they heard Phoenix as she hurried across the hotel lobby. "Henry, some good news. Papa is coming; he is in Singapore and will arrive tomorrow," she said.

Some news to comfort her. *Not for long*, thought Matt.

"That cheered her up. No end, son. Henry, we are going to go back to the hotel now, and we will all meet again tomorrow. I'll call you," said Matt.

————————

The cabana or chalet-style accommodation in the Kuringai hotel met the needs of Matt and Bill. The rooms were spacious enough inside to get their work done during the day and they also featured an open veranda that would be useful in the evenings. The quietness and stillness of the late evening provided a pleasant, tranquil setting. There, outside, they could sit and relax over a few glasses of wine. They decided on rooms that overlooked the lake as it meant they didn't catch the evening wind. It was autumn now, and the wind could blow up off the South Pacific Ocean and bring with it occasional light showers.

Matt and Bill asked Penny and Connie to join them and told them all about the three cases so far. The girls sat and shook their heads in disbelief as they heard the details. They believed Phoenix had a connection to all this somehow. They hoped that with her help, they could start putting more information about the three family members together.

"We could be dealing with the murder of three brothers here," said Matt.

"The first one, father of two sons, Matt?" asked Bill.

"There's still that possibility. We can't be sure, can we?" replied Matt.

Bill clicked his fingers.

"DNA . . . pass me your phone, please, mate," he said, and he moved back inside to make a call. After a few minutes, he returned to the veranda.

"This case, or these cases, gets harder and harder as the time goes on. It's supposed to work the other way around as more evidence comes to light. Anyway, I got hold of an old buddy of mine, Walter. He is going to drill down on the DNA results for me and he will let me have something tomorrow afternoon. I owe him a pint," said Bill.

"Going back to this thing with the names, Bill?" asked Matt. "It seems to me that there's only one person who used his actual name in all this, and that's this David Illya character. Sultan Suleiman, not Solomon. Today, Saul Shamir becomes Saul Illya. I know the server in Ashraf's Indian takeaway in Ribblesdale; he's Bangladeshi, and he's called Samir, not Shamir."

"Matt, for hundreds, maybe thousands of years, the people of the Middle East and Asia have used and changed their names for their convenience. Just look through the history books. They may have reasons to have unique identities, maybe for business or personal reasons. If others are aware that you use a different or alternative name or names, I guess it's okay. But to have a secret identity, yes, that is suspicious."

"We should look through the copies of those business cards again one day. Maybe we will find something else there." Bill offered his opinion.

"But why Shamir, Bill?" asked Matt. "I thought you would know the answer to this one!"

"Shamir," started Bill, "was a mythical creature. It appears more than once in the Old Testament and the Talmud. It is fascinating, Matt. Shamir was a worm-like creature—a horrid, ugly thing. But it could cut through wood, stone, marble, even diamonds by using its vision. The first mention of Shamir is back in the times of Moses. Shamir was one of the ten wonders created on the eve of the first Sabbath. Moses also used it to engrave the breastplate for the high priest of the Israelites, the one that holds the gemstones of the twelve tribes of Israel.

"King Solomon, while building a temple to reflect peace and a place to worship, would not allow any iron tools to be used inside the temple. Solomon knew about this Shamir creature, so he delegated a mission of men to go out and find Shamir and bring it back to cut the stone blocks."

"Sounds fascinating," said Penny. "What happened to Shamir?"

"Like a lot of other articles in Jerusalem, Shamir disappeared after Nebuchadnezzar destroyed the city.

"Now, when not being used, Shamir had to be wrapped in wool and kept in a lead-lined box as lead was the only material that its piercing vision could not penetrate. Does that remind you of anything?"

"Not a thing, mate," said Matt.

Penny and Connie shook their heads.

"Maybe Jerry Siegel used the same research books as me when he created the mineral weapon kryptonite to threaten and harm his hero, Superman. Kryptonite also could not penetrate lead. By the way, Jerry Siegel also used the names Joe Carter and Jerry Ess. Cheers to that, Matt."

Matt thought to himself, *Where did Bill get his knowledge from and where did he store it?*

They finished the bottle of wine and retired for a good night's sleep.

ELEVEN

U nlike their previous visit to a medical examiner, this time, the two detectives had to prepare themselves. They donned clean suits and shoe covers outside the inspection room. Sliding doors opened automatically and the drop in temperature was noticeable. Even for two stalwarts from the north of England.

The medical examiner pulled back the white sheet and exposed a well-tanned, average-sized male body. There were no signs of any bruising on the limbs or torso, but they could see some scratches around the neck area.

Mitch watched and waited for a reaction from Louise. She stood strong.

"Can you confirm the cause of death, please?" asked Matt.

"Yes, it was poison," said the medical examiner.

"Our colleagues mentioned that yesterday," said Matt. He acknowledged Mitch and Louise with a gentle nod of his head towards where they were standing.

Matt pointed at the scratches on the victim's neck. "That's a mess, some sort of struggle, do you think?" he asked.

"It looks like his neck had some kind of thread or wire wrapped around it—two or three times, it seems. We found some fibres around the scars. Also, the victim fought back and tried to pull the yarn away. In doing so, he has scratched himself. We don't think this action was intended to kill him. The aim here was to bring him down and get him into a vulnerable position to enable the attacker to administer the poison," said the examiner.

"We've seen something similar on the last one," said Bill.

"This is what I find strange. Look here," said the examiner.

He beckoned for Matt and Bill to move closer, picked up the right arm of the corpse, and pointed to a very nasty wound on the right forearm.

"See, not a small incision, but brutal. Look at the bruising around the wound." He pointed.

"What could have made such an incision?" asked Mitch, at last contributing.

"Compasses," blurted Bill immediately.

Louise looked vacant.

"You know, the tool for drawing a circle. It has a pencil in one leg and a sharp metal pin in the other leg!"

Bill turned his hand upside-down and illustrated the movement of a pair of compasses with his two fingers.

"Have you identified the poison?" was Matt's next question.

The coroner stared, looked terrified, and took a deep swallow. "Batrax," he said.

"Good God," declared Bill. "Batrachotoxin, the stuff for poison darts from the frogs in South America?"

"Exactly, but we kind of wonder how they got it here?" said the coroner.

Bill knew the answer.

"Easy," exclaimed Bill. "I have read several articles about how the tribes extract it from the frogs. They stab the frog with a long stick and then roast them alive over a fire. As the frog cooks, bubbles of poison form on the frog's skin as the skin blisters. They dip the point of the dart into the bubbles, or they collect the bubbles and let them ferment. However, there is another method and one I suspect is more likely in this case. The tribesmen force a long thin bamboo splinter through the frog's mouth and out of the frog via the back leg. Of course, this causes the frog intense pain, and it secretes a sort of bodily fluid.

"This secretion, almost like perspiration, forms a white foam on the frog's skin. When collected by this method, the toxins can last for up to one year. Put some on the point of the compass, cover the point with a plastic ferrule, and keep it in your tool bag. No one would ever know any differently," explained Bill.

"How much would be needed?" asked Mitch.

"An amount the same as two grains of salt is enough to kill a human in a matter of minutes. There is no known antidote and it would have to be handled by someone who knew what they were doing," Bill finished.

"But where does the poor frog get this deadly poison from in the first place?" asked a confused Louise.

"I thought someone would ask that. A lot of bugs, beetles, and insects carry it throughout the rainforests in South America. The frogs get it when they eat the bugs and beetles. Over the years, they have built up immunity to the poison," continued Bill.

"We also found a trace of botulinum toxin in the blood," said the examiner.

"Oh, very smart," said Bill. "Death occurs in the same way, muscle paralysis. If the Batrax toxicity has worn off and didn't get him in a few minutes, the Botox would do him in a couple of hours. Maybe less, depends on the dosage amount, like any poison."

"Botox," queried Louise.

"Yes, love, botulinum toxin; 'bot' is the bot in Botox. The anti-aging treatment that hundreds of women use every day on the high streets of most major cities all over the world. It works by stopping a chemical messenger that carries the signal for the muscles to relax. It's okay, quite safe when administered properly. But on the other side of the argument, it also needs someone who knows what they are doing—right, doctor?" Bill looked at the medical examiner.

"Completely true, sir," said an impressed examiner.

"So, bat-whatever on the compass point and Botox on the pencil, Bill; is that what you are saying now?" asked Matt.

"Pencil? What pencil?" asked Mitch.

Matt and Bill looked at each other but said nothing.

The coroner stepped forward as he held up a plastic evidence bag.

"This pencil? We found it in the victim's shirt pocket," he said.

"I suspect it is not even lead in there, but something else, and the point will be very sharp. Be careful; they could have covered it with a good coating of lethal botulinum," explained Bill.

"That's just it, sir," said the medical examiner. "There was no lead in it."

Bill now took hold of the pencil and handled it carefully. "Yep, as I thought, an Orenz," said Bill, "the only mechanical pencil, as far as I am aware, that can take a 0.2mm lead. It has an internal sleeve that supports the lead when it is under pressure, touching the surface."

"Or stabbing people," added Louise.

"If they loaded this pencil with a sharpened steel needle, that could easily deliver enough toxin to kill someone in a short time. One nanogram will kill a human in a few hours," said Bill, "and any trace of such a needle now would be nigh on impossible."

"The proverbial haystack, Bill?" asked Matt.

"Exactly, mate," said Bill.

"But where would the murderer get rid of the needle?" asked Mitch.

"With proper planning, Mitch, the murderer knows how to get rid of a three-inch-long piece of thin steel needle. It could have disappeared with the rest of the rubbish or lying in a flower bed in the garden downstairs for all we know," said Matt.

Louise silently mouthed to Mitch, "How did they know about a pencil?"

Mitch, wide-eyed, whispered, "I don't know. How did he know about the frogs in South America? And what's all this about compasses? Have you seen any compasses turn up anywhere, Lou?"

"No, but I'll tell you what. I am booked in for some facial work next week that's getting cancelled, I am telling you," said Louise.

"There is one other question I have. What was the victim wearing, short-sleeved or long-sleeved shirt?" asked Bill.

"He was wearing a short-sleeved shirt. Why?" Louise asked.

"The victim was fighting back. How would the attacker be able to roll up a shirt sleeve and make that wound?" explained Bill.

"Go on, Bill," said Matt.

"He stabbed him. The attacker stabbed the victim. The attacker didn't expect a fight back. I bet he expected to do a better job of wrapping the thread around the neck. He didn't and when the victim fought back, it turned into a brawl.

"That's why there are so many scratches on the floor. They wrestled, and the first chance the attacker got, he stabbed the forearm. Look at the bruising. Plus, don't forget the attacker knows about the poison on the point. He doesn't want to be on the receiving end, does he?" explained Bill.

"Matt, at last, our murderer is slipping up." Bill smiled.

Again, Mitch and Louise stared at each other.

"Where next, Bill?" asked Matt.

"We need to return to the lodge building. By the way, have they traced the delivery van yet?" Bill asked on his way out and now back in his detective role.

At the lodge, Basil was busy tidying up the garden when they all arrived. He signalled to the security to let them in and made the familiar "pen in hand" gesture for them to write in the log.

"You forgot to register yesterday. I added it in after you left," he said.

After an exchange of checking each other's well-being, Bill asked, "Basil, you said there was a meeting planned the other evening after the delivery van brought the new regalia. What time do they usually start and finish?"

"They start around seven and the meetings take about two hours. But Tuesday was the evening of the intended long power cut," replied Basil.

"What?" Matt was open-mouthed.

Bill showed to back off. "You had a power cut, that's unusual for down here, surely, and what do you mean by long? Twenty minutes, half an hour?" asked Bill.

"We have had power cuts on and off for the last ten days. They have always been at different times of the day, anything between ten and twenty minutes. But the one the other night, they said, was going to last much longer, could be up to three hours, they said. It's something to do with a new line for one of the new housing developments being installed and connected to the supply."

"Saul was already here and upstairs, and I told him. He said never mind and he would send a message that they should skip the ceremony and just meet at the resort for dinner," explained Basil.

"What time did this happen, mate?" asked Bill.

"It was between six o'clock and six-fifteen. I remember because Saul phoned me a couple of minutes before the electricity department. He asked me about the cartons that we had received in the afternoon and told me he knew nothing about them and asked what time we could meet up."

"I had to be brief with him, as we were over in Newcastle General visiting Sandra's mum. She's just had some surgery and they don't permit phones in the hospital," explained Basil almost apologetically. "Remember, I said yesterday that the electricity company had phoned us earlier in the afternoon, but they hung up before I got there. Later they apologised for not giving us enough warning."

"Then?" said Matt.

"We left the hospital around a quarter to seven; by the time we drove back, oh, we stopped and picked up some food, it must have been half-past seven. It was when we came back that the security guard told me about the new connection he had to inspect, and he asked me about Saul. I went upstairs, and there he was, laid out on the floor. I shouted down for someone to call the police and ambulance. I thought he was still alive," explained Basil, certainly much more relaxed than yesterday up until this point.

"Do you mind seeing if you can trace that call from the electricity company on your phone for me, please?" said Matt.

"The electricity has always called the landline at the security desk," he said.

"And the power cut?" asked Matt.

"It never happened, apparently," said Basil, "according to what our security informed me."

"Is the temple upstairs open?" asked Bill.

"Yes, I have just been up there getting ready for tonight's meeting. Lodge Macquarie, Scottish third-degree tonight," said Basil.

Matt and Bill made their way upstairs, opened the temple door, and they entered. Both of them walked straight across the black and white chequered floor and to a small wooden table positioned in the middle of the room. On top, in the middle of this small table-like piece of furniture, there was a large heavy book—the Holy Bible. Bill opened the Bible using a page marker sewn into the spine of the book. The opened pages revealed a square and compasses. Matt put a glove on and reached to pick up the compasses; Bill stopped him.

"Hang on, mate; the lodge is closed," said Bill.

"Yes, so?" Matt looked puzzled.

"The compasses' points are open, which suggests to me that these were not the ones used during the last meeting. Any experienced Mason would have noticed the points were in the open and not closed position," said Bill. "So, this suggests that whilst the murderer may be familiar with the inside of a Masonic lodge he is not altogether so familiar with the ritual itself."

"Very good point, Bill; good job I brought you halfway around the world," said Matt.

Matt held up the compasses, looked closely, and sniffed at the points.

"Be careful, mate. I doubt you will see or smell anything now, but better be safe than sorry. Let's get it over to forensics straight away," said Bill.

"If this is the murder weapon, where are the original compasses?" asked Matt.

"Doesn't matter really, does it? Even in a small lodge like this, with two meetings a month, it could be several months before anyone even noticed that the compasses were different. It's just another very convenient way to divert the search for the murder weapon, don't you think?" said Bill.

"We've seen a lot of that over the last few days, haven't we?" said Matt.

"I am now totally convinced that the murderer of all three victims knew them all fairly well. He knew of their movements, their habits, everything he needed to know. He has planned these three murders for months, perhaps even years," said Bill.

Matt gave Louise the evidence bag with the compasses and asked her to get them tested for blood and any traces of batra-whatever.

"But how does a pencil fit in here?" asked Louise. "You said earlier, at the medical examiner's, that there was a point on one side and a clamp for a pencil on the other. I don't see how it would fit."

So Louise was more astute than she had first appeared. She had observed the difference between Masonic compasses and an architect's compasses.

Mitch entered the temple. "Look at the architecture; it's magnificent; look at the roof and the stonework around the windows. Beautiful. What do you say, Lou?"

"Curtains are the wrong colour!" she said. She paid little attention to anything else, as she still examined the compasses in search of a solution to her quandary.

Matt explained they had to return to a meeting at their son's hotel and they would contact them later.

"If you get a trace on the vehicle, please call me," said Matt as he and his companion got in their taxi.

———————————

Henry knew Phoenix was still in shock, but he persuaded her to answer some questions from Matt and Bill. She still didn't know about the fate of her third uncle in Beirut. Penny and Connie joined them in case Phoenix needed some support.

It was now of the utmost importance that Matt and Bill talk to her with no further delay. They all sat on the terrace.

Matt explained; what she had to do now could have a massive outcome on developments in the next few days.

"Phoenix, if you don't mind, may we start where we left off last night when I asked you if you were familiar with the family name Illya?"

She sighed, and after a few seconds, she began: "The Illya family roots have been traced back over a thousand years to the 1099 Siege of Jerusalem. Some claim, even before that. It could go as far back as the 7th century. They were not called Illya in those days but were a very well-respected family from Caesarea with very high regard for discipline, honesty, and integrity. The family moved to Jerusalem as they had some sort of discipline control or administrative power awarded by the military commander. Please don't ask me his name, Umar or Omar, maybe...."

Bill started; Matt stopped him.

"Their job was to reintroduce and maintain order amongst the population after the siege. The legend is that the patriarch of this family, at that time, a guy named Sultan, convinced the authorities to allow him to establish a separate organisation for trading. This was for bringing much-needed food and other materials into the city. He was a smart guy and set up a streamlined procedure where all the goods that entered Caesarea port would be declared as 'Illya'—that is all," explained Phoenix, still somewhat nervous.

"Shipping mark: Illya, Jerusalem," said Matt.

Phoenix nodded her head.

"Over the years—well, actually centuries—that followed, they grew bigger and bigger as they spread throughout the Levant. Their presence can still be seen in many sectors to this day. The name itself was adopted, or rather, inherited by the family.

"Coming forward, because of the Israeli-Arab boycott, they created a separate company called MESOL. This was for their business in the Gulf region and other sensitive areas. In these areas, they did not use the name Illya so much. So, it became a habit to be recognised by other names, especially for some members of the family.

"Now, going back, about fifty years, the key person in those days was Sultan Illya. He married a woman called Leila, and they had four children, three sons and a daughter. The names of the sons were Saul, David, and Suleiman, and they were born in 1971, 73, and 75.

"A daughter, Jamila, was born between David and Suleiman in 1974." Phoenix, now somewhat calmer, was doing a grand job. "Also, not long after the birth of David, some people say that Sultan Illya had an affair with another woman. Some even say that this woman gave birth to an illegitimate son. More than that, I do not know.

"The three brothers grew up very close together. Under the guidance of their father, Sultan, they all developed a very astute business mind. Each of them specialising in a different sector. But they always agreed that property would remain their mainstay.

"The daughter, Jamila, of course, had nothing to worry about. But life for women in the Middle East can, sometimes, be very dull. Through one of her father's projects, she went overseas for some work experience. Unfortunately for Jamila, she got more than experience with work. While she was away, she met an Englishman. He was older than her but very handsome, knowledgeable, charming, and a magnificent lover. Jamila became pregnant by this man, and she gave birth to a daughter, whom she named Tamara."

Matt and Bill exchanged glances at each other.

"She deliberately picked the name, Tamara, after Tamar, for she believed her daughter would grow to be extremely beautiful. Tamar was the name of the only daughter of King David, who was also said to be stunningly beautiful." Phoenix continued her story with confidence. "Jamila also wanted to protect her family from any scandal. A scandal of this nature in the Middle East region can cause a lot of grief and harm for their business in the region.

"As the girl grew up and blossomed, Tamara's father believed one day she might need a second identity. The girl's uncles had become powerful and very influential people.

"Saul, the eldest, had one son. David had no children, and Suleiman had two daughters from his marriage. Suleiman also had a reputation as a womaniser.

"In 2008, Sultan passed away. It was only then that the three Illya brothers found out about the existence of their niece. The father met all three brothers and informed them. The girl's father also invested and joined the Illya Corporation in the interests of his daughter's future.

"As the region prospered, the Illya Corporation expanded, but, as we all know, the world is full of unscrupulous people. Therefore, the agreement was that the family must take action to prevent any harm from coming to the girl, Tamara. She was also now reaching an age where people would start recognising her beauty. There was great concern for her welfare and security as there had been an attempt to kidnap her during a visit she made to Dubai."

Phoenix's voice quivered slightly at this stage of the story, and she bowed her head to recompose herself.

"So, her father considered issuing his daughter with a British passport. But after consideration and because of his own status, he decided against it. Anyway, the solution was that an independent identity would be most suitable. So, they organised to have her issued with a different passport altogether. A Maltese passport. A small price to pay."

Matt looked at Bill; it was all coming together at long last.

"They gave Tamara a new name, and while it changed her identity completely, it would always keep a connection to the name given to her by her mother and her cultural background."

"Tamar, in Hebrew, means date, the fruit or date palm," continued Phoenix. "Now, the flowering plant of the date palm has a different name. They also use the same word for over twelve different species of dates found from Southeast Europe to Southeast Asia. That name is Phoenix. Now, an Arabic word for the description of cultivating or developing a fruit tree could be Istrara. They had the idea to make this word sound more Maltese to Istaza."

She stopped her story and held out her hands like an Indian statue. "So, everyone, here I am. Phoenix Istaza, aka Tamara Illya."

Her smile was radiant.

"Now, I remember, that day in your bedroom, you said Dubai brought back terrible memories for you," said Henry.

Matt looked at Penny. "Her bedroom!" he said.

Penny's eye rolled to the top of her head.

"Phoenix, I find your story fascinating. Thank you. And after hearing your account, I can now relate to this," said Bill.

He held up a piece of paper with an illustration of a MESOL business card. Phoenix opened her clutch purse and held up a similar business card.

"See," she said.

"The image used on this card has perplexed us, Matt and me, for the last few days. Now, after hearing your story, I think I can now explain it. I suspect the ladder shown here, on these cards, is the so-called *immovable ladder*," said Bill.

Matt looked at Penny and Connie.

"In the 18th century, someone positioned a ladder on the roof over the entrance to the Church of the Holy Sepulchre in Jerusalem. It leans permanently up to a window. Nobody knows who put it there, but it has been there ever since. The status quo, established a few years later, meant no one could move this ladder ever again," explained Bill.

"Status quo, Bill?" asked Henry.

"The status quo, in this context, describes a mutual understanding between six different Christian denominations. The understanding itself refers to nine different holy places that are in and around Jerusalem and Bethlehem. The status quo mandates that no one can change any of the nine sites without the agreement of all six of the different denominations. I forget all nine sites now, just as I have also forgotten the six different denominations," explained Bill.

"However, I recall amongst the sites: the tomb of the Virgin Mary is one, and the Church of the Nativity is another. But the one that holds significance for us today is the Deir es-Sultan. It means Monastery of the Sultan and you will find this monastery on the roof of the Church of the Holy Sepulchre."

"Bill, you never cease to amaze us," said Matt.

"Thank you very much, Miss Istaza. The information you provided us with will now make our job so much easier from here on."

"And now, Bill, at long last, we know the whereabouts of Tamara Illya," said Matt.

"One more question, if I may, Miss Istaza. What is the name of your father?" asked Matt.

Phoenix stuttered, "Please, call me Phoenix. My father is Edward Chapman, but most people know him as Sir Rupert Edward Chapman. You can meet him soon, as he is arriving from Singapore this afternoon."

Another surprise for Matt and Bill, and just as Matt was about to talk, his phone rang. A polite finger pointed upwards, saying, "Wait a moment, please."

"Hello, yes, found it. Where? Oh, doesn't matter. Okay, see you outside," Matt spoke into the phone.

"Bill, the local cops have got a lead on this Ribera guy; they're outside the hotel now. Phoenix, thank you very much; we actually met your father a few days ago in Beirut. Girls, Henry, see you later; let's have a beer at sundown on your terrace yonder. Must dash!" said Matt as he rushed out.

Matt and Bill hurried across the hotel lobby.

"Henry, is your father always like this?" asked Phoenix.

As they drove along, the conversation quickly came around to Freemasons. Louise started, "So, what do you guys know about the Freemasons and all that stuff?"

"Well, maybe it's better if we ask you what do *you* know about the Freemasons and all that stuff?" said Bill.

"Well, the story we hear is that a bunch of posh men meet in that old building, and they ride around on goats. When I was young, my mum used to say that building is where naughty girls went, and they would never be seen or heard of again," said Louise.

"Yeah, my mum used to say the same to us, Lou," added Mitch, "about naughty boys, though."

"It's some weird religion, right? All to do with God and the big G in the room, and I know they have to wear a funny apron and have a secret handshake. What's that all about? Really strange," she followed on.

"Tell me something, Louise; are you a member of a gym club here?" asked Bill.

"Yes, I am, sure enough," came her reply.

"And do you have a membership card with your photograph on it?" was Bill's next question.

"Yes, got one," replied Louise.

"Do you mind showing it to me?" asked Bill without hesitation.

Louise immediately turned around and stared at Bill.

"Do you think it is strange, a man you hardly know, asking to see your gym membership card? Isn't it the same?" asked Bill.

"It's like anything that we don't have proper knowledge about, but we seem able to believe or assume whatever it is to be right or wrong. This method is, unfortunately, how most of the world has functioned for the last two or three hundred years. Let's face it. Until this morning, you didn't know that the injections used for Botox treatment come from the most powerful poison on earth," said Bill.

"As far as knowledge of Freemasonry goes, well, it's like any new subject that stimulates one's interest. I always try to encourage people to research that subject for themselves before they form ideas or opinions.

Certainly, where anything that may appear strange or outrageous is concerned," was Matt's contribution.

"Like riding goats around in an old building," said Mitch.

"Exactly," came Matt's reply.

"I can't help thinking if we had the story that Phoenix provided us earlier, we would be ahead of the game now, Bill," said Matt.

"It's always a difficult one to judge," replied Bill. "Look at it like this if it helps. Nostradamus was famous for his verses that predicted future events. Or did they? Every single one of them has only ever reflected historical events with hindsight. No one has ever made a forecast or said to have predicted a future occurrence based on reading any of his verses in advance."

"Do you know, Bill, I actually find some comfort in that? Thanks, mate," said Matt. He slapped Bill on the knee.

Fifteen minutes later, they arrived at a commercial vehicle rental depot.

They entered and Mitch made a quick introduction to Matt and Bill and explained the reason for their visit.

"Do you have any vehicles like the one we are talking about currently in your depot?" asked Matt.

"Yes, we do. Follow me, please," replied the depot manager, and they went through to the rear of the building.

"Over there, we still have three in the yard, all about the same," he said. He pointed towards the vehicles.

"They arrived about two weeks ago. Maybe the one you are asking about is out for the first time. I'd have to check the computer. We let another one out on a six-month rental. That new resort development over by the lake took it," the manager said.

"All the same?" asked Matt.

"Pretty much all the same cosmetics—double rear door, single side door, auto box, diesel. It's a decent van. We have gone through a few of the previous models. They run forever," he said.

Bill and Mitch looked around the vehicles to observe any features that the manager may have overlooked.

"May we see the rental agreement form for this Ribera guy, please?" asked Bill.

"Back in the office," said the manager, and off they all walked.

The manager called it up on his computer screen.

"Yeah, here it is, booked online, last Sunday—maybe Monday, overseas booking. Sometimes there's a delay until it shows up here. There is an email address here—jribera at Telefonica.com.es. Pick-up Monday morning, two named drivers but not listed here, taken full cover, credit card number, that all seems in order. Nothing strange here. Oh, pick up at Newcastle airport but I cannot see any flight arrival details. They will have all the hard copies at the airport branch. I can get copies of the licenses scanned and emailed over for you if you want," explained the manager. He was very helpful.

"That would be a great help. Mitch, leave him your card," said Matt. "And could you let us have a record of the mileage when the hirer collected the vehicle, please; that might also help us."

"You will have it within thirty minutes," said the depot manager.

"Do we need to go back to the lodge building, sir?" asked Mitch.

"I think we are done there, for now, Mitch. Not much we can do until we trace the actual van itself. Keep working on that, please, and let us know," said Matt.

"We will drop you back. Your hotel or the Valide?" asked Mitch.

"The Valide, please," said Matt. They got in the car. "Valide, such an odd name for a resort hotel, or any hotel, come to think about it."

"Something to do with an old rule of the family that is developing it. I had it explained to me when they first started there, but that was two years ago. I didn't understand it then, to be honest with you," said Mitch.

———

As Matt and Bill walked into the reception area, they saw Henry, Phoenix, and another man seated at a low table in the lobby. Matt licked his lips. "Just what I need right now!" he whispered as he noticed the teapot on the table.

It appeared Phoenix had been crying again. She held a handkerchief to her eyes. Henry sat by her side as the other man put his arm around her shoulder.

"Dad, more bad news, I'm afraid," started Henry, "but I think you knew it all along, didn't you?"

Before Matt could answer, Henry said, holding out his arm toward the other man, "Dad, Bill, may I introdu—"

"No need, Henry," interrupted Phoenix. "They've met already. I heard your father say as he left the hotel earlier."

"Sorry, Miss Istaza. I am not with you there," stuttered Matt, very puzzled.

"My father, Sir Rupert Chapman. You said you had met him already, a few days ago," she said as she pointed.

Chapman also looked puzzled. "My dear, I have never met these two gentlemen before in my life," he said.

Matt and Bill once again swapped puzzled looks. They also had never met him before.

They all sat down, and between Matt and Bill, they submitted their account of events to the others.

At the end of the explanation, Chapman asked, "You say that this imposter came to your room, eh? Who announced him to you?"

"The hotel reception called to the room and said he was there, and wanted to come to my room," said Matt.

"Obviously, so that no one would see him meeting you. In case you started referring later to someone else about a meeting in the lobby with Sir Rupert Chapman. If no one observed such a meeting, you don't have any witnesses. What if you were asked to describe my appearance? They deliberately set it up that way to deceive you," he said.

"And he also said what? That the next day, the police brought us the gifts for the girls in some boxes. Poppycock! We saw no gifts. Unless they came later in the week. I left for Singapore the following day. As far as I know, we have never even been contacted by the police," explained Chapman.

"It is correct that old Solly returned to his room to bring the girl's gifts for me to carry back. He said he didn't want them in the restaurant in case of any damage and as we were on our last bottle, he thought it would be convenient."

"So, these boxes could possibly still be on the shelves in the police station until today," added Bill.

"I will get it checked immediately. Leave this with me," said Chapman. Phoenix cried again.

"How did the message we left with the British embassy get in the hands of a Sir Rupert impersonator?" asked Matt.

"Matt, the murderer has planned this for months, could be years. He has all his accomplices in place. He must have known that Suleiman would meet Sir Rupert for dinner. So, he needed to prepare for the contingency. I bet he even had something with Sir Rupert's secretary," explained Bill.

"Hah, funny you should say that. April left us a few days back. She has been with us for over fifteen years, walked on the day," said Chapman.

"Where did the white roller come from?" asked Matt.

"A white Rolls-Royce, in Beirut. I can give you ten places where you can hire one from over the phone for less than a hundred dollars. All those years during the turmoil, these cars have been in storage covered over and never used at all."

"I am sure that this Othman character is involved in this somewhere, Matt," said Bill.

"Hah! Harold Othman!" exclaimed Chapman. "Do you mean the police officer? The detective, or whatever he calls himself," he laughed.

"Yes, he told us he was an inspector," Matt and Bill said together.

"I guess you know him then," said Matt.

"Hahaha, know him? Mr. Baxter, let me ask you a question. Hahaha, have you ever seen the movie *Casablanca*?" asked Chapman.

TWELVE

They all moved onto the terrace. It was a busy time, as people returned back from their daytime sailing adventures. The conversation was quite tricky at first for Phoenix. She informed her father that she had told the others some of the backgrounds of the Illya family and company.

"Phoenix, I have some questions for you, if you don't mind. We need to go back to when you were in England," asked Matt.

"Go ahead," she replied.

"First, do you know why David booked the hotel in Ingleton?" asked Matt.

"David always made his bookings at the last minute. I know he had been somewhere in the same region the previous week; Papa told me he was with him. I recall now that it was the same place where the car repairmen said they came from. After that, he took the train to London, where he stayed for a few days. I also remember something about him going to the studio in Paris for a couple of days. Then I heard he would be back in the north, to meet someone on another project. He said something about a guy from Seattle?"

"Settle. Close to us, thirty miles," said Matt.

"Yes, that's it. He will have looked on the internet and booked a hotel, as near there as he could find, I guess," she explained.

"Next, why were there two power banks in the rental car, and you also had two in your car?"

"Oh, that! Hahaha! Sorry. When he told the office in Dubai that he had to go up north of England, they said to make sure he had an emergency power supply. They said sometimes there is no electricity north of London. They sent me an email with the same story."

"You have shown little grief over David's death. You didn't seem to be upset at all, not like your other two uncles."

"We weren't close, far from it, not since my teenage years. Not like I was with Saul or Solly. It could be because Saul was the eldest, I don't know. David could be quite vulgar towards me, and I didn't like it at all. More than once, I have slapped his face. He was a pervert! Sorry, Papa. I think you saw it as well."

Chapman nodded his head to agree with her.

"We never saw you outside the pub in the early morning. Didn't the noise wake you up?" said Matt.

"I stayed in a room at the back of the building, and I never heard a thing," she explained.

"But later in the day, you heard there had been a murder. Do you remember when we met later that evening?" asked Matt.

"Yes, I heard the news but why would I think this had anything to do with my uncle David?" she said and shrugged her shoulders.

"So why did you go to the hotel in Ingleton the previous evening?" Matt asked.

"Oh, he brought my new package. I have been moving around so much, it never caught up with me, and it was a new month. I needed it. I never went to the hotel; we met where those big warehouse shops are."

"Package?" queried Matt with raised eyebrows.

"My credit cards, health insurance cards, that kind of stuff. There were also some new business cards," replied Phoenix.

"Why was the car abandoned? Left unlocked?"

"He was to meet someone back in your village, and he had been drinking. I brought him over. He said he would get a taxi back. I even scolded him for driving from the hotel to the warehouse area. When he drinks, he doesn't know when to stop. He would have forgotten to lock it. He left the key and his fancy new phone in the toilet at that deserted gas station down the hill," replied Phoenix.

Matt stopped for a moment as his memory went back to the day he went to the petrol station and the strange behaviour by the son when his father mentioned the customer showed him a very fancy smartphone.

"Why did he use your Tamara Illya name on the named driver rental agreement instead of Phoenix?" was Matt's next question.

"He would have booked the car through the office in Dubai. They all knew me as Tamara from when I lived there."

"Why did David have one of your name cards? We traced the address to be in Jerusalem. Is it a coincidence that the street name is Sultan Suleiman—any connection?" asked Matt.

"I recently changed my cell number in Germany and had new cards printed. They were in the parcel that he carried over and he asked for one of my *new* cards," replied Phoenix.

"The address in Jerusalem . . . ?" queried Matt.

Another shrug of her shoulders. "It goes back years. The family always stayed there. I remember it as a small child. I never knew or even thought of any connection between the family and the street name—I still don't," said Phoenix.

"In the back of your car, there was an airline luggage tag from a suitcase. You know, the one they wrap through the handle with the destination code printed. I could only make out BE of the three letters; I assume it was BEY for Beirut."

"Then you would assume wrong, Mr. Holmes," joked Phoenix. "Before I came to England, I was on an assignment in Europe, which I had to cover by land. A lot of it had to be done by train, and my trip started in Belgrade. I took a flight and took that suitcase along. I left the luggage tag in the car when I removed it from the bag after I picked the car up in London after the assignment finished."

Henry imagined how much he could have enjoyed that trip if they had been together.

"What about the key to your car?" asked Matt.

"David was tormenting me. After I parked the car in the pub yard, I wanted to get away. I was so angry, I pressed the stop button and got out of the car. I realised afterwards that I had left the key in the car," stuttered Phoenix, getting emotional.

"Calm down, sweetheart," said her father.

"By the way, my car key turned up after all. The beer delivery men found it when they opened the cellar doors. They said it must have fallen between the space of the two doors." Phoenix unknowingly added more vital information to the case, and the expression on Bill's face showed this.

Matt looked at Bill. Bill held his finger and thumb apart to show a small distance: two centimetres.

"When you talked to the car repairmen, how did you know about the railway tracks that used to run through the old factory? The railway removed them five years ago," Matt asked what he thought was a very important question.

"When I took on the assignment, the company provided me with some old maps of the village and the region. This is quite normal for these projects. I had nothing to do for almost two days and so I had been studying the maps in my room. I remembered about the rail tracks," she replied confidently.

"About your car . . . I think you left a phone in your car, didn't you? And when you found it, did it have a missed call on it?" asked Matt.

"Yes, it did. How do you know that?" asked Phoenix.

Matt remembered Ryan tried to call the German phone number from the card they found on the victim. "Where is David Illya's luggage in all this?" asked Matt.

"David doesn't use luggage. He keeps a toilet bag in his briefcase, and he buys clothes as he needs them. When he leaves a hotel, he donates what he leaves behind. He always has done it, as far as I know."

"Damn fellow! Had no respect for his money," said Chapman.

"So, you went back to the hotel in Ingleton on Saturday, for what purpose exactly?"

"I attended an interview for a job there; I told Bill and Henry about it last week. Glad I didn't get it now. She was a bitch. Sorry, Papa."

"Coming back to the hotel booking for David Illya at the Ingleton hotel. What do you know about that? We understand he had considered extending his stay," said Matt.

"Not much. As I said before, we weren't close. I wanted little to do with him. He was always trying to get me to go to bed with him. When we met that evening, he told me he would extend his hotel stay over the weekend if I stayed with him in his hotel. He was trying to get me to have dinner with him and go back to the hotel that same evening. He said he would drive, and we could get his phone and keys from the gas station on the way."

"That man was a deviant!" exclaimed Chapman, thumping his palm with his fist.

"On Thursday evening, when you came back to the pub, someone had upset you. When I asked if you were all right, you said you were hoping to meet up with someone in London, and then the same night you extended your stay at the pub. Isn't that odd?" asked Matt.

"Not really. I had hoped to meet up with my father before he left London. He had been there all week, and I was angry because, by the time I could reach London, he would have left. That's when I decided to stay on and be at the village festival. I ended up pulling the beer pump, and I met Henry . . . Jimbo!" said Phoenix, smiling at Henry.

"That's all, I think," said Matt. He sat back and took a long drink from his ice-cold beer.

"Thank you, Phoenix. That has been very helpful." Matt stared outside towards the entrance of the hotel as the resort light flickered to life. He had a question in his mind.

Meanwhile, Chapman stood up away from their table as he talked on the phone. After a brief conversation, he sat down at the side of Phoenix.

"I have my people in Beirut going to the police headquarters to check on the gift boxes. There won't be many people around, being Saturday afternoon. With a bit of luck, we will have an answer late this evening or tomorrow morning, afternoon, latest," said Chapman.

"Matt, things are coming together now, same as any other murder enquiry," said Bill.

Matt changed the subject, and he pointed to the illuminated resort sign. "I have meant to ask you, why 'Valide'? It's an odd name for a resort hotel like this. The local police officer tried to explain it to me, but he had forgotten the story."

"Okay, please allow me, Matt. It's fairly straightforward, actually. Valide is the word used to describe the mother of a Sultan dating back to the Ottoman Empire. We kind of adopted it for the Illya hotel chain as an acknowledgement to the old Sultan. Plus, our marketing guys said we needed a one-word name to identify with our properties," explained Chapman.

Bill was itching to add his contribution. "Hafsa Sultan was the first Valide, and she was also the mother of Suleiman the Magnificent," he added.

Matt, Penny, and Connie stared in disbelief.

"Do you see the resort sign, over there above the archway, on the pole? We have our very talented Phoenix to thank for that. She designed it, painted it; I even heard she helped them in the carpentry shop to build the bloody thing." Chapman laughed.

"Oh, Papa, that reminds me. We brought those old bits and pieces over with us. David gave them to me, something you asked for when you met up the week before," said Phoenix.

"Hang on. I'll get it now." Henry jumped up and went to their villa. Connie used the opportunity to refill everyone's glasses.

Henry returned, holding an old canvas bag that he passed to Phoenix's father. He opened the bag, looked inside, then closed it back up and put it on the floor, down by his side.

"Only some old rubbish," he said. The others stared at him.

"I told you." Phoenix gently slapped Henry's arm. "He says it's old rubbish, but I bet it doesn't get thrown out."

"Where did that come from?" asked Matt, very concerned.

"It was in my car last week, just some stuff David passed to me for Papa," replied Phoenix.

"Phoenix, do you mind? I missed that last week when you got your car started," Matt reached out for the bag and looked inside. Something immediately caught his attention.

"Aye, aye, Bill, what do we have here?" He pulled out a twenty-four-inch gauge, which he held high for all to see.

Bill sat upright, and after a couple of seconds, he leaned forward for a closer examination. Matt focused on the brass hinge between the two lengths of the rule. He ran his thumb over it. "Ouch! Very sharp," he said to Bill.

"Careful, Matt! It might need to be checked by forensics," said Bill.

The others looked at each other, bewildered.

"This could well have been the tool used as a weapon for the first attack on David," said Matt. "The brass hinge has been ground sharp, so when it's thrust in the victim's throat, it would choke and lacerate him at the same time—stunned him."

"Is it one of those working ones you explained to me?" asked Penny.

"Yes, it is one of the three first-degree working tools," said Matt, "and goes together with the mallet and the chisel. We already have those in for further forensic examination and we should get the results tomorrow."

"But why would the killer send it over here?" asked Phoenix.

"They, the murderers, have used this opportunity throughout these three cases. If you are not a Freemason and you came across their so-called working tools, what do they mean to you? They only have a symbolic significance to Masons. If you are not aware of that significance, it must be quite easy to masquerade them as something else," said Bill.

"I also think another factor played a part here. I actually believe the killer wants your family to know something," said Bill. "As if they are trying to send you a message."

"Let's see what Sir Rupert's team comes up with on the ones in Beirut," said Matt.

"Ladies and gentlemen, we have all had a very eventful day. We can move inside to the dining room, where I would like to invite you all to join me for dinner," announced Chapman.

The next morning, the phone in Matt's room rang out. "Hello, morning, yes, okay, half an hour, fine. See you in the lobby."

He relayed a similar message to Bill and immediately made a request to room service. Twenty minutes later Matt walked out of the door and as he arrived at reception, a pot of fresh tea was deposited on a small table. Bill joined him.

"Morning . . . what day is it, Matt? I haven't got a clue, what with all this travelling," asked Bill.

"Good morning, Bill; today is Sunday. Work doesn't stop on murder enquires, you know that, mate," said Matt. "They've found the van. By the way, a message from your mate Walter on my phone."

Mitch and Louise arrived. Matt and Bill managed a takeaway cup with the help of the hotel staff, and they got in the car. Once in the car, Matt and Bill talked more about the situation back in England. Matt passed his phone to Bill.

"Hang on; something is wrong here. It looks like Walter has been on the bottle when he sent this message," said Bill. "His message says the DNA from two of the hair samples taken from the brick factory is showing up a higher DNA match than David and Phoenix. Also, there is a third sample from the brick factory, but no match to any of the others."

"Perhaps call him this evening, Bill; we need that cleared up," said Matt. "Come on; we're here."

Moored on the marina of the yacht club, there was row after row of boats and yachts. Over in the corner of the car park was a white van, registration plate 831 ZQA. A couple of uniformed police officers stood guard, accompanied by a man in blue coveralls.

"Have you got a warrant?" asked Bill.

"Here," Louise held it up. "I doubt we need it, though," she said.

"There's the garage guy; he's aware of the situation," she added as they walked over towards the vehicle.

Mitch and Louise examined the outside of the vehicle. Nothing to go on there.

A quick search in the driver and passenger seat area revealed little.

"They will have removed everything," said Bill.

Matt turned around and looked across the marina.

"Look in the back, please, Bill, but I doubt you'll find anything. The important thing for us now is to locate the culprit if he, or they, is still in the region. Who knows; he may have moved on already. Where to next, I wonder?" Matt talked as he looked around the marina area.

"Do people live on some of these?" he asked Mitch.

"Yes, sir; still quite popular, especially if you're a water sports enthusiast.

Many people will be out on Friday afternoon and return on Sunday," replied Mitch.

"Or go somewhere else?" asked Matt. "How long to reach somewhere like Myall Lake on something decent?" Matt pointed to a thirty-five-foot craft.

"Not long; it's only about an hour and a half by road," said Mitch.

"What about Brisbane?" asked Matt. "I tell you why Mitch: all murderers plan their escape before anything else."

"Have you considered something else about this case? How do you think the murderer got away from the building? Let's assume that he came into the compound, hidden in the back of the delivery van. He must have known that his victim would be the first to arrive for the meeting. He arranged for a power cut to the building as part of his plan," said Matt.

"So, it would be dark?" asked Mitch.

Matt looked at Bill and rolled his eyes.

"No, mate. To keep the other members of the club from getting anywhere near the building. The murderer was already hiding upstairs. The delivery guy said they were told they must deliver the cartons upstairs. So, the third person in the van crept upstairs, prepared what he needed and waited," said Matt.

Mitch still looked vacant.

"It means the murderer must have known the victim. There must be a few of them; they go to all this planning—the delivery van, correct positioning of the vehicle at the entrance. The bogus telephone call to divert the caretaker. Then the power cut and a mysterious new line connection. They must even have known the caretaker would be away at the hospital on this evening. With all this precise planning, don't you think they would have thought about their getaway just as carefully?" said Matt.

"Absolutely. One point we have not yet covered, with security on the entrance, or in this case, exit, how did the murderer leave the premises?" added Bill. "Anyway, back here, we need to check with the marina security who is supervising these boats. There must be a registration or something. You can't just come to tie alongside and bunk up for a few nights. In these places, you need to hook up to the auxiliary services to receive power, water, and pump out your toilets."

"I will get on that straight away," said Louise. "Checking the list of occupants, that is. By the way, here's the report on that cardboard carton from our forensics—interesting. Read it."

"Better go back a few days, miss. There's a good chance that they used this for a couple of nights before they moved on," said Matt. "Start from when they picked the van up at the airport."

"It's *they* now then, mate?" said Bill.

"Has to be, Bill, all along; it has to be they. The murderer has had an accomplice all the time. Not just a nephew working as a server in the hotel in Beirut. No, someone has put these murders together with very meticulous planning. To me, it suggests more a partnership than relying on the chance of one person being in the right place at the right time," said Matt.

Matt read the forensic report: "No prints on the skirret but they found traces of white cotton fibres on the inside of the box and get this, traces of human flesh on the piece of string. They are doing more tests to match it to the victim, and they should have the results before six p.m. today." The tone of his voice escalated towards the end of the sentence, and he flicked the paper with the back of his fingertips.

"Bill, Mitch, we need another visit to the lodge. Anything in the back of the van, Bill?"

"Not a thing, Matt: clean as a whistle," came the reply.

They left Louise to go through the residential records of the crafts in the marina and made their way back to the Masonic lodge building.

An enhanced registration procedure was now being used at the security gate. The caretaker had looked at ways to improve security protocols, which is not a bad thing. The security now requires a copy of an identity card to permit entry. The guard took the passports and turned to the newly installed photocopy machine.

"Basil has gone out. He will be back shortly, he said," informed the security guard.

"It's not him we need at this stage," said Matt. "Mitch, during the evening, they found the body. Did you come here?"

"Yes, we reached here about eight-fifteen," he said.

"With whom?" was the next question.

"I came with the super, and the crime scene team was right behind us," said Mitch.

"How many CSIs?"

"Two, I think; no three, no, hang on. Yeah, two . . . maybe three." Mitch had to think.

Matt looked at Bill.

Bill started now. "Better be sure, lad. Think now! Your CSIs, are they clothed up in white boilers?"

"Yes, standard ops," said Mitch. He started concentrating.

"The delivery that came in cardboard boxes . . . where are the boxes?" asked Bill.

"The super told us to remove them and take them to the station," replied Mitch.

"That's fine; so all of them went back. Are you sure?" asked Bill.

Basil arrived, and Matt asked him to go accompany him to the security guard.

"On Tuesday evening, did you leave your post at any time?" asked Matt.

The security guard never replied.

"We change security guards at seven o'clock every day," Basil submitted.

"Do you know if the evening shift guard left his post at the gate for any time on the evening of the murder?" asked Bill.

"Yes, he told me when we came back from the hospital. He had to check on some repair work done to an electrical panel down that lane at the side of the compound. He went with the electrical technician, and he made him sign a form to say the work had been completed," said Basil.

"Where's this panel?" asked Matt.

Basil showed, and they followed him outside and down the side of the compound, where he pointed at a grey panel.

"Can you do me a favour and get on to the electricity company? We need that panel opening, and we need to be here when that happens," said Bill. "Tell them it's police business. Sunday morning, they'll be here in ten minutes, I bet."

"Would they have left the gate open?" They walked back to the outside of the gate.

"I guess so. He can't have been away for five minutes," said Basil.

Matt took out his phone, pressed some keys on the screen, and looked for and found the stopwatch app.

"Probably more than twice as long as what they needed," said Matt.

"Don't forget they can contact each other by message on their phones; just switch the ring tone to mute. It needs less than two minutes if you ask me," said Matt. He passed his phone to Bill. "Ready, Bill? *Go!*" exclaimed Matt.

Matt jogged across to the building. He ran through the garden, just missing the rhododendron sets, which Basil had spent his time tidying a couple of days before. He followed the same route that was explained, and he came to the main entrance of the building. Then, he jogged on the spot for about twenty seconds and then he came back to the gate again.

Matt stopped, bent over, his hands on his knees, and panted for breath. "How long?" he gasped.

"One minute and eighteen seconds," said Bill.

"They know the security guard is a different guy to the afternoon shift. An electricity worker drives his vehicle into the compound to ensure both gates are open; he takes this new guard down the side of the building to the electrical panel. He has to inspect some work. The night shift guard knows nothing about power cuts, bogus or otherwise. The murderer's escape van, driven by the woman, comes into the compound, this time the driver alone. She knows exactly where to stop the vehicle from her earlier visit. Even though there is no one else around to observe what they are doing, the murderer gets in, and they drive out of the compound," said Matt.

"The white suit?" asked Mitch.

"Just in case something didn't go according to plan. The murderer is wearing it. He can hang around and when the CSIs turn up, he just blends in his presence and goes from there."

"You were slow on your jog there and back, and I think you were short on the time you waited at the entrance, Matt. But yes, I also think easily less than two minutes," said Bill.

"So, do you mean to say that the power company technician," said Basil, stuttering, "was the same guy as the afternoon delivery man? The security guard had already changed over so no chance he would recognise him, right?"

"And no new power connection either, mate," said Bill as they turned and walked away.

Mitch took a call. "Okay. I will come over, no problem."

"It's Louise. The guys at the marina have given her what we need."

"Mitch, you go for her and see what she's come up with," said Matt. "We will hang around here for the electricity company to turn up."

"By the way, Mitch, the only way in or out of the lake is down near Swansea Channel, correct?" asked Bill.

"Yes, sir," he replied.

THIRTEEN

The gates to the compound opened, and a large white saloon car drove in without registering at the security gate. Basil was straight over and stopped them. One of the rear doors opened and out stepped a senior uniformed officer. His epaulettes featured a crown and two stars. He approached Matt and Bill and introduced himself as Chief Superintendent Warren Davies. They moved inside the building and Matt explained the connection to the two previous cases.

"It's not so much about the murder weapons," said Matt, "but how they have moved the weapons away from the crime scene. Quite smart, actually."

"We have a lead on the weapons used in Beirut last week. We hope to hear about it later today," he added.

"You are right. The murderer has planned very well, indeed. If I, or any of my team, can assist, please let us know. Our focus is on sorting this out. I am getting my arse kicked from upstairs," said Davies.

Another place where they use the same expression, thought Bill.

"Ultimately, it's not good for the tourist industry around here. We're coming into winter, and that can be a busy time of year in these parts. By the way, I received a phone call about ten minutes ago from the electricity company. Their guys are on the way. They know nothing about power outages out here in the last five years, never mind two weeks. And there have been no new power connections made recently," said Davies.

Davies' car left the compound, and through the same gateway came the technicians. Matt and Bill, accompanied by Basil, took them to inspect the electrical panel.

"Nothing new," said one technician. "Here's the latest update log from control."

The technician pointed to an entry in a logbook and to a white sticker on the inside of the door. The information on both was the same.

Someone had signed the two records. The signatures were hardly readable, but they were similar. It could have been Thomson or Johnson, dated 10 October 2013.

"Have you guys got any records of the power outages that they have been having here recently?" asked Matt.

"Power outs! Here! Nah, mate, you've got that wrong. But sure thing, we will check it out again when we get back and let you know if we find anything," said one technician.

"We had twenty-minute power cuts almost every day for the last couple of weeks," said Basil.

"Must be an electrical fault in your premises, mate. Nothing wrong on the supply side," said the technician.

"Come on, Bill; back to the Valide for us now," said Matt.

Matt phoned his wife. "Yes, love, we are on our way to Henry's hotel. Yes, be about twenty minutes, I reckon. No, I didn't change much at the airport—only two hundred. Ah, okay. I saw a bank opposite the hotel, and there's a small shopping centre there; they will have a money changer. Yes, sure it is, and it's pleasant enough. See you there then, bye," said Matt. He ended his call.

In the lounge near the lobby area, Henry was in conversation with Edward Chapman. Henry believed opportunities lie ahead for him.

"Two more cups, please, lad," said Matt as he approached. "Your mum and Connie are on their way also."

"Phoenix went over to the shops to meet Mum and Connie. They need some ladies' things, so Phoenix volunteered. She knows where to buy that stuff around here," Henry explained.

"Good. Try to take her mind off things. It can't be easy for her," added Bill.

"I expected news from Beirut by now, old chap. So far, nothing. I will give it another hour," said Chapman.

Matt relayed the discoveries of the morning's work to the two of them. Everything was coming together.

Over in the shopping centre, Phoenix showed the two ladies around. It was a rather modest place. Most outlets focused on equipment for water sports activities. There were the usual retail outlets: ready-to-wear, pharmacy, travel agent, car rental, protein supplements, and fancy cakes shop.

"Wasn't that man in the exchange centre helpful, Phoenix?" said Connie. "Are they all as polite and helpful as him around here?"

"The resort development has brought a lot of jobs here, so people are quite pleased. There are plans for more development for the next five, maybe ten, years. Papa was talking to Henry this morning about staying on and doing some work with us," chatted Phoenix as they strolled along.

"But there are always a few people not so happy," said Phoenix. "I used to hear from Saul that there were still a couple of gangsters displeased with what Illya had achieved here. Some American corporation had this development all lined up apparently until Illya Corp. came along and snapped it up. But that's business, I guess."

"Do you know who that man at the counter reminded me of, Connie?" said Penny.

"No, Penny. Who?" Connie asked.

"You were watching the movie on the plane from Dubai. That nice English actor, he played Mr. Banks," said Penny.

Connie only heard half of Penny's sentence.

"Oh! Don't start me off with Mr. Banks. Whenever I hear that name, he's a nuisance. I don't know how Bill puts up with him. Whenever he and his snob of a Spanish wife want to come to stay with us, I would rather tell them we are full. As soon as I see them arrive at the pub..." said Connie with an expression of anguish.

"I am talking about the actor in the Mary Poppins film," said Penny.

"Who are you on about, Connie?" asked Phoenix, using more of her new Yorkshire dialect.

"What's-his-name? Tony Banks stays at our place three or four times a year. Married to that Spanish woman," said Connie.

"Do you mean that little man with the big head, redhead wife? I thought they were the rudest people I have ever met," said Phoenix.

"What do you mean, love?" asked Connie. They stopped walking.

"When I came into the lounge on Tuesday, I said good evening to everyone. All the customers replied, very polite, except for him and his wife. They whispered to each other and looked me up and down like I was some sort of escort. I sat on the barstool and pulled my hemline up and gave them something to talk about." She mimicked it, using the skirt she was wearing. They laughed and continued walking.

"You should have told Bill." Connie said rather scornfully.

"It's nothing. Small-minded people," said Phoenix. "I get that sort of thing sometimes. But, a funny thing, the next morning. I went out to my car, and when I pressed the remote, suddenly, there he was: He appeared at the back of my car, this Banks chap. I asked if I could help him, and he ignored me and walked away; well, almost ran away. His wife was standing outside at the archway entrance. She was smoking one of those long, thin cigarettes. As she followed her husband inside, she stared at me and blew a big puff of smoke my way. Smelled like 'dog muck,' as you say in Copper's Wood," said Phoenix.

More laughter from the three ladies.

"Sweetheart, you must stop calling it Copper's Wood," said Connie, in her headmistress tone of voice.

———

Edward Chapman had received the telephone call from his Beirut office. The police had found two gift boxes from the hotel in their storeroom. Inside they found a block of wood in one box and two pieces of wood that looked like a broken boomerang in the other.

"Those were the exact words he used," said Chapman. "Here, he has sent me some photos."

"You have your guys under control, Edward; I can see why you are a director of ceremonies," said Bill.

Chapman looked startled but only for a moment.

"I guess you found the summons on David," said Chapman.

"Indeed, we did," said Matt. "It was inside his coat pocket."

"Yes, I also attended that meeting," said Chapman. "It was the last time I saw David."

"We would love to attend a meeting someday," said Bill.

"Sadly, I think the days of the Lodge of Illya are over," replied Chapman. "Ah, here are our ladies."

"Bill, Phoenix has just told us about that Tony Banks in our pub last week. Quite rude to her he was," said Connie.

"Who is this Banks guy?" asked Chapman quite suddenly.

"He's been staying at our pub for ages. He's been coming to the region for years, as his company used to supply industrial cleaning chemicals. That's how he got to know the region," said Bill as he looked away at stared vacantly for a few seconds.

"Yes, you're right there, love. Here's a photo from our Christmas dinner that was only four months ago. Quiet guy; it always looks like he has been away on holiday with his suntan. His wife makes more noise than him. She's a bit of a snob—nothing is ever right for her when she comes to our place," said Connie as she passed her phone to Chapman.

Chapman raised his eyebrows—no one noticed.

"How much did you get out of him during the interview, Matt?" asked Bill.

"Not much. They had dinner early in the evening and then went to their room with a bottle of wine to watch some television," said Matt. "You confirmed that Bill, remember?"

"I remember they had dinner in our pub, but now, when I come to think of it, I can't remember selling them a bottle of wine. They could have bought it outside earlier, I suppose. After dinner, they said they went straight upstairs to their room," Bill said slowly, his mind ticked over with other thoughts.

"Did you recognise this Banks character when you first met him, darling?" asked Chapman.

"No, Papa; why should I? I have never seen him before," replied Phoenix.

"Phoenix, you said that you brought your uncle back to Cooper's Wood on Wednesday evening. What time was that? Can you remember?" asked Bill.

"Yes, we left the warehouse place around seven, maybe a few minutes after seven," she replied. "It took me about an hour to get back. I remember because the road is much worse in the dark and it was raining heavily up on the top road, really scary.

"We had to stop at that gas station for David to use the bathroom and let out some of the champagne he had been drinking at the hotel. It was almost in complete darkness, eerie feeling," said Phoenix.

"Did you see the curtain move at the upstairs window, love?" asked Penny.

"No, I couldn't see upstairs. I parked right outside the door. That's where the only light was on. My car is super quiet, so we won't have disturbed them," Phoenix explained.

Matt recalled the interview with the old father at the petrol station a few days ago.

"That was the night of the football, Bill; the old boy and his son shut up a few minutes early that night," added Matt.

"Good girl. They closed around eight, so I would estimate that you reached our place about eight-fifteen or eight-twenty. Where did you drop David?" asked Bill.

"He came to the pub car park with me and started being vulgar and misbehaving with me. He had been touching me all the time I drove over that mountain road. He knew I was not very comfortable driving that dangerous road in the dark. He was a maniac," said Phoenix.

"Do you remember when I came into the pub that evening? I went straight upstairs to my room," said Phoenix.

"Aye, I remember now. And Connie also said that you looked like you had a fight with your boyfriend," said Bill.

"I was so flustered and angry because he was in such a rush. He had left his car key and cell phone in the toilet in the gas station and he insisted I drive him back to collect them. I refused, so he continued tormenting me and touching me while I was driving. When we got out of the car, he was brutal with me, and he even tried to kiss me. I thumped him, but he continued to try to kiss me and persuade me to drive him to get his things." Phoenix was quite anxious as she explained. "That's when I ran off into the pub; I was so upset that I didn't even realise that I had left the key in the car. I hate these keyless starts; it's so easy to leave the key behind," she cried.

"It's okay, love," said Penny as she comforted her and sat by her side. Connie joined on the other side.

"When . . . when I went to the car, the next morning, I found the car locked and assumed David locked it and went off with the key. I said nothing, as I didn't want to get dragged into it. I called David on his cell. Someone answered, but they said nothing back," she explained further.

"Didn't you think to inform us about this at some point?" asked Matt.

"It's a UAE number. I thought it was a poor connection and considered nothing other than that," replied Phoenix, now very distraught.

"I remember what you said earlier, Matt. You said that whoever had done this must have known both the victims personally. There were only two then. Now we can add Saul also, so he knew all three victims. But you also said something far more significant to me than that. You said that the killer never expected that the same coppers who handled the case in England would handle the case in Lebanon. So, he never, ever expected to see us down here on this one," said Bill.

"Phoenix, how are you feeling now?" queried Henry.

"I am okay; it's just whenever I think of him, it gives me the creeps. I still say it was that bastard that tried to kidnap me in Dubai. Can we change the subject, please?" she said.

"I am worried about you, Phoenix. Are you okay—sure?" asked her father.

Phoenix nodded to him and raised a smile that always warmed her father's heart.

"But going back to my car key, Matt. How do you explain that? David, or someone, must have taken it from the car after I ran inside. Yet it turned up when the beer delivery men opened up the cellar a few days later—that's strange, isn't it?" asked Phoenix.

"Hey! The murderer also knows you, Phoenix!" exclaimed Bill.

"*What?*" shouted Phoenix.

"Of course, that is why they didn't just discard the key in the rubbish. If David did take your car key and it was found on him later, it would give the game away. Its discovery anywhere in the vicinity could lead to you and your connection to David," explained Bill.

"Imagine the police find the key to the one and only Porsche in the village. They interview you and ask you to explain how you lost it. No, they couldn't take that risk."

"Why didn't they hold on to it?" asked Connie.

"Good question, love," said Bill; he hesitated. "But what if the cops found it on them?"

"My goodness, the murderers also knew the routine of our pub. That's why they knew to hide the car key in a place that would not be opened up for another week," said Bill with a deep swallow. And in the blink of an eye, it seemed, to Bill, that everything fell into place.

"Papa, you're very quiet over there," said Phoenix. "Are you okay, Papa?"

"Yes, I know, sweetheart, and there is a good reason as I am waiting for the right time," said Chapman.

"The right time for what, sir?" Henry said as he looked around at the others in the group.

"Yes, now is the right time. There is something that I need to tell you. All of you, including you, Phoenix," announced Chapman.

"Last night, we talked about the Illya Corporation and its business, the setup, the history. I also understand that Phoenix has given you some history about the family of Sultan Illya," began Chapman.

"Sultan actually had an affair between the births of David and Jamila. The name of the woman with whom he had an affair was Rana, and she was from mixed parents. Her mother was from Sri Lanka, and her father was from England. From Yorkshire, believe it or not. They had a child, a boy, and he grew up with his mother. Sultan had no time for him at all, and he was never, ever considered a member of the Illya family. He always tried to get on good terms with the other family members. Especially his half-brothers, but they had no time for him. He knew of the wealth of the family, of course.

"Before Sultan died, he thought of a way to get rid of this illegitimate son, once and for all. The old boy didn't want more burden on his other sons after his death. Sultan contacted this other son and got him to agree to accept a rather sizeable amount of, shall we call it, *hush money*. I only found this out myself from the brothers after the old boy passed away.

"I was also told that the funds had to go to a bank somewhere in South America; maybe Colombia. I forget the exact details, but it was for the company's benefit as much as anything else in case anyone ever tried to trace the money.

"This son was very fond of South America, and he spent a lot of time over there—Chile, Colombia, Venezuela, Brazil. He met a woman, and they got married. Her name was Maria. She was South American; I am not too sure about the exact country, come to think about it.

"Later on, we found out that he had used the funds to set up a chemical company in Colombia or Venezuela. They specialised in industrial cleaning chemicals and treatment," said Chapman.

"What was the name of this company? Can you remember?" asked Bill.

"Sorry, I am getting old, but I can find it somewhere in my records, I am sure," said Chapman as he continued:

"Okay, in that case, what was the name of this illegitimate son, please?" asked Bill.

"His name is Anthony Aloysius. Aloysius coming from some Ceylonese Jesuit priest or something. And his surname, he took his grandfather's name, Banks," said Chapman.

"Well, I never," said Matt.

"And that is why I asked Phoenix earlier if she recognised the chap called Banks over in England. Until now, Phoenix did not know of the existence of this person. However, after what I heard earlier, if the chap in Yorkshire last week was the same Banks, for sure he would have recognised Phoenix.

"Something else you should know. It happened a few weeks after we won the Macquarie resort development contract. I was sitting outside with the three brothers. We had just had the ground-breaking ceremony when suddenly, a big four-wheel-drive vehicle came speeding toward us. It stopped inches from knocking all four of us off our seats.

"A man jumped out of the car. The three boys and I were shocked.

They shouted, 'Banks, Anthony Banks, what the hell do you want?' and a few added expletives.

"Banks threatened, 'One day, you three bastards will all die by the sacred tools that you claim put you where you are today. This was our project until the greedy Illya family showed up.' and then, and I remember like it was yesterday," said Chapman.

"He held both his hands around his own neck, and he pointed at each one of them, one after each other," said Chapman, mimicking the action he described. "He got back in the car, and away he went."

"My apologies for the profanity, ladies," said Chapman.

Silence for a few seconds, broken by Bill's voice. "I need to call Walter ASAP," and he looked across at Matt.

Phoenix was visibly shocked. She had absorbed a lot over the last few days, and her father broke up the meeting.

"Henry, please take Phoenix to your room now. If you need anything in the night, do not hesitate to call me," said Chapman.

"Matt, Bill, ladies, we all have a lot to think about, and today has been very hectic. May I offer you some transport back to your hotel and we will meet again tomorrow? My daughter is under a great deal of stress now," said Chapman.

"We have a meeting with the police tomorrow at about nine o'clock. Penny and Connie can come over around lunchtime and spend some time with Phoenix. Girlie stuff, you know," said Matt. "Are you okay with that, girls?"

"It's our pleasure, Edward," said Connie. Both the ladies nodded their heads in agreement.

They all went off. Sure enough, Matt and Bill were now very close to the solution.

FOURTEEN

Henry drove the golf buggy cart along the embankment of the Valide Resort. Chapman pointed out various landmarks and points within the resort grounds as they went along. The maintenance staff was busy trimming the bushes, cutting the grass, and tidying the grounds. The recreation crew had tied a few small motorboats along the quayside. At certain stages, Chapman called a halt to the golf cart and got down to chat with the staff.

Away from work, three ladies relaxed by the pool. They had been through a few hectic days that certainly had taken a toll on them. Phoenix laid back on a sun lounger. Next to her, there was a stack of women's magazines, held in place by a small speaker that emanated music to add to their therapeutic mood.

"Is that a pair of binoculars you have there, Phoenix?" asked Connie.

"Yes," replied Phoenix. "Would you like to use them? I like to watch the boats going out and then try to remember them when they are returning in the evening."

Penny was busy as she read from some *People* and *Cosmopolitan* magazines. In between, she chatted with Phoenix about her younger years. They came to her school life and what it had been like being continually moved around.

"I spent most of my primary school years in Dubai," she explained, "as my mother and some of our other family lived there. Dubai was a booming city during those days. There was so much construction going on, and the MESOL companies were doing very well in that region."

"When was that? What years?" asked Connie.

"It would have been around 2005 to 2006, so I was ten or eleven years old," said Phoenix.

"But didn't you mention you went to school in Paris?" asked Penny.

"Yes, later, as a teenager. I went to one of those girls-only schools since I was about fourteen years old. It was horrible; I hated it. It was in a Paris suburb called Pantin, known as Le Petit Pantin. 'The little puppet' in English. They kept us like puppets. It was very strict. We could not read any girlie magazines, no pop music, only classical music. No boys, of course, not even any contact with boys. When our letters arrived, the staff would open them for examination. It was awful," said Phoenix.

"How did you pass the time?" asked Connie.

"Well, do you know those small thumb drives, pen drives, whatever their name is? In 2010, they started supplying them with a much bigger memory—thirty-two gig, sixty-four gig. One student went back to America and came back with a few of these drives loaded with movies. She got them through the inspection when she came back in. Don't ask me how. I prefer not to think about it," she said.

"So, you spent most of your time watching TV instead of doing your homework. You sound like our Henry," said Penny.

"The trouble was what we had to watch. The stupid girl asked her brother to load the movies onto the drives, and all he put was Laurel and Hardy films!" said Phoenix.

They all laughed.

So that's how Phoenix could entertain Ryan back in England.

Lake Macquarie was busy that day, and a lot of boats made their way through the Swansea Channel. They passed under the Pacific Highway Road bridge, then continued east to go past Blacksmith's Point on the port side and Reid's Mistake Head on the starboard side.

Connie looked through the binoculars, being nosey at the people going out on their boats. Suddenly, she screamed out, "Oh, look who's there! We were just talking about them yesterday," but without revealing the identities of the people she had seen.

"Who?" asked Penny.

"I am sure that's Maria Banks on that boat, over there. There she is, at the back. She looks like 'Lady Muck' as usual. You can tell by her flaming red hair," said Connie.

"Can I have a look, please?" asked Penny.

Connie pointed towards the boat. Penny looked through the binoculars.

"I can't make the woman out now, though. She has her back to us. Oh, hang on. Oh, yes, it looks like her. You're right; you can tell that hair anywhere," said Penny.

"What's the name on the back of the boat?" asked Connie.

"I can't make it out. They are too far away now," said Phoenix.

"Not with these, love," said Penny, looking through the binoculars. "It looks like Panting Marta or something."

Connie took the binoculars again.

"He's there now. That's him, definitely. I would recognise him any-where. Look at the blazer he is wearing. Daft bugger." said Connie. "Shall we shout out to them?"

"They'll never hear you now. Save your breath," said Penny.

"What on earth are they doing here? Big coincidence, don't you think?" asked Connie.

"Sorry if I sound like my husband, but I don't believe in coincidences, not to that extent," said Penny.

Not long after, and they were under the road bridge and out of view. Penny took out her phone and called her husband.

―――――――――――

"Mitch, Louise, can you both join us at the hotel, please? My wife says she has some interesting information for us," said Matt.

They reached the hotel and went to the terrace. Henry and Chapman had already returned, and they were all seated together.

Connie told Matt and Bill what they had seen earlier. But she since had second thoughts and doubted that it was Anthony and Maria Banks, after all.

"It was them. I am sure of it," contributed Penny.

"Louise, have you got that list of occupants from the marina where we found the van?" asked Matt.

Louise passed the list to Matt. "We've checked all the entries; nothing," she said.

"Maybe we were looking for the wrong name," said Matt.

"How big is the lake?" asked Bill.

"One hundred and ten square kilometres," said Mitch.

"Bloody hell, Mitch; that's the same size as Manchester. Shoreline?" Bill asked.

"One hundred and seventy kilometres," replied Mitch.

"There must be more than one marina," exclaimed Bill.

"For God's sake, Mitch! Do you mean to tell me that your team hasn't checked all the marinas around the lake?" asked Matt.

Mitch put his cup down and walked over to a quiet corner on the terrace to make a phone call.

"Edward, can you lay your hands on a map of this region, please?" asked Matt.

"Certainly, but how far are you looking? Brisbane is about a nine-hour drive north from here. Sydney is three hours south," he said.

"Up to Brisbane should be fine for now," said Matt.

Mitch finished his call.

"Our guys have been phoning around all the marinas on the lake since Friday morning. It's not easy to get the information over the weekend; it will be easier today," said Mitch.

"Matt, Bill, this is our hotel manager, Marcus. I asked him to join us as he does a lot of sailing, fishing, and that sort of thing. He goes out every weekend he can get a chance and knows this lake area very well indeed," explained Chapman as he was doing the introduction.

"Sir Rupert has already spoken to me about this whole dreadful affair. It is awful for him and his daughter. She is such a sweet young lady. If I can help, please, you only have to ask," said Marcus.

"How long have you known Phoenix?" asked Matt.

"I have known her since she was a small girl going to school in Dubai. I was working in their hotel there," replied Marcus.

"Sir, most of the boats of fifty and sixty feet will moor at Marmong Point. They have the best facilities and services, but they are northwest of the lake. Where did you go yesterday?" said Marcus.

Bill remembered the location and explained it to Marcus.

"Near Belmont; that would be the Lake Macquarie Yacht Club," Marcus said. He knew it. "Yes, your guy is smart. He deliberately left the van there to throw you off the scent. The Marmong Point on the northwest side would have been more suitable for him," explained Marcus.

"Marcus, I have a question for you, if you don't mind," said Bill. "Imagine if we had this sixty-footer, and we wanted to go to somewhere such as Brisbane or Sydney; is it possible?"

"Yes, sir. It is only a matter of time involved. If I wanted to go north, I would go for about five hours to Forster. There is a small marina there inside the entrance to the lake. Stay one night there and then aim for Port Macquarie the next day; maybe another six hours," said Marcus.

"Sorry, I'm confused; come back here. Why?" asked Bill.

"No, Port Macquarie is farther north. It is about halfway between Lake Macquarie and Brisbane," explained Marcus.

"Bill, I am sure that Banks would go back to South America, so he will want to sell the boat," said Matt.

"Sell the boat?" asked Marcus. "For sure, he will go to Port Macquarie. The sea sports and activities start there, and it gets more popular as you go north to Brisbane and the Gold Coast. If he is looking for a quick sale, the port is where to go. When do you think he will leave?"

"We understand he may have departed about two hours ago, but we don't know if he went north or south. This is the problem," said Bill.

"It's not a problem at all. He will have gone north. There is a storm coming up from Tasmania, and it funnels up through the Tasmanian Sea here. One of those unexplained weather phenomena. It is due to reach Sydney tomorrow afternoon. If he reaches Forster tonight by nightfall and sets off tomorrow at daybreak, he will be in Port Macquarie by midday, easy," explained Marcus.

"Mate, you've been more help than the coppers," said Bill. He smiled across at Mitch.

"But Bill, if he sells the boat at Port Macquarie, then what?" asked Matt.

Mitch came back into the conversation. "There are plenty of flights from Port Macky to Brisbane. From there he can get a connection and come back to Sydney, Melbourne, or even go to Singapore, Rio, anywhere."

"Come on, guys! We have to stop him wherever he is heading!" said Matt.

"My suggestion is that we get over to this Marmong marina and start there," said Bill. "It's about an hour's drive, you say, Marcus."

Marcus nodded his head.

"What if we go across the lake, Marcus?" asked Chapman, and he pointed to a speed boat moored up alongside the resort waterfront.

"That's a fibre-glass Go-fast, sir; it can reach eighty knots. I can get you there in half an hour, sooner if not for the speed restriction on the lake," said Marcus.

It was a four-seater. Henry stayed back with the ladies. The two police officers couldn't understand what was happening.

"Mitch, can you get a colleague to meet us at this Marmong there?" asked Matt.

"Never mind. Mitch, get inside; you'll be okay. Help your colleague, Louise, come on," said Marcus.

"I'm okay here with the ladies if it's all the same with you. There are sharks in these waters," said a timid Louise.

Louise did her bit and untied the shoreline. Marcus took the craft through a 180-degree turn that made it feel as if the boat would capsize. The boat levelled on the lake surface, and he powered up the throttle. They were off. A steady thirty knots as he pulled away from the Swansea channel, and then he powered it up to fifty knots.

"Come on, Bill. I know you can't wait to tell us," Matt said.

Bill looked over at the controls.

"If he can get it to around 40 knots, that is just over 70 kilometres per hour," said Bill.

"Tell me, how do you calculate that, please?" asked Chapman.

"Double it and take 10 percent off the total. So, 80 kilometres less 8 equals 72 kilometres per hour," explained Bill.

"I will not let you take part in our pub quizzes when we get back!" Bill shouted at Matt as the engines roared, "I'm giving you all the answers on this trip!"

"If the lake is 22 kilometres long and 8 kilometres wide, it means we have to go about 24 kilometres. We can be there in about twenty minutes," said Bill, "but there is no rush anyway as our target has already left."

"What if he has left something behind?" asked Matt.

"Where? How do we know where he stayed this time?" asked Bill.

"With a bit of luck, we can get hold of the management and see if they left anything behind," said Matt.

"Do you think he may have left some notes or travel details behind?" asked Chapman.

"It's a good possibility, Edward. Bill, we have seen complacency sneak in on this one. What do you think?" asked Matt.

"I think all those years I have been telling you about doing your job are paying off, mate," replied Bill. He winked at his friend.

Back on the terrace, the four ladies were together with Henry. They thought it was late enough for a Monday afternoon, so they opened a bottle of wine. They sat around and chatted away about girlie stuff. Henry wished he had gone along in the speedboat.

"Yes, there have been reports of sharks in the lake. Quite a few, but don't forget this is the largest coastal saltwater lake in Australia. It is 15 metres deep in some places, so if a shark came swimming up the channel here, he is going to feel pretty much at home, don't you think?" said Louise.

Penny's phone rang out. "Hello. Oh! Hello, Bill. Hang on. It looked like Panting Marta, could have been Maria, of course, *Panting Maria*. Uh, cheeky! I knew you would say that, Bill Cooper. Wait until I talk to your wife!" said Penny and she closed the call.

"Your husband is terrible, Connie. He is saying rude things about the boat name *Panting Maria*," said Penny.

"It can't be *Panting Maria*," said Louise. "It sounds like Maria, whoever she is, is getting a damn good rogering."

Three of the four ladies laughed; Phoenix appeared perplexed. *What on earth is a rogering?* she thought to herself.

Over in Marmong Point, the team of investigators had met with the operations manager.

"We have the name of the boat as *Panting Maria* but that is because we saw the name on the back from a distance," said Bill.

"Panting, panting, I can't work that one out; even *Painting Maria* wouldn't work," said the manager. His name was Cliff.

He looked through a book of boat names.

"What about *Parting Maria*?" asked Mitch. "Seeing as they were leaving? Nah, sorry about that, fellas."

"*Farting Maria* is probably more like it if you saw the amount of red wine she can put away," added Bill.

"Just a minute," said Marcus. "You said this Maria woman is from South America somewhere?"

"Yes, but I am not sure if Colombia, Brazil, or Chile. or wherever," stuttered Chapman.

"In Spanish, *el placer Maria* means Maria's pleasure or happiness," said Marcus.

"No 'el' in the name, according to the girls," said Bill.

Marcus clapped his hands!

"O, *Prazer Maria*! Portuguese, you can drop the *o*, so *Prazer Maria*; it means the same," said Marcus.

Cliff typed P R A Z E R on his computer keyboard.

"This is networked. It links all the marinas around the lake. Here we are, *Prazer Maria*. The owner is Maria Rodriguez. Yes, I remember them; odd couple. They stayed in that hotel over on Stockland Road, left earlier today. He's happy; he sold his boat. It cost a fortune to keep it here. They only came down twice a year, although since Christmas, they've been here twice," explained Cliff.

Cliff provided the story without being asked questions, observed Matt.

"This might appear to sound a strange question, but would you happen to still have their rubbish, their garbage, from when they left?" asked Matt.

"For sure, if they left it before they departed. It will still be at the side of the service connection in the bin there. Today is Monday, so our contractor doesn't come in until late afternoon, berth No. C17," said Cliff.

No sooner the berth number was revealed and Matt was through the door.

"Cliff, do you know when they arrived here? When did you first see them come on the marina?" asked Bill.

"That would be in our security logs. We keep a record of when owners are present and taking their vessel out or they book in for maintenance. Stuff like that," said Cliff.

Matt returned, holding a bundle of papers in his hands.

"Look at this; there's three of them. The other guy's name is Raul de Guzman. Here's something. Hang on," said Matt as he unfolded a paper.

"You said he sold the boat. Do you have any details, please?" asked Bill.

"Nah, mate. I only know he sold it to a bloke in Red Head. He showed me the paper, and we had a friendly laugh because he was teasing his wife. Mind you, she didn't find it one bit funny," said Cliff.

"Yes, I can guess," said Bill.

"Forster marina to Red Head is twenty minutes by car," said Marcus.

"I told you complacency would kick in, Bill," said Matt.

Matt smoothed out the papers he had found.

"How far is Forster from here, Cliff?" asked Matt.

"I reckon a good two and a half hours by road and I would say it is going to be close to eighty or ninety miles, over the water. At a steady twenty-five knots, you'd be looking at four hours," replied Cliff as he studied a coastline map hanging on the wall behind him.

"Brisbane to Auckland and then the afternoon Latam Airlines to Buenos Aires. I was looking at flights online last night. Matt, I remember you found a piece of notepaper with a scribbled note in the hotel in Beirut. Have you kept it in your wallet by any chance?" asked Bill.

Matt opened his wallet and read out, "4M8001625; we thought it was a hotel booking reference."

"4M, Latam Airlines, Argentina," shouted Bill. "Bingo!"

"Once he is in South America, we will never see him again," said Chapman.

As the others focused their attention on the flight booking, Mitch concentrated on the paper.

"Wait a minute," Mitch exclaimed. "Cliff, did you say they have gone to Forster as the buyer of the boat is in Red Head?"

"Yes, mate. He showed me the paper he wrote it down on," said Cliff.

"Was there any street address shown, or only the place?" asked Mitch.

"Just that, mate. Red Head and what looked like a phone number," said Cliff.

Mitch stared at Cliff, and Cliff's face drained before a smirk appeared on his face.

"No," said Cliff. "It can't be; surely not."

Mitch turned to look at the others present and announced, "It's not Red Head; it's Redhead, here, about ten kilometres away! The other side of where your Kuringai Hotel is, Matt."

Matt stood speechless; Bill looked at the piece of paper and started laughing. Chapman stared at Bill.

"Sorry, sorry. I recognise the handwriting; it's the wife's. Maria must have written it down over the phone, and she wrote Red Head," said Bill.

"So how do you know it should be Redhead?" Bill queried.

"Look at this. Someone also wrote Seaview Malays rest. It's a restaurant over there. A mate of mine from Penang owns it," said Mitch.

"My goodness, what a blunder," said Bill.

"That means they either come back here for the sale or dump the boat at Forster without selling it and continue with their plan of escape," said Matt.

"They will come back," said Cliff. "She wears the pants there, and she loves it here. Their first plan was to leave last Wednesday, then Friday; then it became Saturday. You mark my words. They have the berth paid until the end of the month."

"So, let's get this clear, they get to Forster, realise their mistake, so they turn around and come back here. He has still got a buyer for his boat, and it will cost a few dollars to change the tickets to departing from Sydney. They still need to get to Auckland to catch the flight to Buenos Aires," said Mitch.

"Let's get back to the hotel and make our plans," said Chapman. "Come on, Marcus."

Back on the terrace, Mitch stood away from the group and after he closed a phone call:

"Okay, the manager at Forster Marina didn't have a clue what I was talking about. I also spoke to my friend Balan, the owner of the Malaysian restaurant in Redhead. He has arranged the boat for a mate of his and he is expecting to meet them at the Lake Macquarie yacht club marina later this evening. Balan says he has only ever spoken to a lady, but her English wasn't so good," said Mitch.

"Mitch, it is important that when they arrive at the Forster marina, the manager there does not inform him that someone has been making enquiries. That could screw our next move completely," said Bill.

"The manager understood. They will have to stay there tonight and set off early tomorrow morning if they decide to come back. The marina manager will call me and let me know their plans," replied Mitch.

"Is there any chance you can get an offshore patrol to tip us off when they get nearby, Mitch?" asked Bill.

"Yes, I have thought about that and put a call into Central already. Central will let me know," said Mitch. "By the way, the super is coming over. He says he would like to meet you guys."

About an hour later, Chief Superintendent Warren Davies arrived at the hotel. There was a discussion between the two local police officers and Matt and Bill. Chapman also sat with them. They agreed on a plan.

A very pleasant evening for everyone, under the circumstances. Mitch and Louise departed as they had to make certain arrangements.

Henry and Phoenix were deep in discussion. She hoped for an end to the whole situation, sooner rather than later. Matt, Bill, and wives returned to enjoy some time alone in their own hotel.

The next morning, breakfast was over. It was around ten o'clock.

Matt's phone rang. The police informed him that the *Prazer Maria* left Forster Marina at six-thirty that morning. The coastguards were aware of the situation, and soon a helicopter would be in the sky.

Warren Davies returned to the hotel. He was with two other gentlemen from the Lebanese embassy who had flown in from Canberra.

Mitch came to join Matt and Bill. "We received a message from Tomaree a few minutes ago, and the chopper patrol has picked him up. They're about twelve kilometres away, so about twenty minutes before they will enter the lake. The patrols are on the way," said Mitch.

"The weather has slowed them down a bit this morning; the storm has moved north quicker than forecast. But they are close to the coastline. They will still reach a good twenty knots," explained Mitch.

"Phoenix, are you okay?" asked Chapman.

"Yes, I am fine. Thank you, Papa," she said as she stood up.

In the distance, the lake's horizon turned into splashes of white foam as several highspeed boats headed towards the resort. The sound of high-octane engines got louder and louder as the boats neared. As they arrived at the Valide quayside, the air filled with the smell of ethanol.

Just then, there was the noise of a commotion coming from the hotel lobby and the noise spread through onto the terrace. Marcus tried frantically to keep the people away from the waterfront. Fortunately, Mitch had arranged for a few uniform police officers in case of any disturbance. It was the press. But the mobilisation of so many police and coastguard patrol boats stimulated interest for everyone.

Phoenix and her father climbed down onto one of the police patrol boats. Henry offered to go with Phoenix, but she thought it better if he stayed back. Matt and Bill boarded another boat. Warren Davies and the Lebanese embassy officials boarded another. The boats pulled away from the quayside and moved toward Swansea Bridge. All four crafts pointed to the sea. Positioned between the police boats were two coastguard patrol boats. Surely, they didn't expect them to make a run for it. Several other boats, waiting to leave the lake, switched off their engines and stood idle to see what was about to happen. This position was an ideal setup. Swansea Bridge has narrow spaces between the supports. This makes it quite difficult to observe the other side of the bridge when entering from the sea.

The *Prazer Maria* now moved much slower as it passed under the bridge. As the vessel appeared into the lake, the engines of the four police patrol boats roared with power. Just enough to thrust them into a position where the *Prazer Maria* could not proceed. The police patrol boats set their engines to idle. Chief Superintendent Warren Davies walked to the front of one of the patrol boats. Fadi, the Lebanese official, stood nearby him. Bill walked to the front of another of the patrol boats. They both held a megaphone in their hand.

"Good morning, Mr. Banks," said CS Davies. His voice echoed through the megaphone.

"Don't look so worried. I have brought your old friend to say hello." Davies pointed over to Bill on the other patrol boat.

"Hello, Tony," said Bill. "I wish I could say it was nice to see you here."

Matt appeared. "Or should we say Sadiq Al Bunuk?" said Matt, and he pointed to another patrol boat.

"Or Juan Riberas?" said Chapman.

"Are you Anthony Aloysius Banks?" asked CS Davies.

"Yes, I am. Is there a problem?" replied Banks.

"Mr. Banks, we will now take you to Lake Macquarie Yacht Club and onto Belmont Police station. You face charges of the murder of Mr. David Illya in Cooper's Wood, England, and Mr. Saul Illya in Belmont, Australia. Mr. Fadi Boussari joined us from the Lebanese embassy in Canberra. You are a suspect for the murder of Mr. Suleiman Illya in Beirut, Lebanon," said the chief superintendent.

As Davies spoke to Banks, one of the police patrol boats, the fourth vessel, had positioned itself alongside. Two police officers had boarded, and one fastened a pair of handcuffs onto Tony Banks. The other officer was already at the controls of the *Prazer Maria*. Maria herself was frantic, and she constantly shouted out Spanish expletives. She paced up and down the side of their boat as she gesticulated and pointed several times at the occupants of the police patrol boats. The police boats revved up their engine whilst still idle to drown out

Maria's voice and anger her even more until she was also in handcuffs.

Before the boats started moving, Phoenix appeared on the front deck of the patrol boat. She grabbed the megaphone from her father.

"I knew there was something evil about you the day I met you and that bitch of a wife of yours. That was two weeks ago, and you have made our lives hell since then," she said.

Banks responded, but the engine noises made it difficult to hear his voice. But Phoenix picked up something.

"Just let me be an Illya," or so it sounded.

"Mr. Banks, members of the Illya family are kind and generous people. They are compassionate and loving people. My grandfather would never expect or accept any of his children to do what you have done, and so you can never be an Illya." Phoenix expressed her emotions and started to cry.

She turned around and hugged her father as the patrol boats started moving across. CS Davies signalled to the skipper of the boat with Chapman and Phoenix aboard to return them to the resort. Davies and the other patrols made their way to the yacht club.

Once back onshore at the Valide, Henry, Penny, and Connie greeted and hugged Phoenix. Edward Chapman, in a very emotional state, continued to support his daughter. It had been a very traumatic experience.

About three hours later, Matt and Bill returned to the hotel and, of course, went straight to the terrace. It had been an extremely stressful day, and they both felt that they deserved a beer, let alone needed one.

The storm, as predicted the day before by Marcus, had reached the lake region, and Phoenix took a nap in the afternoon. Still shaken and emotional, Penny and Connie stayed with her in the villa at the resort. Henry spent the afternoon with Edward Chapman and left the ladies alone to rest.

Matt and Bill were both seated when Chapman caught sight of them and joined them. Not long afterwards, the three ladies joined them. They were keen to hear what had happened at the police station.

"It's all pretty much as we have revealed over the last few days. It has been a matter of fitting it all together," stated Matt.

Matt's raised right arm showed the server he needed another bottle. "That never touched the sides!" remarked Matt.

"Bring two buckets of beer here, please; three, make it three," said Chapman to the server.

"Right," Matt started the full explanation. "Maria, Anthony Banks' wife, is originally from Colombia. The story that Edward provided is quite accurate. In 2006, the Illya Corporation paid a substantial amount of money to Banks. Five million dollars. Not bad for go-away or keep-away money.

"Banks had been trying to negotiate a higher amount for several years. They heard about old Sultan's illness and Maria convinced Tony to take the money whilst he had the chance. They used the funds to set up a chemical processing company in Colombia, which they called AMBIC, Anthony Maria Banks Industrial Chemicals.

"Banks' grandfather is from Settle and there are still some members of the family living in the region, two of whom own a construction company. They do barn conversions, housing remodelling, and that sort of stuff. On that Wednesday evening, David thought he was going to a meeting with the owners of the construction company.

"The local council had recently approved the redevelopment plans, so it was to discuss an investment opportunity. The idea is to renovate the old factory into a shopping centre and sports hall. Indoor football and squash, that sort of thing," said Matt.

"Baldwins," said Chapman, "I met them with David when I was over there the other week."

"That name rings a bell," said Matt as he glanced across at Bill.

"It was easy to convince David to meet in the evening. Baldwin told him that their MD had just flown into Leeds airport and had to drive to Scotland early the next morning. It seemed plausible to David, I guess."

"Poor, gullible David," said Phoenix. She changed her tune somewhat. "If only I had known."

"Tony Banks hid in the darkness with his wife. They knew David would recognise him and they didn't want to take the chance that he may recognise Maria."

"Well, one of these Baldwin guys met David and brought him through into the factory yard at the rear. Once there, Tony and Maria attacked David.

"A sudden stab to the throat with the sharpened hinge on the twenty-four-inch gauge and David went down instantly. He gasped for breath. David had unknowingly contributed to his downfall by consuming a little too much champagne at the hotel. Banks then delivered several blows to the head using the mallet and chisel as had been previously suspected.

"But, after the attack, the murderers made a mistake. They used some of their industrial-grade chemicals to clean the surfaces of the tools. It left a trace on the surface and after analysis, back in the UK, we discovered a cleansing agent that is a prohibited substance in the UK. We received a report from Ryan in the UK earlier this morning," explained Matt.

"By cleaning these two articles, they thought the police would overlook the old tools. There are still plenty of old brick makers' tools lying around in the yard. The only difference being the other tools have rusted over. The cleansing agent they used brought the tools up almost like new. Banks didn't notice. It was too dark, as there was no illumination in the yard," explained Bill.

"Now, a bit of their own planning that went slightly wrong in finding Phoenix's car key. Maria passed David's passport and wallet to Baldwin to remove David's ID. He then tossed what he thought was an empty wallet away, probably thinking it would appear like a mugging. This Baldwin guy didn't hang around, as a car waited for him, standing by outside.

"Maria and Banks now had to think of a change of plan as they knew they had to get rid of the car key. If the police found it, they would be straight on to Phoenix. This would then provide the connection between Phoenix and David. Fortunately for us, Maria stopped her search when she came across this car key and she missed the lodge summons.

"Tony and Maria made their way back to the pub. First, they went to the car park. The car was still unlocked. David had never even locked the car. Their initial idea was to leave the key in the car and make it appear as though Phoenix had overlooked it. But they realised it would have David's fingerprints. Also, as they looked in the car, they came across a canvas bag. This is how they thought to get rid of the twenty-four-inch gauge and they put it in the bag. Obviously, they expected Phoenix to return to London and on to Paris and they realised if they concealed the key, there would be a good possibility that this would provide a delay during the police's search of vehicles in the car park itself. Then they made their way around the back of the building to the lounge entrance on the other side.

"Just before they went inside, Banks saw the wooden cellar doors. He told his wife to push the key in between the gap in the wooden doors. They knew very well that the beer delivery wouldn't be for almost another week. There was a good chance the police, at some stage, would search the pub premises as they investigated the case. And if they did, they would find a car key that, by that time, someone would surely have reported as lost.

"Our constables didn't find anything during the search of the pub rooms, and they were unable to get in Phoenix's car to search inside there. I searched it when the technicians opened it up. I was so focused on finding David's luggage, I missed the canvas bag stuffed under the front seat," said Matt.

"How on earth could they manage all this in the dark?" asked Connie.

"Practice, love. Another reason they had made frequent visits was so they could practice what they had to do in the dark. Baldwin had got duplicate keys cut on a previous visit to survey the site. On the night itself, Maria had already prepared the tools inside the yard," said Bill.

"The odd thing is, no one quite understands why David went alone into such a place in darkness to meet people he didn't even know," added Matt.

"It doesn't surprise me at all, Matthew. David could be quite a scoundrel, but he was fearless at times and a bloody fool at others," added Chapman.

"The abandoned car, the two power banks, his phone, and car key? What about all those?" asked Penny.

"It was as Phoenix explained to us the other evening," said Matt, smiling across at her.

"The Banks couple left the hotel on Friday morning. They planned, or hoped, that Phoenix would drive away with the last of the murder weapons. Banks left for Beirut and Maria continued onto Australia, all planned weeks in advance," explained Matt.

"Why was he around my car that morning I told you about?" asked Phoenix.

"Do you remember why I was nosing around your car that day when the technicians arrived? I was looking for evidence of someone else. Banks was checking the back of your vehicle for David's luggage or anything else he could tie his arrival to. He wanted to be sure David was in town." explained Matt.

"What about Beirut?" asked Penny.

Bill's turn. "Murder number two. The brother of the first victim, which we did not know, three days after the first murder. When we first started on this one, we seriously suspected the involvement of Harold Othman. We were wrong. He wasn't an accomplice at all. Banks, heard from his own people how incompetent Harold is. It was because of Harold's incompetence that Banks murdered Suleiman in Beirut. Harold Othman's elder brother is something to do with the ministry of the interior, so Harold has a job for life. A classic example of cronyism if ever we heard one."

"Banks had his associates, his accomplices, there. He gave us the name: Al Nadri or El Nadhi. Perhaps you have heard of them, Edward," said Bill, "and it seems they also had an axe to grind with MESOL or the Illya family.

Chapman nodded his head and remained silent.

"They provided the bogus security guard and everything else. This accomplice has financially rewarded all the people they needed in the hotel for months," continued Bill. "The Beirut Qasr Hotel is notorious for paying low wages for extended shifts of duty, apparently.

"But the way the police handled this whole situation, it smelled of something very fishy. Even corrupt, as they simply did not follow basic police routines. Or they disguised procedures to appear that they were under processing.

"Here, Banks saw an ideal opportunity. It was a piece of cake to book the two adjacent rooms, 1401 and 1403. He booked in the hotel as Amin Sadiq Albunuk and used the Dubai address exactly for the reason we suggested. It gave him just enough time to make his escape on Sunday morning. Even the reception clerk accepted that Albunuk used a local ID card when he registered.

"The murder was exactly as we outlined. Banks also knew Suleiman had the habit of buying a pair of porcelain dolls for Sir Rupert's twin daughter's birthday. He would hide the murder weapons in the boxes that originally contained the dolls. He even went to the courier company the previous day to eyeball the size of the boxes that contained the dolls. He knew from the hotel that they were waiting to be picked up by Sultan Suleiman.

"Banks admitted that he almost slipped up when he left the murder weapons in Suleiman's room. After the police and television reporters had gone, he waited for things to die down and in the early hours, he went back into room 1401 after he left the adjoining door in his room open. He started to pack the weapons into the boxes after he removed the dolls but he made a mistake as he broke the wooden square on the corner of the wooden table.

"He thought he was smart. He had already unlocked the adjoining door from his side, 1403, so he took the boxes and the weapons into his own room and finished the rewrapping job there. After he finished, he returned the repacked boxes to 1401, locked the adjoining room door and went back to his own room, where he by now had kept the two dolls. Just as the key logs showed. However, he overlooked cleaning up the wooden splinters that he had caused when in 1401.

"Next, the plumb rule, my goodness! He made the most noise about the fact that he had to import it from Dubai. He couldn't get a wooden one here, as most builders use what they know as a vertical level these days."

"Banks kept the plumb rule in 1403 overnight. His accomplice returned early the next morning. This time as hotel maintenance, in his builder's overalls and carrying a canvas tool bag. He met Banks in his room, picked up the plumb rule, put the dolls in the canvas tool bag and he then walked out through the rear staff door. It was six o'clock in the morning; there was very few staff around in the hotel for anyone to think twice about why a maintenance guy was in the hotel. A lot of hotel maintenance happens during the night. The police never even started a search of the rooms and hotel area until Sunday morning."

"Why didn't the police open the boxes?" asked Connie.

Bill shrugged his shoulders and screwed up his face. "We understand Banks' accomplice, after he dropped him at the airport, returned to the hotel as the security officer. He arranged with a police officer to store the dolls boxes, concealing the weapons, in the police storage as objects are withdrawn from the crime scene, no longer relevant—porcelain dolls as it said on the packaging from the doll maker. The rewrapping showed they had been examined once already. They were archived. Othman's staff would never even question it.

"Banks left for Australia and looking at the mileage and petrol receipts from the rental, this De Guzman guy and Maria met him at Sydney airport. Maria had arrived a few days earlier, who came here straight from the UK to make sure everything was all set up," explained Bill. "However, here, we missed a vital connection. When we searched 1403, we found a necktie. This tie had a crest of the Royal Institute of Chemists and the letters A M B I C embroidered," admitted Bill, rather sheepishly.

"I remember you had a momentary thought when you saw that, Bill, was it old age or out of practice, mate," laughed Matt.

"Must be a bit of both," replied Bill.

"Finally, murder number three. Saul Shamir, or Saul Illya, was found murdered upstairs in a Masonic lodge building. This murder, like the other two, has been very well planned and uses two of the most toxic substances in the world. Upon arrival in Australia on Monday morning, Tony joined Maria and took rooms at a nearby hotel. Their accomplice, this time, this guy called De Guzman, Maria's brother, stayed on the boat in Marmong Point."

"The following day, Tuesday, all three of them go to the lodge in a hired van. As Maria diverts Basil away to the security, using a bogus telephone call, Banks quickly jumps out of the side door of the van and walks into the building.

"Banks put the murder weapons in place and had a white ME suit ready for his getaway. He removed the yarn from the skirret and put the skirret back in the box. He removed the original compasses from the Bible and placed them in the drawer on the same table.

"Saul came in and wondered what the cartons were. He phoned Basil and asked to meet him after the meeting. Banks, in hiding, then sent a message to De Guzman, who made a phone call to inform the security that there would be quite a lengthy power outage. When Saul heard this news, he told Basil they would cancel the ceremonial meeting and they would just meet for dinner at the resort.

"Moments after this phone call, Banks attacked Saul. He jumped him from behind and wrapped the yarn around his neck and forced him down. He dragged Saul across the clothing room. Saul fought back, but Banks stabbed his forearm with the compasses. This was a brutal infliction, and enough poison would have entered Saul's body to kill him. But to make sure, Banks then took out a mechanical pencil and pushed the top of the pencil to extend a fine needle coated with a lethal dose of botulinum. He plunged the needlepoint into the same open wound. A very evil method indeed.

"Next he took the yarn and wrapped and tied it around the carton that he used to smuggle in his white ME suit. He removed the needle from the pencil and trapped it between two of the floorboards. It could be months before anyone finds it, if at all ever; a 0.2mm thin strand of steel? He then wiped the compasses and put them in the Bible to replace the ones he had removed earlier.

"But as with most cases like this, complacency had set in. Mistake number one. He overlooked that none of the other cartons in the cupboards were tied with any yarn or string. They were all folded closed. Mistake number two. He removed the needle from the pencil but placed the pencil in Saul's shirt pocket for it to appear as, well, a pencil. But this is quite an unusual pencil and only takes 0.2mm leads. Obviously after discovering the replacement leads were not available, Banks took a chance and left the pencil with no lead. The ME spotted it. Any copper worth his salt would see something odd about these two events. And mistake number three, he left the compasses in the Bible with open points. They should have been closed, as the lodge was closed," Matt explained as he opened his next bottle.

"Now, De Guzman, he is a chemical engineer from their company in Colombia. He has access to just about any toxic substance that may originate in that part of the world.

"He got the tools in, both prepared with the lethal dose of poison, carried the cartons into the lodge. He was the bogus electrician and anything else needed throughout. We also believe they may have involved him in the other murders in one way or another. The police will start on him later to find out more of his story."

"The getaway from the lodge building, exactly as we described earlier," said Matt. "One piece of the puzzle that we couldn't find here was how the power cuts at the lodge building were happening? Well . . . this afternoon, the local police arrested a guy by the name of Estaban De Guzman. He has been working with the New South Wales Electricity board as a lineman for the last ten years. They even made use of his official vehicle in the evening for the getaway. Banks certainly knows how to seize on an opportunity."

"By the way." Matt looked around at everyone present. "*Albunuk* is an Arabic word for riverbank, just as *Ribera* means the same in Spanish.

"But as we said earlier. If it wasn't for us following all three cases, other investigators could have overlooked these connections. He could quite easily have gotten away with it.

"Now, yesterday evening Bill made a telephone call to his DNA contact back in the UK, and he confirmed to us what we assumed was an error in his first report but two of the samples found at the factory had a greater match than the match shown for David and Phoenix, Bill," said Matt.

"Basically, the Y DNA, or the Y chromosome, gets passed on from father to son. Two brothers will have the same Y DNA and the variation in the full DNA is down to a number of other reasons. It doesn't work the same with father to daughter or uncle to niece. If you have three or four hours spare, I will explain it to you," said Bill as he raised his bottle.

"So, there you have it. Thanks to everyone. Bill, I couldn't have done it without you. Thanks to you girls, Penny and Connie, for accompanying us. Thanks to Henry for being with Phoenix and to you, Edward, or Sir Rupert. Now, if no one objects, I am going to get pissed," said Matt, "and

Phoenix, I do not mean get angry!" he said.

And so, just as on so many previous gatherings, they all sat together. They all had their own subjects and topics to discuss with each other and for the first time, Matt didn't feel he had to keep an eye on the movements of his son's latest love. That young woman who may have appeared so different to others, in so many ways. A young woman, so well experienced in many aspects of life and yet so naïve in many others. But then again, not many young women have been raised in such unusual circumstances as Phoenix Istaza aka Tamara Illya.

As the drinks flowed with a subdued yet jovial mood and with total innocence, Matt took out his Peterson's rusticated Jekyll & Hyde and started to fill it with his favourite squadron leader tobacco. Surely, the resort management would make an exception to their no-smoking rule.

"Sorry, Mr. Baxter . . . no exceptions, I'm afraid . . ." Phoenix had that wicked but charming smile on her face as she reached across and removed his pipe.

"Please, call me Matt," he replied.

ABOUT THE AUTHOR

William Wendyll has spent over half of his life away from his birth-place, Sheffield, England. First, at the young age of twenty-two he started traveling internationally for his career before he decided to permanently live abroad in 1988, when he moved to Dubai.

He has lived in the United Arab Emirates, Singapore, Thailand and the Philippines before deciding to settle with his wife and children in their favourite country, Malaysia. During this time, he has taken up contract work in the United Arab Emirates, Bahrain, Saudi Arabia, Kuwait, Poland and twice in the United States of America.

William admits that whilst this lighthearted novel shows a unique topic of a particularly debatable subject, it also reflects many of his own travel and lifetime experiences. Indeed, although all buildings and characters are fictitious, there once was a man who refused to drink tea made in a cup, there once was a hotel room with the light switch awkwardly fitted at the entrance, there once was a publican, who knew a tremendous amount of trivial knowledge. And there once was a young man who fell in love with a beautiful girl, gave up everything and traveled halfway around the world to be with his sweetheart.